A Little Walk in the Park

It was a beautiful fall morning in Russellville, Georgia. The sun was sitting on top of the pine trees that circled the high school. This was a small town about 100 miles southeast of Atlanta. ~~The population hadn't changed much in the last 50 years~~. The red brick school house was probably 75 years old; the flag pole out front flew "Old Glory" and the Georgia state flag, both proudly flapping in the gentle breeze from the west. A red and white two-tone Chevrolet Silverado pickup slowed to make a right hand turn into the gravel parking lot. It was only 7:30 a.m.; the teachers and staff were the only other people to arrive ahead of Shawn McLeod. This was the first day of his senior year and he wanted to be early. As he parked his pickup and exited, he noticed a small gray car entering the big semi-circle driveway out front of the school. He knew the car well; it belonged to Mrs. Bradberry. He had loaded groceries in her car for almost five years now. Shawn worked part-time at the local grocery and dry goods store owned by Mr. Peterman, so he knew everybody in this small Georgia town of about 4000 people. He closed the door to his pickup and looked back at the small gray car.

Shawn was tall and slim and had brown eyes and hair and was dressed in a typical country boy plaid shirt, jeans and of course, his western boots and belt. He was a good student. His parents had told him that he would have to quit his part-time job at Mr. Peterman's store, if he didn't keep his grades up, so Shawn's grades were good, mostly A's.

The little gray car stopped near the front door and out stepped a beautiful teenage girl with long caramel blonde hair wearing a white blouse and blue jeans. She ~~just~~ stood beside the car for a few minutes and was apparently listening to Mrs. Bradberry. Now, Shawn knew that Mrs. Bradberry didn't have a teenage daughter, so he wondered who this pretty young lady could be. He walked over to the rear of the small gray car and stopped. He wanted to meet this new girl in town. He waited patiently for Mrs. Bradberry to explain to the young lady that the principal's name was Mr. Bowen and his office was the first door on the right and that he would show her where to register for school. Then Mrs. Bradberry noticed Shawn standing near the rear of her car.

"Shawn," she called "This is my granddaughter, Dani. Would you mind showing her around?"

Shawn snapped to attention and said, "I would be honored to be her tour guide, Mrs. Bradberry, as long as she agrees to go with me to the movies on Friday night."

Dani turned toward Shawn and gave him a big smile, showing her dimples;

she was beautiful. "I'd love that, if you don't mind being with a country girl," she said.

"I love country girls!" Shawn replied. He extended his left arm for Dani and they walked toward the front door.

"Is Dani your real name or is it a nick-name?" asked Shawn.

"It's my real name," said Dani. "My Dad wanted a boy, but he got a tomboy instead," she continued.

As the couple entered the big open doors Shawn said, "We have some extra time; why don't I show you off, I mean around?"

"Sure, sounds good to me," Dani replied. So Shawn gave Dani the tour and introduced her to the teachers as they worked their way down the long hall, then to the cafeteria, gym, and football field.

"What brings you to Russellville?" Shawn asked.

"My mother was killed in a car wreck a few months back, and Dad was afraid to leave me home by myself. He's a traveling salesman for a large corporation, and we live in the country. He is gone for a couple of weeks at a time so he decided to bring me here to live with my grandparents and finish high school." she said.

"I'm very sorry, I had no idea that you had suffered such a loss," said Shawn.

"It's alright," said Dani, "I know you didn't know," she continued.

"Well, we better get back to the office and get you signed up!" said Shawn. On the way back to the office Shawn said, "I can drive you to and from school each day if you don't mind riding in a pickup."

"I love pickups," said Dani. "We lived on a farm. I drove dad's pickup and his tractor, and I know how to fix fences, feed cows, shoot guns, and climb trees. I'm a country girl, remember," she continued. Shawn in all his eighteen years of living had never met anyone so kind, sweet and beautiful, as this new girl. He had just broken up with a girl named Lyn; she had a real mean streak and was never pleased by anything-complaining was the overpowering drive in her life. As he walked down the hall with Dani he wondered why he had even dated Lyn at all.

"I'll introduce you to Mr. Bowen, our principal and Miss Jones, his secretary." said Shawn.

Miss Jones worked out a schedule for Dani and she and Mr. Bowen welcomed her to school. Mr. Bowen even introduced her to the entire student body during the morning announcements over the intercom. Shawn was happy that he and Dani would have the same homeroom, lunch break and final class of the day together. After school Shawn drove Dani to her grandparent's home and said he would pick her up at 7:45 the next morning. She thanked him for being so helpful. Shawn drove back to his home and told his mother about his very special new friend while he changed clothes for his after school job at Mr. Peterman's store. Over the next few months Shawn and Dani became very close; they dated on the weekends and spent as much time together as they could. Shawn's parents and his two little sisters all liked Dani a lot and he finally got to meet her father at the harvest festival. He wasn't a real big man, had a full beard, but a big smile always seemed to be on his face.

"I'm fresh out of traveling salesman jokes," said Shawn.

"That's alright," her father said. "I've heard enough of them to last me a lifetime," he continued.

Dani's grandparents liked Shawn a lot and her father was very impressed with this fine young man that his daughter had become so attached to after moving to Russellville.

Chapter 2

As winter turned to spring and the trees sprouted new leaves, the grass turned green and the flowers blossomed, so did the feelings of this young couple. ~~They had kissed and held hands, but nothing of a serious nature had taken place.~~ Shawn had tried to be as nice to Dani as he could. He could only imagine how terrible it must have been to lose her mother in such a tragic way and at a young age.

On Friday night, ~~after work~~ Shawn picked Dani up to go to the movies. They had to drive about 30 miles to Macon because Russellville didn't have a movie theater.

A few stores, a post office, the train depot, a gas station, a garage, Mr. Peterman's store and city hall was all they had on main street. The only employer in town was the Barton Manufacturing Co. Mr. Barton, the owner and founder, had started the company from scratch over 50 years ago. The company manufactured small camping trailers and sold them nationwide. The company stressed quality workmanship and personal service. Shawn's former girlfriend, Lyn, was Mr. Barton's granddaughter. I guess rich and spoiled runs together.

Shawn was hoping to get a job at the plant after college and spend his life in his little hometown. Most of the other graduates of Russellville High School move away to Macon, Atlanta, or Augusta, but Shawn planned to stay.

On March 25th Shawn called Dani to tell her he would be late for their date. It was Saturday and the customers were still lined up at Mr. Peterman's grocery store. He normally closed at 7 p.m. during the week and 8 p.m. on Saturday, but as long as the customers were coming in he would stay open.

Dani told Shaw, "Don't worry if it is too late to come over after work. We can spend Sunday together."

Dani was so kind and easy to please. Shawn remembered how spoiled Lyn, his former girlfriend, had been. One night he was 15 minutes late and she used a string of four letter words to show her anger.

The next morning Shawn picked Dani up early. Shawn apologized for missing their regular Saturday night date and thanked her for being so understanding.

Dani just smiled and said, "It's alright."

Shawn could tell Dani had been crying. "What's wrong?" Shawn asked.

Dani said, "Nothing, I will be alright."

Shawn was concerned so he asked again and Dani said, "today would have been my mother's birthday and I would like to go put flowers on her grave."

Shawn said, "Sure, let's go."

Dani explained it's a long drive, about two hours each way. Shawn said that he would be glad to take her. He needed to call his parents and tell them so they would not worry about him. After a quick phone call, Dani and Shawn drove to Mountaindale and arrived just in time to catch her father in the driveway.

Dani's father gave Dani a big hug ~~and said "Good morning~~" and he told Shawn he was grateful for the way he had taken care of his daughter.

"It's been the greatest pleasure of my life, sir," said Shawn.

Dani's father took them out to eat at the Mountainside Diner. After leaving the diner, the three drove to a small church just a couple of miles beyond Dani's home.

It was about 2:30 p m and the sun caused the tall pine trees to cast a shadow on the white walls of the little country church. The mood turned somber as the three exited Mr. Bradbury's car and approached the cemetery behind the little church.

Dani squeezed Shawn's hand as the three walked slowly to a single grave next to the main path. Dani's father had brought a large bouquet of flowers to place near the large headstone that read: 'The most wonderful darling of a wife and mother. Thank you, God, for sharing her with us!'

Mary Elizabeth Bradberry

March 26, 1965 - ~~January~~ June 25, ~~2008~~ 2005 OK

Dani kneeled at her mother's grave and sobbed as Shawn knelt beside her and placed his arm around her. Mr. Bradberry knelt beside Dani and then he kissed the gravestone.

"She would have been forty today," said Dani's father.

"It's my fault," cried Dani. "If only, I had put her checkbook back in her purse!"

"It's not your fault, honey. How many times do I have to tell you that?" he asked.

They had not noticed the arrival of another person now standing quietly behind them. It was Reverend Stone, the pastor of the church.

"Excuse me. I was riding by and saw you, and I wanted to say hello," The pastor said.

Dani's father thanked him for stopping.

Reverend Stone was a tall, older man with a slim build wearing a dark blue suit and red tie. His salt and pepper hair gave him the appearance of maturity and his peaceful voice and smile showed strength and kindness.

Reverend Stone knelt next to Dani and put his arm around her and pulled her to his side. "Dani, your mother would not want you to suffer like this," he said.

Dani cried, "I loved her so much!"

Shawn held Dani's hand.

As Dani cried, tears ran down her beautiful face and dripped on her mother's grave. Mr. Bradberry stood and helped Dani to her feet and held her in his arms.

"Dani, come with me," a voice rang out from behind them. It was Mrs. Stone, the pastor's wife. "We have a surprise for you," she said.

Mrs. Stone was also graying like Reverend Stone and she had the softest voice and the kindest smile on earth. Dani rose to her feet and hugged Mrs. Stone. The Stones had been a strong influence on Dani all her life.

The Stones had graciously offered to let Dani live with them while her father was on the road but Mr. Bradberry felt she would be better off in Russellville away from the place where her mother was killed.

Mrs. Stone led Dani toward the front door of the little church.

In the meanwhile, Mr. Bradberry had introduced Shawn to Reverend Stone. The two shook hands as Dani's father remarked, "This fine young man has done wonders for Dani and I am very grateful."

As the group entered the church, the first thing Dani noticed was a new piano. Her mother had played piano in the church as long as she could remember. Mrs. Stone told Dani that the piano was dedicated to her mother. As Dani walked toward the shiny new piano, she saw a picture of her mother on top and a plaque that read: "In memory of Mary Elizabeth Bradberry, a beautiful inspiration to us all!"

Dani was grateful that the church had honored her mother's memory in such a special way. The Stones had arrived at just the right time and knew how to handle any crisis.

After another round of hugs, Shawn, Dani and her father drove back to the Bradberry home.

"I'm moving to Birmingham," said Mr. Bradberry. "I can't live here anymore. It's too lonely without you and your mother. I have been offered a fair price for the place and after it sells, I will give you the cash from the equity."

Dani looked around at the place that had been her home for nearly 18 years.

"You can have the money for college," said her father.

Dani took Shawn by the hand as she walked toward the small country home and reminisced about the flowers, trees, fields and fences. It was home. She thought about the good times, the porch swing, the rocking chairs and the rope swing that hung from a large oak tree on the north side of the house. She could visualize her mother on her knees, working in the many flowerbeds. She could see her father teaching her how to ride her bike. She wondered how all of this had come to such an end.

Her father responded, "I'm going to lease an apartment. Living alone and traveling most of the time, I don't need anything else."

Dani hugged her father and told him that whatever he decided would be all right with her.

It was a long drive back to Russellville. It was getting dark as they arrived at Dani's grandparents' home. Shawn had driven home with Dani pressed up against him with her head on his shoulder. He had found an FM station out of Atlanta on his pickup's radio and had simply let the soothing music take the place of conversation.

After exiting Shawn's Silverado and walking to the porch, Dani turned to hug Shawn. "I want to thank you for taking me home today," she said.

"It was my pleasure," Shawn replied.

As Dani reached for the old screen door with her right hand, her left hand still held on to Shawn. A note attached to the door with a piece of tape indicated that her grandparents had gone to church and would be back around 8:00 p m.

"Well, we're home alone," Dani remarked. "Come in and keep me company." Dani led Shawn into the simple, but neat country home of her grandparents. Dani led Shawn down the hall to her bedroom and opened the door and led Shawn inside. After closing and locking the door behind them, she hugged and kissed him. Until now, their relationship had only been hugging, kissing and holding hands, but in the darkness of the bedroom, they made warm, passionate love. An hour later as their tired, spent bodies were still wrapped in each other's arms, Dani's mind ran through the events of the day.

Shawn's conscience was bothering him. He felt that he had taken advantage of Dani in her time of grief, but he loved Dani and if it were wrong to make love to her, he would make it up to her.

As the two exhausted lovers held each other, the sound of a car entering the driveway brought them back to earth. They hurried around the room retrieving their clothes and getting dressed. Shawn dressed first and grabbed Dani and kissed her good night. He raced to the front door. "I'll see you in the morning," he whispered as he hurried through the house.

"Well, I'm glad you love birds made it back safely," her grandfather remarked.

"Yes, yes, we just got back. Dani is getting ready for school tomorrow," said Shawn. "I hope you two had a good trip together," said Dani's grandmother, Gracie. "We had a great time," Shawn responded as he opened the door to his pickup and then drove away. Dani had been listening at the window and decided to go straight to the shower.

That night as Shawn lay in bed, all he could think about was that he and Dani had made love and what a beautiful experience it had been. He had had sex several times before with his former girlfriend, Lyn, but this was very different. It wasn't just sex, it was love!

The next morning as he pulled into the driveway, he wondered if her grandparents had figured out what had happened the night before and would meet him at the door with a shotgun. To his relief, Dani was dressed and ready to go, waiting for him on the front porch steps.

She ran to Shawn, as he opened the door and jumped in his lap and said "Good morning, darling," and gave him a big kiss.

Shawn closed the door and drove away.

Arriving at school, Shawn saw Donald Anderson, but because they were the richest family in town and his father ran the bank, Shawn called him "The Donald."

Shawn pulled up beside Donald's car and said, "Donald, meet my girlfriend, Dani. Dani, meet my richest friend, Donald."

Donald smiled and said "Hi" to Dani.

Then Donald said, "Wow! You are much too pretty for Shawn. How did he get lucky enough to snare you?"

Dani responded, "Actually I snared him right here in this very parking lot the first day of school."

Shawn laughed and said, "See what I got for being early?"

Dani asked Donald," Just how rich are you?"

"Extremely rich, my dear. If you will just dump old Shawn here, I'll show you my castle and jewels," said The Donald.

Dani responded, "I guess for the time being, I'll just stick with my little poor country boy, but if he gives me any trouble, I'll keep your offer in mind."

Then Shawn asked, "What are you doing here? I thought you were going to a big private school in Atlanta."

Donald answered, "The private school I was attending threw me out for getting my classmates drunk and inciting a small riot."

"It's for the best, Donald," Shawn said. "You need to graduate from a little place like Russellville so you can say you had a modest beginning."

"Modest or not, I'm here. I just hope Mr. Bowen, our beloved principal, feels like forgiving me for my past," said The Donald.

The Donald was dating Shawn's old girlfriend, Lyn, a strange event considering they were such good friends.

Chapter 3

When graduation time arrived Shawn had saved about $2000.00, but he won a small scholarship from the F.F.A. (Future Farmers of America) and figured he would commute and live at home and maybe still work Saturdays for Mr. Peterman. Dani had received a check from her father for nearly $25,000.00 from the sale of their home in Mountaindale. Dani also owned an old log cabin and a few acres near Mountaindale that had been left to her by her grandfather.

The young couple decided to commute to Macon College and Dani said she would share some of her money with Shawn to help him.

The two young lover's plans would soon be put on hold. Dani had been holding back a secret praying she was wrong, but a trip to the doctor confirmed that she was pregnant. Several mornings she had experienced morning sickness, but she had just written it off as stress. A week before graduation Dani finally told Shawn that she was expecting.

He took the news well.

"I don't really need a college education anyway, because I can get a job with Mr. Barton, and help him build campers."

Shawn told Dani that he didn't want to leave Russellville. It's home. Shawn had already thought about asking Mr. Barton for a job someday so it would be now instead of after college.

Dani said, "We can use the money my father gave me for college to pay down on a house."

The wedding was only a few weeks after they graduated from high school; they were man and wife.

Shawn's family and Dani's family had agreed to help them.

The young couple spent their honeymoon at Jekyll Island off the coast of Georgia. The next weekend they returned to north Georgia to visit the old mountain cabin Dani's grandfather had left her in his will. It was a typical old mountain style log cabin with a stone fireplace. It had a front porch with four rocking chairs and a porch swing on one end. A mountain stream supplied running water for the cabin by filling a tank up stream. The electrical service had been disconnected for years so Shawn and Dani used candles for light.

When they returned home Shawn went to see Mr. Barton, and he gave Shawn a job at his manufacturing plant.

The young couple had been living with Shawn's parents, but now that Mr. Barton had given him a job, Shawn and Dani decided to look for a home of their own. A small town like Russellville didn't have a lot of homes for sale, and they realized they couldn't afford a new home, so they looked for an old home they could remodel.

Mr. Peterman told them about a ~~two-bedroom~~ home on the edge of town. Dani and Shawn went to see the old house and fell in love with it. It wasn't very big, but it was beautiful; the property was shaped like a triangle. It bordered the railroad on the south side, US Highway 80 on the north and a country road on the east. A semi-circular pond circled the south side of the house and a deck on the back extended out over the water.

Flowers, trees and shrubs were everywhere, but the house needed a lot of work. The paint was peeling, and some of the windows were broken. Shawn had helped his father paint and roof their home, so the repairs didn't scare him.

Mr. Peterman called the owner and she agreed to cut the price from $50,000 to $40,000, just for them. Shawn and Dani would have to acquire a loan from the bank to pay the balance.

The trip to the bank went well. The town's banker agreed to loan them the money they needed. Shawn, his father, and even Dani worked evenings and weekends to get the house livable. Neighbors and friends gave them furniture and Shawn's parents bought them a new refrigerator and living room furniture.

Dani's grandparents gave them an old china cabinet that was over 100 years old. Shawn's mom helped Dani make curtains and Shawn's dad helped Shawn put on the new roof. Work on the little house was progressing slowly, but surely.

Dani's father came to spend the weekend with them and reworked the plumbing and wiring.

As Dani's due date neared, lots of preparation went into the nursery for the new baby. The doctors had told them that the baby would be a girl. Shawn hoped she would look just like her mom. It was hard to believe he had only known Dani for a little over a year. He could have never predicted that morning when he drove into the high school parking lot how much his life would change.

The next Monday morning as he drove into the Barton Manufacturing Company parking lot, he noticed a strange car parked at the front door. Shawn entered the building as usual and proceeded to Mr. Barton's office. Shawn made it a policy to arrive thirty minutes early and to ask Mr. Barton if he needed any help before the workday began. Shawn also went by Mr. Barton's office before he left for the day to help Mr. Barton lock up the building.

Mr. Barton appreciated Shawn's help and bragged about him to his son-in-law, who just happened to be the plant manager, Buddy Strange. Buddy was also the father of Lyn, Shawn's ex-girlfriend.

As Shawn ~~entered the building, he~~ heard a long tirade of cursing from Mr. Barton's office. Shawn recognized the voice right away. It was Buddy Strange having one of his temper tantrums. Apparently, Buddy had purchased a new car and he wanted Mr. Barton to pay for it. ~~A heated argument was in progress as Shawn entered the building~~.

Shawn walked to the door of the office and said, "I'm sorry. I didn't mean to interrupt. I'll just go open the doors and set up the stockroom."

Mr. Barton told Buddy that Shawn is the kind of man that works his way to top by always being early and the last to leave. He said, "You could learn a lot from this young man."

Shawn appreciated the compliment from Mr. Barton, but the evil look on Buddy's face spoke volumes. He did not appreciate being down-rated by a teenager.

In the short time Shawn had dated Buddy's daughter, he had never met him until he went to work at the plant. Lyn always walked out the door when he drove up. He had met Lyn's mom at Mr. Peterman's store and she appeared very nice. Lyn, on the other hand, acted more like her father. She could not put five words together without cursing.

Mr. Barton yelled "Now take that new car back to the dealer in Macon and get your old car back."

~~Buddy responded by telling Mr. Barton that he had bought the car for his spoiled daughter, because she wanted it.~~

~~"Carla's van is only a year old and she loves it," said Mr. Barton.~~

Buddy yelled back, "I can't take it back. I had a little accident with it Saturday night and bent the fender."

Mr. Barton just shook his head in disbelief and said, "Well, then half of the cost will come out of your and Carla's retirement account, and the rest will be deducted weekly from your salary."

Buddy retorted, "My salary isn't large enough now and I can hardly support my family."

Mr. Barton replied, "You should have thought of that before you bought a new car you can't afford."

Buddy, still yelling at Mr. Barton asked, "Why can't I get a raise?"

Mr. Barton then replied, "Buddy, you don't earn half the salary you receive now. You come in late and leave early. In between those times, you take afternoon naps."

Buddy yelled back, "If you would let me run this dump, I'd raise the price on our inventory, and we all could live better."

Mr. Barton responded, "You can't raise the prices. Our sales are off, and have you looked at the price of gasoline lately?"

Buddy said, "Who cares?"

Mr. Barton said, "I care. When the price of gasoline is up, people do not buy things like campers, so we can't raise the prices. It's a wonder we are selling what we are."

Buddy went on with his tirade. "If we're so broke, why did you hire 'Wonder Boy'?" As Buddy was yelling, he pointed at Shawn.

Mr. Barton said, "He's one of the best workers here, and I can depend on him."

Buddy, still yelling, said, "I'm tired of living like a beggar with my superior education. I could make this place work."

Mr. Barton told Buddy, "If you would stop ~~your~~ drinking and hanging out at the strip joints ~~in Bentonville~~, not to mention the gambling ~~with his friends in Macon,~~ you could live well on your salary."

Buddy told Mr. Barton, "What I do is none of your damn business."

Mr. Barton fired back at Buddy, "It is my business because you work for me, and you are married to my daughter. ~~You are supposed to be plant manager, a job you don't deserve~~, and it's my business when I have to give my daughter money to pay your bills because you gambled yours away."

Shawn backed slowly out of the office and proceeded to open the shop, and then checked the work orders. The camping trailers they built were sold under the brand name 'Fantasy Quest'.

Shawn was busy at work when the other employees arrived. Suddenly, Shawn heard a voice behind him.

"I see they are at it again," said Jerry.

Shawn turned to see Jerry Allen, another employee, standing behind him. "Good morning, Jerry, how are you doing?"

Jerry said, "Good morning," as well and then looked back at the two men arguing in the office. "I don't know why Mr. Barton puts up with that worthless son-in-law of his," said Jerry.

Jerry was mid-thirties, a little on the heavy side, with black hair and a well-groomed beard. He had worked for Mr. Barton for over ten years. Jerry really liked Mr. Barton and appreciated his job. Mr. Barton had hired Jerry after he had lost part of his left hand in a farming accident. Jerry never let his handicap slow him down and he had a good sense of humor. When someone needed help, they would yell "I need half a hand over here" and Jerry would stop whatever he was doing to help them.

Shawn's feelings were hurt by the way Buddy referred to him as 'Wonder Boy'. It was Shawn's father that had convinced him to come to work early and be the last to leave. Employers remember these things when it's time for raises and promotions.

Shawn had a wife and a baby on the way at only nineteen years of age and he had acquired a lot of responsibilities. He knew he had to do the best he could to support his family.

Suddenly the door to Mr. Barton's office slammed shut and Buddy stormed out ~~mumbling something under his breath. Buddy walked quickly out the front door of the warehouse~~ and sped away in the new car.

Mrs. Barton ~~had just entered the parking lot, but~~ stopped suddenly to let the hothead out.

Mrs. Barton, better known as "Mrs. Alice" to the employees and her friends, handled the books for the company. She was small but had a big heart and smile to go with it. Like Mr. Barton, she was mid-sixties and she wore her gray hair in a ponytail at work.

Shawn went home each day during the lunch hour break. He got to see Dani, plus get a little work done on the house. It was a good thing that they lived only about a mile from the plant.

As Christmas approached, Shawn worked extra hard to finish the work on their little home. In the predawn hours of December 28th, Dani woke Shawn and said it was time to go to the hospital. After a trip to the hospital in Macon, they became the proud parents of Mary Elizabeth McLeod, seven pounds and eight ounces with blonde hair and blue eyes like her mother. They named her after Dani's mother.

As the sun came up that morning, the magnitude of his responsibilities became very apparent to Shawn. As Shawn held little Elizabeth in his arms, he leaned over and kissed Dani and said, "This is the most beautiful gift any one could give me. Thank you." Dani was so happy tears of joy and sadness ran down her face. She was thinking about her mother and how excited she would have been to hold this precious child.

Shawn's parents and little sisters arrived and were very excited about the new baby. Dani's father called from a motel in Memphis after being paged by Shawn. He was delighted to hear they had named the baby after Dani's mom. Shawn had also called Mr. Barton to tell him the good news and to tell him he would be late for work. Mr. Barton said, "Just take the day off, Dad!" Mr. Barton was a wonderful boss. It was Friday and the plant normally shut down at noon so the employees could cash their paychecks and shop or pay bills. Mr. Barton's plant worked eight and half hour days Monday through Thursday and only four hours on Friday. ~~Shawn thanked Mr. Barton for allowing him to be off and promised to be back at work on Monday.~~

Shawn's mom and little sisters spent the afternoon at the hospital with Dani and the new baby. Shawn and his Dad drove back to Russellville to put the finishing touches on the nursery. The heating unit was making a strange noise so Shawn's Dad called the gas company and they sent out a repairman. After checking the heating unit, the repairman said "Four hundred dollars will fix it right." Shawn knew he didn't have that much in his account. Then the repairman said, "Ninety days same as cash." Shawn signed the repair order and gave him a check for one hundred dollars. The responsibilities of being a husband, father and homeowner were beginning to set in.

The next morning it was cold, but sunny when Shawn, Dani and the baby pulled into the driveway of their little home. Shawn's parents were waiting to help get the family out of the cold. Shawn's mom had prepared a nice hot meal for them. Shawn's mom asked his Dad "What's wrong with the water heater?" Shawn's Dad checked the water heater and the news wasn't good. The safety switch had tripped and the tank was leaking.

After enjoying the meal together, Shawn and his Dad drove to Bentonville to buy a water heater. Shawn's Dad wrote a check for the water heater. Shawn called Dani's father and he said he would install it the next day.

Shawn said, "I have a wife, a child, and a house, and I'm broke."

Shawn's father replied, "Welcome to the father's club, Son."

On Sunday, everybody in Russellville dropped by to see Elizabeth.

As a new year began, Shawn worked hard for Mr. Barton. After work and on the weekends, he worked on his home. Little Elizabeth was growing and Dani did her best to be a good wife and mother. Dani started working part time for Mr. Peterman and Shawn's mom took care of the baby. Shawn dropped by Mr. Peterman's store on Saturday morning and asked him how his new employee was doing. Mr. Peterman answered "Just fine."

"I noticed you are the one carrying the groceries to the car. Your former employee did that for you" said Shawn.

Mr. Peterman smiled and said, "That's alright, she's a lot prettier than my former employee."

They all had a good laugh over Mr. Peterman's comments.

Suddenly, the door opened and in walked Sheriff Sam Giles with a sad look on his face. Sheriff Giles said, "Mr. Barton died just before daybreak this morning. He had a heart attack."

Shawn was deeply saddened by the news. ~~Mr. Barton had become a second father to him~~. The entire McLeod family did everything they could to help Mrs. Barton during her time of grief. This little town had lost one of its most important and popular citizens. Even the bank closed for his funeral.

Mrs. Barton told the employees that she would try to continue operating the plant until she could sell it. She asked for everyone's cooperation. Part of the deal would be to continue their employment. The employees pledged their support and agreed to help her in any way they could.

The next day, Mrs. Barton asked Shawn and Jerry to come to the office. She wanted to show them how to open the safe and pay the delivery people because she was going to Texas for a few weeks. She had decided to visit her sister for a while and she didn't trust Buddy to handle the cash.

The next day, Mrs. Barton's daughter drove her to the Atlanta airport for her flight to Texas. Employee morale was really low after Mr. Barton died. The crew tried to stay upbeat but with Mrs. Barton gone and Buddy drinking and harassing the employees, it was hard to focus on their work. Several prospective buyers came to see the business but after trying to deal with Buddy, they all left and didn't return.

Then one night the phone rang ~~and woke up little Elizabeth. She had been napping on the sofa and Dani got up to check on her while~~ Shawn answered the phone. The caller was "The Donald" as Shawn called him. He wanted to know more about the mountain cabin they owned. Shawn explained it belonged to Dani and the place is old, run down and secluded.

"That's perfect," said Donald. He asked, "Would Dani allow him and some friends to borrow it over the weekend?"

Dani said, "It would be all right with her."

Shawn gave Donald the directions.

As Shawn put the phone back on the receiver he said to Dani "Can you imagine some rich folks spending the weekend in that old run down shack?"

They both had a good laugh ~~about it~~, and ~~then~~ Shawn helped Dani fix some soup and sandwiches for the evening meal.

As they sat down to eat ~~and watch television~~, Shawn asked Dani about her grandfather, the one who left her the mountain land and cabin.

She told Shawn, "I never knew him. He was a Canadian, and after my grandmother died, he abandoned the cabin and went back to Canada."

As Shawn got up to get the coffee pot, Dani told Shawn, "I have several relatives who live only a few miles north of the Canadian border."

Shawn asked "Are they rich?"

Dani laughed and said, "No, I don't think so, but maybe we should go visit them someday."

Shawn said, "On our salaries, if it didn't take, but a thousand dollars to go around the world, we couldn't get out of town."

The next morning when Shawn arrived at work, he saw Buddy pacing back and forth in front of the building. When Buddy saw Shawn pulling into the parking lot, he rushed over to Shawn and said, "I need some money from the company vault."

Shawn didn't know what to do. Mrs. Barton had told him she didn't trust Buddy and didn't want him in the safe. He explained to Buddy that he couldn't open the safe, unless Jerry was present, and then only, if Mrs. Barton instructed him to do so.

Buddy stomped his foot on the sidewalk and said, "I don't give a damn what that old bat said. I need some cash, and I need it now."

Shawn unlocked the front door and entered the building. Buddy followed close behind. Shawn tried to ignore Buddy as he walked around the plant turning on the lights and opening the work trays.

As Buddy became enraged, he picked up a crowbar from a tool tray and drew it back over his shoulder, shouting, "You open that damn safe or that cute little wife of yours won't recognize you when you get home."

As Shawn turned to face Buddy, he saw Jerry rushing up behind him. Jerry grabbed the crowbar from Buddy's hands and asked him, what he thought he was doing.

Jerry asked, "Have you lost your mind?"

Buddy, completely surprised by Jerry's actions, ran out the front door.

Jerry turned to Shawn and asked, "How did all that get started?"

Shawn told Jerry that Buddy got angry, because he refused to open the safe for him. As Shawn spoke, they could hear Buddy racing out of the parking lot in his new car.

"Now what do we do?" Jerry asked.

Shawn suggested that they just let it go and hopefully when Buddy sobered up, he would realize what an idiot he was and maybe would act better for a change.

The other employees starting milling in and Jerry and Shawn explained to them what had taken place earlier that morning. None of them were shocked. Since Mr. Barton died, Buddy's poor behavior had gone from bad to worse. One of the other employees asked Jerry if anyone was serious about buying the business. Jerry told them that every time someone was interested in the plant, Buddy would open his big drunk mouth and scare the potential buyer away. Shawn said he did not see how the business would ever sell as long as Buddy was around. Shawn commented that maybe Buddy would act better when Mrs. Barton returned from her trip. The other employees just rolled their eyes in unison.

"I wonder how such nice people like the Bartons wound up with such a jerk for a son-in-law" said Shawn.

Chapter 4

Sheriff Giles pulled into the parking lot and parked near the front door.

"Howdy, Sheriff, can I help you?" asked Jerry, ~~as he cleaned his hands with a towel.~~

"Well, Jerry, I'm here on official business," said Sheriff Giles.

Jerry asked, "Is Mrs. Alice all right?"

"Actually, we got a call from Buddy saying you tried to assault him!" said the Sheriff.

Shawn saw Jerry talking to Sheriff Giles and walked to the front door to see if something was wrong.

As Shawn approached, Jerry turned and said, "Tell the Sheriff what happened this morning."

Shawn told him that Buddy had threatened him with a crowbar and demanded that he open the company safe.

The Sheriff just shook his head and said that Buddy called the office and claimed that Jerry had assaulted him.

Shawn spoke up. "That's a lie, Sheriff. Jerry came up behind him and grabbed the crowbar out of his hands."

"I had a feeling that he was lying," said the Sheriff. "I've known both of you since you were kids and I can't imagine either of you doing anything like that."

"Sheriff, Buddy was drunk and has been acting real crazy lately. What can we do about it?" asked Jerry.

The Sheriff stated that he would call Buddy and ask him not to go to the plant again until Mrs. Barton returned.

"Thank you, Sheriff," said Shawn.

"You don't have to thank me. That's what I get paid for," stated the Sheriff.

~~Sheriff Giles told Shawn and Jerry to call him, if Buddy came back to the plant today.~~ Sheriff Giles got into his patrol car and drove away.

Jerry said, "What are we going to do? The future of this business and our jobs are at stake."

Shawn said, "I can't see how they could sell the business with Buddy getting drunk and acting crazy."

Jerry said, "I don't know."

Mr. Olivetti, the welder and fabricator, asked "Why don't we, the employees, try to borrow the money to buy the company for ourselves?"

Everybody just stared at each other.

Shawn asked, "Could we do that?"

Jerry said, "That was a good question and it might work."

Mr. Olivetti said, "It was worth a try."

Jerry asked, "Anybody know a banker?"

As they all turned and looked at Shawn, Shawn related that he does not know the banker well enough to borrow a million dollars.

Jerry suggested that they talk with Mrs. Barton and see, if she would be willing to finance it for them.

Shawn exclaimed, "Wow! You mean we could own our own business!"

Mr. Olivetti said, "It was possible."

Jerry suggested that they keep this possibility among themselves, and not say anything to Buddy about it

The two weeks Mrs. Barton was gone was hard on the employees. Without Mrs. Barton to keep the books and records straight, and without Mr. Barton to order the materials, oversee sales and keep an eye on Buddy, the production was falling behind.

On Monday morning Mrs. Barton thanked everyone for taking care of the business while she was away. The employees welcomed her back, but decided to wait until the next day to bring up the subject of the employees buying the business.

On Tuesday morning, Jerry asked Mrs. Barton, if she would consider selling the business to the employees.

Mrs. Barton smiled and said, "Yes, I love the idea."

Then Jerry asked, "Mrs. Barton would also consider financing the business as well?"
you

Smiling, Mrs. Barton said, "I would have to think about it."

Mrs. Barton called for Buddy to come to the office. When Buddy reached her office, she was boiling mad about him threatening Shawn. Of course, Buddy denied everything.

Over the next few days, every employee did their best to show Mrs. Barton they could run the business and wanted her to see them at their very best.

Chapter 5

Little Elizabeth was growing and exploring every inch of the young family's home. Dani was still working part time at Mr. Peterman's store and Shawn's Mom and sisters were baby-sitting little Elizabeth.

Shawn and Dani's income was consumed by the normal daily upkeep of the young family. One night as Shawn was sitting in his recliner, he wondered about the possibility of the employees buying the plant.

~~Buddy had done~~ nothing since he married the ~~Barton's daughter~~. Shawn looked out into space, as a tinge of fear and doubt came over him. "What, if we fail?"

The fear subsided as Dani entered the room holding the baby. Shawn ~~pulled Dani and Elizabeth close and~~ gave them a hug.

After putting the baby to bed, Dani sat down beside Shaw and told him that the stove had quit working.

Shawn replied, "It's about the only thing we haven't replaced!"

Dani said, "I'm sorry."

Shawn said, "He would have to see, if ninety days same as cash, is still available at the Bentonville Gas Company."

Dani told Shawn she knows that he has his hands full with all the repairs at the house and the situation at the plant.

Shawn told Dani not to worry. He told her things will be fine after ~~they~~ we finish the house.

On Friday afternoon, Mrs. Barton called all of the employees to the office. As usual, Buddy had grabbed his paycheck and left early. Mrs. Barton told the group that she had given a lot of thought to financing the business for them. She stated that there might be a problem with the idea. Mr. Barton's will left the business to her and their daughter, Carla. Mrs. Barton expressed her fear that Buddy would probably want the business sold for cash. Mrs. Barton said that Carla would only agree to the financing, if Buddy gets to be chief administrator of the company.

Jerry stood up and said, "I would never agree to have Buddy involved in this business. He has never contributed one thing to help this company.

Mr. Olivetti agreed with Jerry. Everyone else confirmed that they didn't want Buddy involved in any way.

Mrs. Barton stated that she liked the idea of financing the business. She felt that, if she sold it for cash, Buddy would squander her daughter's half in a matter of months.

Mrs. Barton told them she would talk with Carla again on this matter.

As the employees left, Shawn stayed behind to clean up the shop and lock the doors. He could hear loud voices coming from the office. He could tell that the loud voice was Buddy's. Shawn entered the office.

Buddy shouted, "Get the hell out of here; this is none of your damn business."

Mrs. Barton said, "Buddy, I do not want to hear anything you have to say, because you are obviously drunk."

Buddy retorted, "What I do on my time is none of your business."

She replied, "When you are on my property, it becomes my business."

Buddy responded, "Half of the business belongs to ~~him and his~~ wife and that ~~she was~~ not going to cheat them out of it."

"According to the will, I don't have to sell the business, but I can't depend on my son-in-law to run it for me, so that's the only reason I would consider selling it," Mrs. Barton replied to Buddy.

Buddy informed her, "I have heard of your "scheme" to finance the business to the dummies who work there. I will not stand for it".

To which Mrs. Barton told him, "If you had tried to help run the business as you should, I would turn it over to you, but since you are so unreliable, that was out of the question."

Buddy was inflamed by these remarks.

~~Mrs. Barton responded, "You get drunk every night, you cheat on your wife, and you gamble away your money,"~~

Buddy yelled, "If you try to cheat me, I'll sue."

~~"You will never get your hands on this business," said Mrs. Barton.~~

~~Buddy retorted, "Don't be so sure!"~~

~~Mrs. Barton informed Buddy, "The will gave her authority over her daughter's share of the company for as long as I deem it necessary."~~

~~Buddy said, "You wouldn't dare!"~~

~~Mrs. Barton told him, "I could sell the company and put Carla's share in a trust fund, so you would only waste it one monthly check at a time."~~

At which Buddy turned and walked out of the building.

Mrs. Barton started crying. Mrs. Barton told Shawn that she just doesn't understand Buddy.

When Shawn arrived at his home, Elizabeth was playing on the floor and Dani was on the phone.

During the meal, Dani explained that she had been on the phone with her aunt and uncle from Canada.

"By the way, how is your aunt and uncle?" asked Shawn.

Dani said, "They are fine. We need to visit them one day."

Dani informed him, "We received a registered letter in the mail today from the Harmony Gas Line Company."

Dani handed Shawn the letter.

Shawn opened the letter and read out loud, "We deeply regret having to inform you that your home is too close to our intrastate gas pipe line. You have 90 days to move your home or it will be demolished and removed at your expense. Sincerely, George P. Sloppy, General Manager, Harmony Gas Lines of America."

"What! A gas line runs through our property!" Shawn yelled. "I can't believe it. I could lose my job and a gas pipe line company says move your house or we will tear it down! I can't believe it!"

Dani walked over to Shawn and gave him a hug. She said, "I'm sure it's just a mistake, don't worry!"

Shawn called his father.

His father said, "I will have a lawyer check it out."

On Monday morning the lawyer checked the records. He found them to be correct. The odd shape of the property meant there was no other part of the property the house could be moved to. The power lines, railroad, highway, county dirt road, gas line easements, and the pond would make relocating the house on this property impossible.

On Tuesday, Shawn's father suggested they move their house out to the farm.

Shawn said, "That's a great idea, I would appreciate that Dad!"

That night Shawn finally drifted off to sleep around midnight. Then at 2:30 a.m. the phone rang. As Shawn sprung from his bed to grab the phone he could hear sirens screaming in the background. Jerry yelled "The plants on fire, that rotten bastard must have decided to burn it to get the insurance!"

Shawn raced toward town. As he approached the plant, flashing lights and fire trucks were everywhere. He parked and ran toward the fire.

A Sheriff's deputy was telling people to say back for their own safety.

Shawn shouted to the deputy, "I work here, and I have the keys to everything!"

The deputy responded, "OK, go tell the chief, but be careful!"

The large metal building was completely engulfed in flames. Shawn saw Chief Dennis and yelled, "I have the keys to everything and I can show you where the natural gas shut off is!"

Chief Dennis yelled back, "We have already entered the property, and we are pouring water on it from all sides, but, we can use some help. We are trying to save some of the campers out back!"

Shawn yelled, "I'll be glad to help!"

He helped move the last few trailers and then remembered the pontoon boat that was stored in the building near the rear fence. He asked for help to save the boat and several volunteers followed him, but when he opened the door the boat was gone.

He shouted, "I don't understand. I've worked here over a year and that boat was always here!"

Shawn heard a familiar voice yell, "Well maybe the tooth fairy got it!"

Shawn saw his friend the Donald wearing a fire fighter uniform.

Shawn said, "I didn't know you were a fireman!"

The Donald responded, "On top of being the most exciting guy in Russellville, I'm also a fire fighter!"

Then Shawn focused on the boat and explained to the Donald about it being missing.

Donald pointed his flash light toward the ground and said, "These tire tracks are fresh; I would say it was moved in the last 24 hours."

Then Shawn heard, "Our future just went up in flames!"

Shawn turned around to see Jerry standing behind him.

Shawn asked, "How did you know about the fire?"

Jerry replied, "I heard the sirens and turned on my police scanner."

Jerry said, "I couldn't believe my ears when I heard the location of the fire."

Then Chief Dennis yelled, "Better move back, the paint room could explode!"

After moving across the street Shawn said, "This building has been here all my life, I'm going to miss it!"

Jerry said, "I can't imagine Russellville without Barton Manufacturing Company!"

Sheriff Giles approached Jerry and asked if he could help comfort Mrs. Barton. Mrs. Barton just arrived and was very distraught.

Then the sheriff said, "I need to talk to you."

The two walked over behind a large van.

Sheriff Giles said, "This fire was probably arson, the back door and rear gate were left open, and the state fire Marshal is on the way here from Atlanta to do an investigation."

Shawn asked, "Why would anyone want to destroy the only industry in town?"

The Sheriff replied, "That's what I wanted to ask you."

Shawn said, "The only unhappy person here would be Buddy Strange!"

The Sheriff responded, "Yes, Buddy had been a problem for the Barton's for as long as I can remember!"

Shawn said, "Sheriff, I'll be glad to help anyway I can."

The Sheriff replied, "I appreciate it, Shawn."

Then Shawn went to check on Mrs. Barton sitting on the porch steps of an old house across the street.

She was sobbing. As Shawn approached Mrs. Barton, Shawn gave her a hug.

Mrs. Barton said, "I just can't believe it, first I lose my husband and now I've lost the business we spent our lives building!"

Jerry said, "Mrs. Alice, you don't need to be here. We need to drive you home!"

Jerry helped Mrs. Barton to her car and drove her home and Shawn followed.

When they pulled into Mrs. Barton's driveway, Shawn couldn't help but notice the pontoon boat parked behind Mrs. Barton's house.

Shawn asked, "Is that boat yours?" as he pointed toward the pontoon boat.

Mrs. Barton replied, "No. That belongs to Buddy. He must have brought it over here last night."

Shawn and Jerry drove back to the smoldering ruins! When they arrived they saw Carla, Mrs. Barton's daughter, standing beside her car. They stopped and told her that they had just driven Mrs. Barton home.

She said, "I will go spend the day with her," and she drove away.

Shawn asked Jerry, "Did you notice the pontoon boat had been moved from the storage building?"

Jerry replied, "Yes, Buddy moves it around, but I don't think that would prove Buddy was involved in the fire."

Reporters from Bentonville, Macon, and Augusta were taking pictures and interviewing bystanders.

Jerry said, "I don't think I would say anything about the missing boat, because the insurance company might not pay, if they think the fire was arson."

Shawn responded, "You are right, that could happen."

Mrs. Barton will need all the help she can get, if she plans to rebuild and the sooner the investigation is complete, the better." said Jerry.

When the fire Marshal arrived, he placed yellow 'Do Not Enter' ribbons at all of the entrances to the plant. The fire Marshal also photographed the entire location.

Shawn decided to go home to Dani and the baby. When Shawn arrived at home Dani met him at the door with a big hug.

Shawn looked tired and depressed as he said, "It looks like I just lost my job.

Dani said, "You look tired and you smell like smoke, why don't you take a shower and I will fix some sandwiches."

Dani was still trying to cook with the malfunctioning old stove.

Shawn and Dani had just finished the sandwiches when the phone rang. The call was from Jerry. He informed Shawn that the fire Marshal had asked all of the employees to meet at the Sheriff's office at 3 p.m. for debriefing. Shawn thanked him for calling and relayed the information to Dani.

Dani asked, "Do you think Buddy had something to do with the fire?"

Shawn replied, "I wouldn't be the least bit shocked."

Dani asked, "How is Mrs. Barton, have you seen her?"

Shawn replied, "Yes, she arrived about an hour after I got there, but Jerry and I took her home and Carla is going to spend the day with her."

Shawn thought for a moment about Mrs. Barton. He said, "I want to go to Mrs. Barton's house, and I would like for you and Elizabeth to come with me."

Dani said, "That's a great idea, let's go!"

When they arrived at Mrs. Barton's, Carla welcomed them in. Carla was very nice to them and when Shawn introduced her to Dani, she gave her a big hug and then asked if she could hold little Elizabeth.

Carla said, "What a beautiful baby girl!"

Mrs. Barton walked into the foyer holding some papers. She walked over to little Elizabeth and kissed her face and said, "She is so precious," and she then gave Dani a hug and said, "Let's have some ice cream."

As everyone enjoyed the ice cream, Mrs. Barton passed around pictures of the Barton Manufacturing building when it was new. Mrs. Barton exclaimed, "You know what! I'm going to rebuild this business. It's our family legacy and I'm not going to let a fire destroy it!"

The doorbell rang. It was Sheriff Giles and he said, "I'm sorry to disturb you, but I need to talk to Mrs. Barton."

Mrs. Barton walked to the front door and invited the Sheriff into the kitchen for some ice cream.

Sheriff Giles said "No, thank you; you know, we cops are partial to doughnuts." Then Sheriff Giles said, "I just came by to tell you how sorry I am about the loss of your business, and to offer my help to you and your family."

Mrs. Barton said, "Thank you, Sheriff."

Sheriff Giles said, "We are having a meeting at my office at 3 p.m. to interview all of the employees, but I can't find Buddy."

Carla, slowly looked up and said, "I don't think he even came home last night. He's been very depressed lately."

Sheriff Giles said, "I need to contact him."

Carla said, "I have called his cell phone all morning, but he hasn't answered."

Mrs. Barton said, "Why are you holding a meeting?"

The Sheriff said, "It's just a formality, Mrs. Barton. Anytime you have a fire of this magnitude, it's normal to have the fire Marshal question the employees."

Then the Sheriff bid everyone a good day and left!

Shawn said, "I guess we better be going."

Shawn took Dani and Elizabeth home and then drove to the Sheriff's office. Jerry pulled into the parking lot right behind him.

Shawn asked, "Have you heard any more news about the fire?"

Jerry said, "A gasoline tank behind the building was used to torch the factory."

"So somebody broke in," said Shawn.

Jerry said, "No! Neither of the locks nor chains was cut; they were opened with a key. So whoever set the fire to the building had the keys. Only five people have keys. Mrs. Barton, Mr. Olivetti, you, Buddy and me."

Shawn said, "I'm convinced that it was Buddy. He had the keys, he had the motive and he moved his boat just before the fire."

Shawn told Jerry, "The pontoon boat is at Mrs. Barton's house. Mrs. Barton said Buddy had left it during the night."

Shawn and Jerry entered the Sheriff's office and greeted the other employees. The only person missing was Buddy!

The Sheriff introduced the fire Marshal and then took a seat next to Jerry. The fire Marshal thanked everyone for coming. He went into detail about how fires of this nature are almost always accidental, but an investigation is important to ascertain what happened, so they can be prevented in the future. He said in this case, there was some evidence it could be arson.

He explained there was no evidence of forced entry and that the fire had been started with gasoline. He continued to explain that the gasoline tank at the rear of the building had been left on and the hose was extended. This is why we need your help. Only someone with the company keys could have entered the building without damaging the locks or chains.

The Marshal spoke for an hour before issuing all of the employees his card and an envelope addressed to the Marshal. He asked them to call him or write to him if they thought of anything that might help the investigation.

Shawn thought about the pontoon boat being moved, but didn't say anything about it at the time.

The fire Marshal asked if they had any comments or questions. After the meeting ended, the employees gathered in the parking lot and discussed what had just transpired. All of them were in agreement that Buddy's behavior and actions appeared suspicious.

Shawn drove home. He wondered about the future.

When Shawn arrived home, his father was talking to Dani at the front door. Shawn filled him in on the events of the day. Mr. McLeod told him that he would help them. His father also explained to Shawn that it was his duty as a responsible citizen to tell the fire Marshal about the boat being moved.

Shawn immediately called Sheriff Giles with the boat information and asked if he would relay the information to the fire Marshal. Sheriff Giles thanked Shawn for coming forward about the boat being moved.

Shawn wondered how he and Dani would survive. He had lost his job, he had to move his house, and the stove had broken down.

Dani called him to eat. She apologized for the simple meal, but the stove problem dictated the menu at times. After they ate, Dani turned on the television. The lead story was the Barton Manufacturing Company fire. They watched intently as the reporter tried to interview Chief Dennis. His statement was brief. He stated, "We received the call just before three a.m. When we arrived on the scene, the entire plant was engulfed in flames and it is a complete loss!"

The camera continued to move back and forth.

Dani cried out, "Look, it's you, Shawn!"

As the darkness fell on Russellville, the smoke from the tragic fire could still be seen in the distant sky. The McLeod family decided to turn in early, but sleep would not come for Shawn, as he wondered how he could support his family. He wondered, even if Mrs. Barton did rebuild, it might be a year before the plant would reopen. He also worried about moving the house. As the night gave way to sunlight, Shawn finally fell asleep.

The next day Buddy was questioned concerning the fire. Of course, he denied any involvement.

Shawn's father hired him to paint his large barn and Dani continued working part time for Mr. Peterman. Her salary wasn't much, but it was better than nothing. Mrs. Barton contacted the employees and gave them a severance check. The money wasn't a lot, but it helped.

Meanwhile, the Sheriff and fire Marshal questioned Buddy several times, but he kept proclaiming his innocence. Mrs. Barton's insurance company had refused to pay the claim until the investigation was finalized.

Chapter 6

Shawn tried to get an extension on moving the house, but to no avail. He paid the last payment on the furnace and he planned to get a new stove on credit, but

Shawn had no job. The walls were beginning to close in on him. A letter from Dani's father arrived with a two hundred dollar check, and they were very appreciative. Shawn wasn't able to provide for his family and his pride was hurt.

As the reflection of a full moon danced off the pond, the McLeod family lay sleeping in their beds. There was total silence except for a dog barking in the distance. Nothing could have prepared this little family for what would take place as the little town of Russellville slept.

K A --B O O O M M!!! An explosion rocked the small wood frame home. Instantly, Shawn found himself on the floor. Dazed and shocked, he tried to figure out what had happened! He could hear Elizabeth screaming in the pitch black darkness, but he could not see a thing. Shawn struggled to get to his feet, as he realized Dani was lying on top of him. He grabbed her in the darkness screaming, "Are you all right?"

Dani had been knocked out by the explosion.

Shawn cried out to Dani asking her if she was OK.

Suddenly, he heard her groaning.

The door to the hall was blown open and flames were rushing in as Shawn rolled Dani over on her side.

Realizing the house was in flames, Shawn once again heard Elizabeth's cries. Shawn quickly crawled on his hands and knees to her baby bed and pulled her over the side rails. He returned to Dani, as she continued to moan and gasp for air. Shawn realized their only hope was to climb out the bedroom window. The pond was only a few feet away, so he was afraid to drop Elizabeth outside first for fear she would go to the pond and fall in. He had to get Dani out first.

The smoke was so thick he could barely see the window just a short distance away. Shawn licked Dani's face with his tongue, as it was the only wet thing available. Dani began to cough and shake. Shawn laid Elizabeth beside Dani and grabbed their bed and flipped it on its side against the open door to shield them from the flames. He tried to open the window, but apparently the fresh paint had it stuck. He grabbed one of his boots and broke the window and then he threw a blanket over the windowsill to protect them from the shattered glass.

Dani was beginning to regain consciousness and started screaming for Shawn and the baby. Shawn helped her toward the window with his left arm, as he grabbed Elizabeth with the right.

Dani shouted, "What's wrong?"

Shawn yelled, "The house is on fire."

The driver of an eighteen-wheeler stopped his rig on the shoulder of the road and ran toward the pond. As he neared the house, he heard the glass shattering and helped Dani out of the window, and took Elizabeth, screaming in fear, from Shawn's arms.

Shawn climbed out of the window and his feet landed on the broken glass from the shattered window. The truck driver helped them to safety as the flames began to pour from the broken window. Shawn could hear the sound of sirens. Apparently, the neighbors had called the fire department.

The truck driver from Minnesota did everything he could to comfort them. Then, he ran back to his truck and brought a couple of fresh tee shirts from his travel bag to wash the soot from their faces and to wrap Shawn's bleeding feet.

Trucker

The truck asked, "Had everyone gotten out of the house safely?"

To which Dani replied, "Yes," and thanked him for saving their lives.

As the fire truck arrived, the driver met them and informed them that everybody was out of the house, but that they needed medical attention.

Shawn, Dani and Elizabeth were huddled together about one hundred feet from the western corner of the house. As several firemen manned the hoses, water was sprayed on the small house consumed by the flames.

Shawn's friend, The Donald, arrived and checked on Shawn and his family. Donald had taken an emergency paramedic course and he quickly realized Dani was going into shock. He administered oxygen to her, as Shawn held Elizabeth.

An ambulance arrived on the scene and the paramedics on board took over the medical care for Shawn and his family. Within minutes, the young family was on their way to the Macon hospital.

The truck driver walked back to his rig and continued on his way. This was all in a day's work for one of these unsung heroes!

Shawn held Dani's hand and held Elizabeth in his lap as the ambulance raced toward the hospital. As the ambulance arrived at the hospital, Shawn's parents followed them into the driveway. The 911 operators had notified them of the fire at their son's house. In a small town, everybody knew everybody.

As the rear door of the ambulance is opened, Shawn's mother and father were there to help. His parents are very concerned even though the 911 operators had told them they had not been seriously injured. When it's your kids, it's serious!

Shawn's mother took the baby from Shawn and his father helped Shawn walk to the waiting wheel chair, but Dani was brought in on a stretcher still receiving oxygen from a bottle beside her. Everyone's attention was on Dani. Even though she was conscious, she was slow to respond and her eyes looked like they were glazed over.

As the young family was rushed to the emergency room, a doctor and nurse cleaned and stitched up the cuts on Shawn's feet. He told them to check on Dani, but they said we need to stop the bleeding and that she had a medical team giving her treatment. Shawn's concern was for his wife and child.

After the baby was examined and found to be fine, the nurse let Mrs. McLeod take her to the waiting room. Shawn was worried about Dani, she looked so pale. A nurse brought Shawn a wheelchair. He wheeled himself to Dani's side, and held her hand! Shawn knew something wasn't right. He squeezed her hand and got no response. He asked the doctor, "What was wrong?"

Dr. Wayne informed him, "Dani's blood pressure was low."

Shawn had been asked by one of the paramedics in the ambulance, if she had any medical problems in her past. Shawn realized that he didn't know. Dani had said very little to him about her medical history.

Dr. Wayne's phone rang, and as he talked, the hospital intercom was paging Dr. Hughes. Dr. Hughes had been Dani's doctor when Elizabeth was born.

Dr. Wayne ended his call with "Thank you, that's what I figured." He asked Shawn, "Why didn't you tell me that Dani was pregnant?"

Shawn was speechless, as he gazed back at Dani and squeezed her hand. Shawn told the doctor he did not know Dani was pregnant.

Dr. Wayne could tell by the surprised look on Shawn's face that Dani had not told her husband that they were expecting another child.

Dani tried to raise her head and pull the oxygen mask from her face. With a strained voice she told Shawn that she was waiting for the right moment to tell him the news. Shawn told her, it's all right. He leaned over the side of the bed rail and kissed Dani's face.

Dr. Wayne asked Shawn to wait outside while they examine Dani. A nurse pushed Shawn's wheel chair out of the emergency room and down the hall to the waiting room.

When Shawn arrived at the waiting room, Elizabeth reached for her daddy, as he held the baby close.

Mrs. McLeod told him, "I had taken Dani to see Dr. Hughes a couple of weeks ago." Shawn questioned his mom, "Why wasn't I informed earlier?"

Mrs. McLeod looked down at the floor and said, "Dani wanted to wait a few days. She was hoping the situation would improve, but instead it got worse when the plant burned and then the letter from the gas company came in the mail. It just didn't seem like the right time to break this kind of news to you. Mr. McLeod asked about Dani's condition since the doctors had not informed them of her status as yet.

Shawn said, "Dani's blood pressure is low."

Shawn's father asked, "What happened? How did the fire start?"

To which Shawn replied, "I'm not sure, dad. We were asleep, and suddenly I was on the floor and Dani was on top of me. It was complete darkness."

Shawn paused just for a second as he relived the horrible ordeal. "Obviously, there must have been an explosion!" said Shawn.

He surmised that it must have been the stove.

Shawn's mom was so grateful that they all got out of the house alive.

Mr. McLeod replied, "Thank God for looking after you and your family."

Elizabeth fell asleep in Shawn's arms as the early morning sun shone through the windows of the hospital waiting room. While Elizabeth slept, the waiting room became very quiet, except for the hospital paging system, which never seemed to quit!

A couple of hours passed before Dr. Wayne and Dr. Hughes entered the room. You could tell by the look on their faces that they had bad news. Dr. Hughes told the family that Dani is fine, but she had a miscarriage. Dr. Wayne sadly shook his head and told them that they did everything they could to save the baby and told Shawn how sorry he was. Dr. Hughes informed them that Dani would have to stay a~~ couple of days~~ in the hospital; she needed a lot of rest and love.

To which Shawn replied, "She was going to get plenty of both!"

Shawn's heart was broken by the loss of the baby. He felt as though he had brought his problems home and unnecessarily worried Dani.

Shawn asked the doctors, if he could see Dani and the doctors agreed, but for only a short while since she had been given a sedative and needed the rest. Shawn gently handed the sleeping Elizabeth to his mom. His father wheeled him to the room where Dani was resting comfortably. While balancing on one foot, he stood by Dani's bed, leaned over and kissed her face and whispered, "I love you!"

Dani's only reaction was to gently squeeze his hand. Apparently, the sedative was taking effect.

As the I-V in her right arm gave her the medication and fluids she needed, Shawn thought, "If only I had replaced that old stove, none of this would have happened." He mumbled, "I will never forgive myself for letting this happen."

Shawn was still wearing his pajamas and with his feet in bandages, refusing to leave Dani's side. Shawn's parents took Elizabeth with them to their home, so they could get some clothes for Shawn and to relieve Mrs. Perkins. They had called Mrs. Perkins in the middle of the night to come and stay with Shawn's little sisters, when they rushed to the hospital.

Several days went by before Shawn brought Dani to his parent's house. Shawn and his little family would stay in his old bedroom until he could get a job and find a new place of their own.

The next day they drove back to their former home. The home had been completely destroyed. Only ashes, a foundation and charred remnants of the appliances remained. They left the baby in her child seat, as they exited the Chevy pickup to view the remains of what had been their first home.

As they stood there and stared at what was once their home, a Ford Crown Victoria pulled up behind them. It was Sheriff Giles. He removed his hat and told them he was sorry about their loss. The two of them thanked the Sheriff for his thoughtfulness.

Shawn ~~related to~~ told the Sheriff about the explosion. "There was a violent jolt and then total darkness. It happened so fast, I just didn't know what was going on," said Shawn.

"I hate to bother you, but the State Fire Marshal wants to interview you before they complete their investigation, so when you feel up to it, just let me know," said the Sheriff.

"Why is the Fire Marshal investigating this?" asked Shawn.

The Sheriff stated, "Any fire that resulted from an explosion must be investigated by the Fire Marshal's office."

Shawn thought that the old stove was the culprit and told the Sheriff that the stove had been giving them trouble.

Sheriff Giles once again told Shawn, "Give me a call, when you are up to it and I will set up a meeting with the Fire Marshal."

Shawn looked back at the remains of their home and remarked, "It took over a year to fix the old house up, but in only a few short minutes, it was gone."

Dani told Shawn at least one good thing came out of it, "We don't have to worry about moving."

Sheriff Giles then asked them, "Was it true that the gas line company had told them that the house had to be moved?"

They told the Sheriff, "It was true."

They had received a letter from the company a few weeks ago demanding that they move the house, because it was too close to an intrastate pipeline.

Sheriff Giles said, "The talk was, that it was a strange coincidence that Shawn's place of employment and his home both exploded in the middle of the night, within a few weeks of each other."

"Sheriff, do you honestly think I had anything to do with either fire?" asked Shawn.

The Sheriff shook his head and told him, "No, I don't."

Dani looked completely shocked at the implied accusations and said, "I can't imagine any one being so cruel as to accuse us. One fire took our income and the other our home and our baby!"

Dani began to sob.

Sheriff Giles apologized for upsetting her.

Shawn thanked him for believing him.

Sheriff Giles reminded him once again to speak with the Fire Marshal as soon as possible.

Shawn asked the Sheriff to contact the Fire Marshal right away and tell him, "I will meet with him anytime he wished."

The young couple left behind the ruins of what was once their happy home.

As they pulled out of the driveway heading east toward town, Shawn wanted to talk with the banker who financed their home. Mr. Anderson welcomed them into his office and expressed his condolences on their loss.

Mr. Anderson asked, "Have you contacted the insurance company yet?"

Shawn said, "No."

Mr. Anderson told them, "It was time to start the paper work on their settlement." Shawn asked Mr. Anderson for his help in filing the papers.

Mr. Anderson asked them about their insurance policy.

Shawn said, "It was lost in the fire."

Mr. Anderson said, "I think I might have a copy of the policy with your loan papers."

Mr. Anderson walked over to a file cabinet to look for the papers.

As Mr. Anderson read the policy, he informed them, "You had only enough insurance to cover the loan and the twenty thousand dollars you put down was gone. At least, you still have your land, and it will be paid for. I could make you a new loan to rebuild and the land should cover the down payment."

Shawn then explained to Mr. Anderson about the pipeline easement, and reminded him that he has also lost his job at Barton Manufacturing.

Mr. Anderson put his hands together in a ball and said, "I forgot you had lost your job."

As Mr. Anderson is thinking, Shawn and Dani look at each other.

Finally, Mr. Anderson said, "It's been a bad month for the McLeod family, hasn't it?"

Shawn is looking at floor and thinking that he is now unemployed and homeless.

Dani leaned over and whispered to Shawn, "We're not completely homeless;

we still have our mountain cabin."

Shawn smiled and replied, "You're right, we still have our mountain home."

This got Mr. Anderson's attention and he said, "My son loved that place. Would you consider selling the cabin and land?"

Dani looked at Shawn and then at Mr. Anderson and said, "No sir. It belonged to my grandfather and I plan to keep it."

Mr. Anderson arose from his desk and started to walk away to make copies of the security deed, insurance policy and closing statement for them and call the insurance company.

Shawn looked at Dani and said, "I had forgotten about the cabin," and laughed as he remarked, "We might become hillbillies."

When Mr. Anderson returned to his office with the copies of the papers, they thanked him for his help and left.

As Shawn opened the door to the pickup for Dani, an angry looking old lady driving by in a large black car shouted out the window, "You should be in jail, you damn arsonist!"

Shawn froze in his tracks. He couldn't believe what the woman had said; he felt his heart miss a few beats! As he turned toward her, the angry old lady just drove away still cursing and hollering.

Dani was placing the baby in her car seat and rushed to Shawn's side and gave him a hug telling him not to pay any attention to that old big mouth.

Shawn said, "I've lived here all my life and I've never given anyone any reason to believe I would do anything so awful."

Dani told him, "The only reason that old lady was driving, was, because she lost her broom!"

Not a word was spoken, as the young couple drove back to Shawn's parent's home. Shawn's folks were at work and his sisters were in school. Shawn just sat in his dad's big recliner and looked into space, as Elizabeth played on the floor.

Dani fixed a big cup of hot chocolate for Shawn. She sat down in his lap and said, "Don't let that old witch bother you. If I see her again, I'll slap her down and cut that wart off her nose."

Shawn exploded in laughter, as he envisioned what Dani had said. Dani had a way with words and Shawn surely needed something to cheer him up.

The next morning they met with the Fire Marshals at the Sheriff's office. The Marshals put Shawn's mind at ease. They explained the fire had apparently been caused by a leak. They had examined all of the gas-powered appliances, especially the stove, and ruled them out as the source of the explosion. One of the Marshals told them, if the stove had exploded, it would have been blown to bits!

The Marshals informed them that the fire would be ruled accidental. They explained that a forty-year-old house could have developed a crack in the piping.

The insurance company issued a check to pay off the mortgage at the bank. The balance would be used to pay off a few bills, with only a few hundred dollars left.

Over the next few days, several people shouted insults at Shawn. I guess the explosion and fire at his workplace and shortly thereafter at his house was too much of a coincidence for a few gossipers.

Chapter 7

Shawn had been looking for employment and was having no success. Everywhere he went, he was turned away.

They continued to live with Shawn's parents and his father tried to get him on at the feed mill where he worked, but had failed. One night as everyone else slept, Shawn quietly got up and walked through the house and out the front door and sat down on the red brick steps. The moon was peeking through a sporadic wall of clouds, as he looked across the front yard toward the white picket fence that bordered the driveway from the road. All he could think was what am I am going to do? I can't find a job. Apparently, the rumors had spread far and wide about the fire at the plant and at his home.

In his lowest moment of grief, He thought Dani and Elizabeth are so beautiful; Dani could marry a rich guy! As he sat there in the predawn hours on the front porch of his parent's home with his elbows on his knees and his face in his hands. How could all of this happen to me was the thought prancing through his mind. Just then he felt a soft hand wind its way inside of his, as he opened his eyes to see his loving wife on her knees beside him.

"Let's just leave here and start over in Mountaindale," said Dani in such a sweet soft voice. "No matter what happens, I will always love you."

This was exactly what Shawn needed.

Dani said, "We need a change of scenery and that old fashion log cabin with the stone fireplace would look pretty nice."

Shawn was jolted from his thoughts of despair and said to her, "Let's go!"

Shawn stood up and reached out to Dani and the young couple quietly made their way back into the house and made love in the peaceful darkness of Shawn's old bedroom.

As the morning sun rose in the east, Shawn's mom prepared a delicious country breakfast. Shawn woke from what had been only a short nap with Dani on her side pressed up against him and her head on his chest. He thought about how lucky he was to have such a kind, loving and beautiful wife, child and family. He thought his precious wife was right; it's time for the kid that always swore he would never leave his little hometown to pack up and go. He remembered all the times he and his father had fished and hunted on this very farm. His mind went back in time as he remembered jumping in the creek with his friends on hot days from a rope that hung from an old oak tree. He thought about how simple life had been for him. He had always said he would never leave, but the peaceful upbringing of his past had collided head-on with the reality of the present and he knew that his life would never be the same again.

As Shawn lay in his bed with Dani still sleeping, he saw little Elizabeth standing in her bed reaching for him. She wanted to join them. Shawn reached for her and helped her over the top rail of her crib and laid her ~~on the other side of his~~ chest. Little Elizabeth just eased off back to sleep.

About half an hour later, Dani awoke. She reached over and hugged Shawn and the baby.

Shawn whispered, "Did you mean what you said last night about going to the mountains?"

Dani responded, "As long as we are together, I don't care where we are!"

Shawn said, "Well, we don't have much to pack."

They laughed, as Elizabeth awoke. They made their way to the breakfast table where they were greeted by Shawn's parents. Shawn's sisters were sleeping late.

His mom and dad sensed something was about to happen. Maybe there's some kind of mental telepathy between people that love each other so much.

Shawn decided to wait until after breakfast to tell his parents about the decision to move, but Shawn's mom sensing something was wrong asked, "Is everything all right?"

Shawn winked at Dani and said, 'Ham, eggs, toast, grits and coffee, can't get much better than that!"

His mother reached over with her left hand and placed it on Shawn's right hand and gave him a mother's look of concern.

Shawn looked back at Dani, as if asking for support, and said, "We're moving to the mountains!"

His mother and father just sat there and stared at them in disbelief. "The mountains!" his parents exclaimed in unison.

Shawn said, "Yes, we have decided. After all the calamities here, maybe we could use a change of scenery!"

"The mountains!" Shawn's mother repeated.

Shawn turned to his mother and reminded them of the little cabin and a few acres of land Dani's grandfather left her only a few miles from her old home in Mountaindale.

Dani squeezed Shawn's hand to show her support and Shawn went on to say that he and Dani have decided to pack what few possessions they have left and become hillbillies!

Shawn's parents just sat there staring at him.

Shawn's little sisters came running into the dining room. Both came over and kissed little Elizabeth and sat down. It suddenly occurred to them that all four adults in the room were sitting around the table staring at each other.

Kristy and Misty sensed something was wrong. Kristy spoke first, 'What's going on?"

Shawn responded, "Nothing is wrong," as he tried to look normal while pouring syrup on his eggs.

"We're moving to Mountaindale," said Dani as she took the syrup bottle from Shawn.

"The mountains?" the twins said in unison.

Misty smiled and said; "Now I'll get my own bedroom back!"

The twins high-fived each other as the four adults looked shocked at their reaction.

Shawn explained that they could live in the cabin and try to find employment in north Georgia.

His father responded, "Son, eventually, the Barton Manufacturing plant will be rebuilt and you will get your old job back."

Shawn said, "Dani and I need a fresh start." and asked the two of them, "Please try to understand."

Shawn's mother rose from her chair after noticing Shawn's syrup filled plate and exchanged it for a new one. She reassured him that he had their love and support in whatever decision they made. Shawn's dad stared at Shawn's mom, as he nodded his head in agreement.

As the family began to eat their breakfast, the room was unusually quiet; only the twins were talking and playing with Elizabeth. The family, mostly nibbled at their food.

Finally the silence was broken by Shawn's mom as she asked, "Does that old cabin have electric power?"

Shawn told her, "Donald had the power turned on, so he could use it on the weekends."

After breakfast, Shawn and Dani boxed up what few clothes and possessions they had, and put them in the back of Shawn's Silverado. Shawn's mom gave them fresh sheets, pillowcases, towels, blankets, dishes, silverware and everything else she could think of.

About ten o'clock a.m., the little family was ready to take off, when Shawn's mom came to the door. She was carrying a homemade patchwork quilt. As she handed it to Shawn, she told him, "You will need something warm for those cool mountain nights."

His mother tried to smile, but you could tell she was sad.

Shawn's father told them, "If you need anything, just call us."

Kristy and Misty came down the stairs and gave him some pictures.

Misty said, "We brought you some pictures, so you won't forget us."

Shawn hugged his sisters and said, "I could never forget my little sisters."

Then, it was hugs and kisses all around, as the family prepared to say goodbye and begin their trip to the mountains. Even Rocket, the family's golden retriever, looked as if he knew this was an important event.

As they drove away, everybody was waving and calling out "goodbye."

As the red and white pickup disappeared down the road, Shawn's mother broke down and cried. Shawn's father held her in his arms and told her, "Don't cry. I don't think they will stay up there too long."

Shawn's mom cried, "Why, why, why did everything go wrong? I just don't understand."

Shawn's father said, "Honey, please don't cry. It's only a little over two hundred miles to Mountaindale. It's not like they are moving to Canada or something."

~~The twins are sad, too, and they hold on to mom and dad~~.

Then Mr. McLeod said, "Honey, are you going to cry when we finally get rid of these pesky twins?"

Suddenly they all start laughing, but Shawn's mom still felt the pain in her heart and soul for Shawn and his family.

Mr. McLeod said, "For all we know, they might come home next week."

As Shawn turned right onto Highway 80, he glanced back to see the big red barn. It's the only thing you can see from the highway of their family farm. Dani, realizing how hard this must be for Shawn, and kissed his face and told him she loved him.

Shawn could feel an extra ton of responsibility resting on his shoulders. They were starting the journey to the next chapter in their lives. An hour and half went by before they reached Athens, Georgia, home of the Bull Dawgs! Shawn was thinking after junior college, his mother had wanted him to attend the University of Georgia and now those plans were gone like the wind. He had a family to think about and these foolish thoughts about what might have been. were over.

The young family arrived at their destination around three o'clock that afternoon. As Shawn slowed to turn onto the dirt road leading to the cabin, he noticed several white wooden stakes with a red ribbon on top along the path. As the winding road curled back and forth, he saw more of the white stakes with red ribbons. As the young family reached the old log cabin, they saw that the front porch light was on, as if to welcome them.

Dani kept watch over Elizabeth while Shawn unloaded the pickup. There was barely enough level land around the cabin to park a car.

As Shawn continued unloading the boxes, he remembered seeing an equipment rental place just down the road and decided to rent a backhoe and level the ground around the cabin so little Elizabeth would have room to play.

After unloading the boxes, Shawn walked out the front door to take a good look at the scenery and saw another white stake just off the corner of the cabin. Shawn wondered what the stakes were for as he looked down the mountainside and realized they were in a straight row. The power companies have a clear path that runs up the side of the mountains. The power poles that carry electricity to the people ran right down the middle of the clear path and the white stakes he had noticed while driving along the winding road to the cabin were actually in a straight line and ran by the log cabin. He thought the power company must be going to install another set of power lines.

Meanwhile, Dani was happy the refrigerator still worked, but was a little apprehensive about lighting the old gas stove. Fortunately, Shawn's mom had given them an old microwave oven she could use until the old gas stove could be thoroughly checked out.

Dani was unpacking the boxes and Shawn took over the job of watching Elizabeth. Shawn's mom had given them a box of groceries including a canned ham. Dani opened the ham and put it in the microwave, as Elizabeth played and Shawn began to wonder what kind of jobs were available in the area.

As the afternoon sun dropped down behind the mountains, Shawn, Dani and Elizabeth enjoyed ham sandwiches while sitting on the front porch steps admiring the beautiful scenery. Afterwards, Dani busily paced back and forth putting things in their right place until the boxes were empty. Shawn had brought his old television from his room, but forgot the antenna. He figured he would get it on the next trip to see his parents. The precious few dollars they had would have to be spent very carefully.

The living conditions were primitive at best, compared to current standards. The cabin consisted of two large rooms, one served as a big living room, kitchen and dining room and the other had two big beds for sleeping. The only other room was a small half bath that had been added on later.

The water supply came from a holding tank that was filled by a mountain stream. The pressure wasn't very strong, but you didn't get a water bill each month. They would need to buy bottled water to drink and for cooking. An old antique bathtub sat in one corner of the bedroom. It was the only bathing facility. In cold weather, water would have to be heated in a kettle over the fireplace or in a pot on top of the gas stove. Shawn knew he needed to update the wiring and plumbing and he figured Dani's father could help. It was going to be tough, but they were young and had been raised in the country and weren't afraid of work.

The old cabin had pull chain lights and few receptacles. The cabin had only one exterior door that entered from the front and only four very small windows. You pay attention to these things after surviving a home fire. Some of the boards on the front porch were rotten and others warped and sagging. The two best things about the cabin were the big stone fireplace and no payments.

The next morning the sun rose like a fireball in front of the little cabin. The young family had ham and toast for breakfast. After breakfast, scrubbing and cleaning became the agenda of the day. Around noon the little family decided to celebrate a little and drove over to the Mountaindale Diner for a nice meal.

On the way back they stopped at a small country grocery store and bought milk, bread, coffee, eggs, bacon and bottled water. The mountainside hardware store was just a short distance from the road that led to the cabin. Shawn noticed they had a tractor-loader-backhoe with a big "For Rent" sign on it parked just inside the fenced yard.

The hardware store was closed on Sunday, but Shawn thought about renting that backhoe to level the property around the cabin. As they rode on by, the next thing Shawn noticed was an old U-Move-It F-700 Ford van body truck with a "For Sale" sign on it. Shawn had moved everything they owned in the back of his pickup. He certainly didn't need a big moving van.

All afternoon Dani cleaned and scrubbed and swept up the old cabin. Shawn nailed down the boards on the porch and replaced what he could. The tools he kept behind the seat of his pickup really came in handy.

Little Elizabeth played with her toys in the back of Shawn's truck; the bed of his pickup had become a playpen.

Dani called Shawn. She wanted him to build a fire in the fireplace so they could heat some water for the bathtub. Dani didn't want to use the gas stove until it was thoroughly checked out by the gas company. Shawn turned the water faucet on over the antique tub and partially filled it with water. After the water began to boil in the pot over the fireplace, he poured it in the tub. After everyone bathed, Shawn pulled the plug at the bottom of the tub to drain the water.

On Monday morning the family went job hunting. Dani introduced Shawn to every business owner she knew, but nobody was hiring.

Shawn was very disappointed by the end of the day. He had only applied for two jobs in his life and got both of them. Dani could see the discouragement in Shawn's eyes, so she put her arms around him, as they drove back to the little cabin.

All Shawn could think about was the few hundred dollars they had left that would only last a short time.

As they reached the road to the cabin, they had to wait for a big semi-truck hauling two large track-type trenching machines to come by before making the turn from the highway. Shawn noticed something familiar on the door of the big truck. The sign said, Harmony Gas Pipeline Company.

The next morning the family rode down the mountain to check on the backhoe that was for rent. The family arrived at the rental place and Shawn noticed the rundown condition of the building. It was old and rusty and the paint was peeling. Shawn and his family walked in the open front door.

"Good morning, young folks," said an older man as he lit his pipe.

"Good morning," said Shawn, as he reached the sales counter.

The man introduced himself as Doc Hamrick. His long gray beard and tired eyes showed signs of a hard life.

Shawn asked him about renting the backhoe.

Mr. Hamrick told Shawn he normally charged one hundred fifty dollars a day, if it comes back in one piece.

Dani asked, "Mr. Hamrick, are you a real doctor?"

He smiled and said, "No, I used to build docks around the Mountaindale Lake and that gave him the nickname, "Doc."

Shawn asked, "Mr. Hamrick, do you need any help?"

Mr. Hamrick said, "I could use some help with painting and fixing the sliding door that hangs up."

Shawn told him he would be happy to paint the building and do the repairs, if he would lend him his backhoe.

Mr. Hamrick asked them where they lived and Dani told him they have moved into the old cabin, number eight, on Hope Mountain, just up the road.

Mr. Hamrick took a drag off his pipe and asked if it is the cabin the Canadian family lived in years ago.

Dani smiled and told him that they were her grandparents.

Mr. Hamrick related to her that he and her grandfather were good friends.

Dani said, "That's great."

Mr. Hamrick said, "I still miss them."

Dani replied, "Thank you for remembering them."

Mr. Hamrick took a big puff from his pipe and said, "If you will paint this run down old building and do the other repairs, I'll let you use that backhoe for a whole week."

Shawn told him, "You have a deal," as he reached to shake hands with Mr. Hamrick.

Then Mr. Hamrick turned to face Dani and said, "I sure would like some stew. I was wondering, if your folks taught you how to cook."

Dani smiling said, "I'll cook you anything you want, just show me the way to the kitchen."

Shawn went straight to work scraping and cleaning the siding and Dani cooked while Mr. Hamrick entertained Elizabeth. Mr. Hamrick gave little Elizabeth some of the toys from the hardware store's shelves and the toy tractors and dump trucks fascinated her.

When Friday came, the Mountaindale hardware and rental store looked good as new again. As everyone stood admiring the new paint job, Mr. Hamrick handed Shawn the keys to the 580H Case backhoe. He told Shawn not to rush; he could use it for as long as he needed. In the course of a week Shawn, Dani and Elizabeth had found a new friend.

Dani followed Shawn, as he drove the big yellow backhoe up the road to the cabin, with all the flashing lights, it looked like a parade. Elizabeth was very excited and kicked her feet and hollered, as she watched her dad drive the big tractor. When they turned off the main road onto the simple dirt and gravel road leading to the cabin, they saw several men standing in the middle of the road, looking at a large piece of paper, but one of them motioned for Shawn to stop. The man had a big fuzzy red beard and was wearing a construction type hard hat. When Shawn was sure Dani was safely off the road, he stopped the large tractor and shut off the engine, so he could hear what the man had to say.

The man introduced himself as George Felton from the Harmony Gas Line Company. Shawn froze, and he couldn't say a thing. This man apparently worked for the same gas line company that sent them a letter telling them they would have to move their home back in Russellville.

The man asked, "Do you live in the cabin at the top of the ridge?" and pointed to their home.

Shawn said, "Yes."

He told Shawn, "The gas company is running a natural gas line right by the cabin."

Shawn just sat there and looked at the man. your

Mr. Felton said, "We should be coming by their cabin by Monday afternoon or Tuesday morning."

Shawn hit the start button and the backhoe surged forward full throttle. He motioned for Dani to follow, as he sped away from his encounter with the pipeline crew. Shawn was determined, pipeline or no pipeline, to level an area around the cabin.

As the winding road finally reached their cabin, ~~he parked the six-ton tractor near the side of the cabin a~~nd *he* started digging ~~into the wall of the mountain that ran around the cabin~~. He soon realized he was digging more rock than dirt and figured he would eventually need to dig a hole to bury the rocks. Shawn was glad he had grown up on a farm and had acquired skills like operating tractors.

As Shawn worked, Dani and the baby watched. Elizabeth seemed to be fascinated by the big yellow tractor. As Shawn dug at the wall of the mountain behind the cabin, he remembered that Mr. Hamrick had said the trail that ran by the old cabin was over one hundred years old. Mr. Hamrick also said that the trail had been used as a path the old stagecoach line used over a century before.

As darkness began to fall, he realized it would be a good time to dig a hole and bury the rocks. Then it occurred to him, to bury them along the path of the white markers. Maybe it was time for a little revenge against the Harmony Pipeline Company.

A light rain began to fall, as he dug the hole for the rocks. He couldn't wait to see the gas line crew hit his little surprise.

The gentle rain that continued to fall helped to settle the dust. Operating the backhoe had been a relaxing escape from his troubles and he had enjoyed it. He stopped to reposition the backhoe, and he noticed a bunch of what he thought was broken glass and something black like rotten wood. He was apparently uncovering something someone else had buried many years before. The rain was beginning to wet his legs and feet, so he decided to call it a day.

He then turned the engine *off* and ~~switched~~ the lights off, before climbing down from the backhoe, and walked toward the cabin.

It had been a long day. The gentle rain falling on the little cabin's tin roof helped the little family to drift off to sleep.

Chapter 8

Early Sunday morning, Dani woke up first and decided to make a pot of coffee. As Dani poured a cup, she decided to look at the hole Shawn had dug the night before. As she moved closer to get a better look, she saw bright yellow sparkling something scattered around the hole and the glittering of broken glass Shawn had told her about the night before. She got down on her knees to get a better look. She dropped her coffee cup, as she leaned over to pick up a diamond studded gold bracelet.

She thought, "Could this be real?"

Then she saw gold coins and what appeared to be diamonds. She tried to wipe some of the dirt off of them with her housecoat to see, if they were real. After cleaning another coin she saw the date '1852'. Then she became excited, as she wildly clawed at the objects still partially buried in the hole. It was full of gold coins, rings, bracelets, and diamonds. Apparently, the broken glass Shawn had seen the night before was actually diamonds. She held some in her hands and moved them around to see the unmistakable glitter of diamonds.

Dani was in shock. All she could do was gaze at the beautiful gold and diamonds as the early morning sun reflected off of them. She grabbed two hands full of the diamonds and coins and then walked toward the cabin. The only thing she could say was "my, my, my!" She slowly made one-step at a time and then across the old wooden porch to the front door, she walked in a dazed condition.

She was thinking, "Is this real or am I dreaming?"

She managed to push the heavy wooden door open with her foot and then walked across the room toward the bedroom. As she entered the bedroom she said, "my, my, my!"

Shawn and little Elizabeth were still sleeping soundly, as Dani walked up to them with her hands full of treasure. Dani took her knee and bumped the bed several times. Shawn finally woke up and opened one eye just a little.

Dani whispered, "Shawn, are you awake?"

Shawn's eyelid fell shut and he mumbled, "No."

Dani whispered a little louder, "Shawn, honey, I need to show you something!"

Shawn's eyes are still shut tight as he mumbled, "Can it wait till spring!"

Dani was still trying to wake Shawn up without waking little Elizabeth. Dani leaned over and kissed Shawn's face and whispered in his ear, "Honey, if you don't want any of these gold coins or diamonds, I'll just keep them for myself!"

Then she turned and walked out of the bedroom and waited.

Suddenly, she heard Shawn's footsteps as he raced toward the living room.

Shawn asked, "What did you say?"

Shawn only had one eye half open and was standing on one foot as he tried to focus on Dani.

Dani laid the gold coins, diamonds, and jewelry on the round oak table and said, "Unless this is fake, our financial problems are over!"

Shawn, still trying to focus, grabbed one of the gold coins and examined it. They were still covered in dirt, so he raced over to the water bucket on a counter top used to wash dishes and scrubbed it clean with a dish cloth. Shawn couldn't believe his eyes, as he ran back across the floor to get more coins from the table. Then Shawn yelled, "Where did you find these?"

Dani said, "That hole you dug is full of them and lots of these!" as she spoke she showed him a hand full of diamonds, some loose, and some mounted to bracelets and rings.

Shawn, who has by now managed to open both eyes wide open yelled, "The hole I dug in the yard?"

Dani replied, "Yes, that's the one!"

Shawn ran out the front door, then stopped suddenly, and turned around and said, "Please slap me!"

Dani stood there looking at him and said, "Why do you want me to slap you?"

Shawn yelled, "So I'll know, I'm not dreaming!"

Dani gently slapped Shawn and said, "Like this?"

Shawn said, "Yes, thank you!" and then he ran out the front door, across the porch and jumped in the hole! Shawn's facial expression is one of extreme shock as he grabbed hand full after hand full of gold coins and diamond jewelry.

Dani yelled, "Are you sure it's real?" and she joined him in the hole.

Shawn started digging by hand at the bottom of the hole and yelled, "Diamonds, gold jewelry, gold coins, silver bracelets, and look, even gold bars. How did it get here?"

Dani yelled, "Who cares!"

Shawn yelled, "We're rich, rich, rich, rich!"

The young couple started clawing at the dirt to recover even more valuables. A lot of black rotten wood and rusty tin was mixed with the bounty.

Dani yelled, "Who would have buried such a valuable treasure?"

Shawn replied, "Maybe your grandparents didn't trust banks!"

Dani kept rubbing the dirt off of the coins and yelled, "The coins are all dated before the 1860's."

It quickly became apparent to the young couple that their lives would be in for a big change.

Shawn said, "I thought your grandparents were just average working people. You never told me they were rich!"

Dani responded, "They were poor, I'm sure this didn't belong to them."

Shawn replied, "So they worked and toiled to survive and had millions of dollars worth of treasure buried 12 feet from their front door!"

Dani yelled, "I guess so, unless they were saving for a rainy day."

Shawn and Dani continued to remove handful after handful of valuables from the bottom of the hole.

Shawn yelled, "We need a box or something!"

Dani yelled, "The trash can on the porch would be perfect!"

Shawn jumped from the hole, grabbed the trashcan and poured the contents out on the ground. Dani started throwing the bounty up on the bank of the hole and Shawn put it in the big green trashcan. An hour went by, as the young couple filled the trash can with the treasure from the hole.

Shawn asked, "If your grandparents didn't put this here, then who did?"

Dani said, "I have no idea, but I'm glad they did!"

Shawn stopped for a second and said, "So all of the coins are dated before 1860?"

Dani stopped and said, "It must have been before the Civil War!"

"That's it!" yelled Shawn.

"That's what?" asked Dani

"This must be the lost Confederate gold shipment!" said Shawn.

Dani said, "It's not just gold, there is diamonds, jewelry, silver, rubies of all varieties."

Shawn said, "I know, I know. You see, the southerners were desperate for more guns, supplies and ammunition and appealed to the people to collect any and all valuables including gold coin, gold bars and even jewelry to be used to buy the supplies and ammunition for our soldiers."

Dani said, "Well, I guess that would answer why all of the coins were minted before 1860!"

Shawn said, "They formed a mule drawn wagon train to ship the treasure through the mountains to a ship on the coast!"

Dani said, "Hey, you're right, I remember studying about that in history class."

Shawn explained, "When the Union soldiers ambushed the wagon train, all they found were rocks!"

Dani said, "Apparently, the Confederate soldiers realized they were being followed by the Union soldiers and buried the gold and treasure along this path through the mountains!"

Shawn said, "Now that we have it, is it ours?"

Dani froze for a minute and then said, "I'm not sure, the government could take it from us!"

Shawn said, "We could just hide this stuff and sell a little here and there and live very happily ever after!"

"We will have to keep this a secret until we figure out what to do!" said Dani

Just then they heard crying from the house. Little Elizabeth had woken and was letting them know regardless of how rich they were, she was still boss!

Shawn laughed and said, "The secret's out!"

Dani climbed from the hole and went to take care of little Elizabeth, while Shawn continued to fill the trashcan with valuables.

In a few minutes Dani yelled, from the porch, "I need to get dressed and so do you, big guy!"

Shawn had been so excited he just jumped in the hole wearing a pair of briefs and an Atlanta Falcons tee shirt. He decided Dani was right, so he climbed out of the hole and put on a pair of jeans and his boots.

Dani asked, "Are you hungry?"

Shawn replied, "No, I'm too excited!"

After taking care of little Elizabeth's needs, Dani rejoined the treasure hunt. Shawn said, "I still don't believe it!"

Dani responded, "Do you want me to slap you again?"

Shawn replied, "No, no that's o.k.!"

Dani asked, "How much do you think this is worth?"

Shawn froze in his tracks and yelled, "The pipeline!"

Dani stopped suddenly and looked at Shawn and yelled, "Oh no!"

Shawn yelled, "I forgot that pipeline crew will be here tomorrow evening!

"Or Tuesday morning!" said Dani.

Shawn said, "Can they take this from us?"

Dani replied, "I'm not sure!"

The young couple just stood there looking at each other for a few seconds.

Then Dani said, "It's still our land. I remember my mom telling me that even though the power company had an easement to run the power lines through our land, the land still belongs to us!"

Shawn just stood there like a totem pole looking at Dani.

Dani said, "Oh no, if they find even a few pieces of this stuff, they will figure it out!"

Shawn replied, "You're right, we've got to remove every bit of it before they get here!"

Dani asked, "Can the government take it?"

As the two talked, they busily loaded more and more of the treasure into the big green plastic trashcan.

"The government." This isn't government land!" shouted Shawn.

Dani said, "If this treasure is the lost Confederate gold shipment, the government might confiscate it!"

The couple stopped frozen in their tracks and just looked at each other.

Then Shawn said, "You're right. The government would take candy from a baby and they could take it from us!"

Dani asked, "Which government, the state or federal government?"

Shawn replied, "Probably both of them!"

Dani asked, "What are we going to do?"

Shawn replied, "I'm not sure!"

The couple's demeanor changed dramatically as they stared into each other's eyes.

Finally Dani spoke, "If they take it, will we get a finder's fee or reward?"

Shawn just shook his head and said, "Probably not, maybe a plaque, or ribbon."

Dani looked shocked as she said, "So, all of this could just be confiscated by the government!"

The young couple stopped and reached out to each other and embraced in a big hug. For just a moment the young couple just held each other in silence.

Then a smirk came over Shawn's face. He said, "Not, if they don't find it!"

Dani looked up at Shawn and asked, "What do you mean? The pipeline crew will be here in a day or two and they will figure out what happened?"

Then Shawn asked, "How far across the Canadian border do your relatives live?"

Dani just stared at Shawn for a moment and then said, "You mean we could load up all of this beautiful stuff and take off to Canada, just like we were going on a vacation!"

Shawn said, "You said you would like to go see them, didn't you?"

Dani smiled and said, "Yes, yes I did say that!"

"If we can get it to Canada, all of this beautiful stuff will be ours!" said Shawn, as his face lit up with excitement.

Dani stared at Shawn in disbelief and said, "You could be right, neither the state of Georgia, nor the Federal government has any authority in Canada!"

The young couple just continued to stare at each other.

After a moment Dani said, "But we don't have enough money to go to Canada!"

Shawn smiled and said, "So, we could pawn a few discreet items along the way at pawn shops!"

"Are you serious?" asked Dani.

Shawn responded, "I lost my job, we lost our home, and the money your father gave us to pay down on it and now we can't find a job and we live in this dump. Yes, I'm serious!"

"But if we go, we may never be able to come back!" said Dani, with a serious look on her face.

"We can have anything we want. We could live in Canada and be rich!" said Shawn, as he held Dani close to him.

Dani had her doubts as she said, "But what about my dad and your family?"

Shawn smiled and said, "They can come and visit as often as they like!"

As Dani gazed back at the valuables in the trashcan she said, "It's a heck of an idea."

Shawn said, "It's simple. We can stay here and starve or go to Canada and be rich!"

"Elizabeth could have anything she wants," said Dani with a big smile.

The magnitude of the moment had not completely registered in the heart and minds of the young couple.

They went to work and by noon the big green trashcan was so full they couldn't lift it, so they dragged it to the porch. As the sun set in the west and the shadows reached down through the mountains Shawn and Dani had filled and dumped the trash can several times. One corner of the main room was filled about four feet high. Shawn fired up the backhoe again to uncover more of the buried treasure. He uncovered dozens of gold bars. There was so much gold at the bottom of the hole you couldn't count it all. Shawn and Dani realized it would be hard to remove all of the gold before the line crew arrived for work the next morning. Shawn turned the backhoe around and loaded the gold bars in the front bucket. The more he loaded, the more he found. Shawn thought there must be hundreds of them. How were they going to transport so much gold all the way to Canada? He knew his Chevy pickup couldn't carry such a heavy load.

Shawn told Dani, "We are going to need a bigger truck!"

Dani asked, "Can we rent one?"

Shawn shook his head and said, "No, we don't have a credit card and besides if we rent a truck, we would have to return it, so no one would know where we took the gold, or be arrested for stealing the truck!"

Dani said, "I know. Do you remember seeing that old moving van for sale just down the road from Mr. Hamrick's place?"

Shawn's face lit up as he said, "Hey, you're right, that should do it, but what do we use for money?"

"It's old and rusty looking, how much could it be?" asked Dani.

Shawn looked doubtful as he said, "I don't know, but we have less than $800.00 and the gas for the trip to Canada would be more than that."

Dani said, "The sign said 'for sale or trade;' maybe we could 'trade' him something."

Shawn replied, "I can't think of anything we own that would be valuable enough to trade for a truck."

Dani said, "Let's go talk to the owner, maybe he will finance part of the money."

Shawn once again gave his doubtful look as he said, "I don't think he would, but it's worth a try."

Upon arrival at the location of the old moving van, Shawn got out and looked it over. It was probably over 20 years old, but it still looked pretty solid. It reminded Shawn of his father's old farm truck. As the McLeod's examined the old moving van, an older man wearing blue jean overalls and a checkered shirt arrived in a small cloud of dust. He was driving an old golf cart with bulldog stickers on the sides.

The man said, "Howdy folks, you interested in a good used moving van?"

Shawn said, "We need to do some moving, but we don't have a lot of money."

"Don't need much," the man said.

Shawn said, "How much?"

The older man scratched his beard and sad, "Thirty five hundred dollars cash would take it home."

"Would you be willing to finance it?" asked Dani, as she got out of the pickup holding little Elizabeth.

The older man took a cigar out of his pocket and said, "No ma'm, I don't finance and my bank don't sell trucks."

Dani said, "The sign said, sell or trade."

The man smiled and said, "Thompson's my name, and trading is my game."

Dani said, "We have a very nice Silverado here, Mr. Thompson."

Shawn exclaimed, "Oh no! Not my Silverado, I couldn't live without it!"

Mr. Thompson said, "Well, that's a shame. I could use a nice pick up."

Dani said, "It's a deal, Mr. Thompson!"

Shawn pulled Dani close to him and said, "My Silverado for that piece of junk, are you crazy!"

Dani pulled Shawn even closer and whispered, "When we get where we are going, we can buy a hundred Silverado's, new ones!"

Mr. Thompson spoke, "This truck is not junk, young man, it runs like a new one, paints faded, but it runs great!"

"I'm sure with a nice coat of "gold" paint it would look new again!" said Dani.

Shawn felt a little faint as he thought about trading his nice clean beautiful red and white Silverado for an old faded moving van. But even he realized, it was the answer to their problem. Shawn just couldn't say the words, so Dani gave him a hug and said, "It's a deal!"

Mr. Thompson said, "Great, I'll just run back to the house and get my title."

Mr. Thompson jumped on his old golf cart and spun the wheels as he made a sharp U-turn toward his home.

As Mr. Thompson raced away on his golf cart, Dani did her best to comfort Shawn.

"It's exactly what we need," said Dani, as she gave Shawn another hug.

"I must have carried five million tons of groceries to people's cars to pay for my beautiful Silverado!" said Shawn.

He couldn't believe he had just agreed to trade it for what looked more like a rolling signboard. The faded red and white paint and the U-Move-It logo on the doors, made the old truck look like a refugee from the depression.

In a few minutes Mr. Thompson returned, with another round of dust and said, "Please forgive my rudeness, I'm Raymond Thompson."

Mr. Thompson reached out and shook hands with Shawn and then with Dani.

Shawn is still speechless, so Dani said, "We're the McLeod's. I'm Dani and this is Elizabeth, and this handsome guy here is Shawn, my wonderful husband!"

At this moment Shawn couldn't smile without showing his clinched teeth like an angered bulldog!

Mr. Thompson said, "Cheer up, young man, this old truck may not be pretty, but it runs like new!"

Shawn finally squeaks out, "Yea, I'm the lucky one!"

Finally Shawn shuffled over to his pickup, opened the console and removed the title. He then turned and looked at Dani and Elizabeth; nothing had hurt him more since he lost his Captain Mercury decoder ring when he was six years old!

Dani flashed her eyes and whispered, "I love you!"

Then Dani handed Shawn an ink pen she had picked up from Mr. Thompson's paper work, now laying on the hood of the poor ill-fated Chevy truck. No living breathing man on earth looked as pale as Shawn did as he scribbled a twisted version of Shawn Patrick McLeod where it said 'seller' on the back of the title.

There is a bond between a country boy and his pickup truck that challenges every known force on earth. ~~Shawn had a lump in his throat the size of Stone Mountain, as he handed Mr. Thompson the title.~~ ~~It would take five gallons of testosterone to help him get over this one event without crying like a sissy~~! He had bought his Chevy pickup from his pal, the Donald's father. It was only three years old and still like new when he drove it home. To trade it off for a mangy old moving van was almost more that he could stand, but he knew they needed the truck for the trip to Canada.

After removing little Elizabeth's child safety seat and all of their personal items from the Chevy pickup, the young family said goodbye to Mr. Thompson and climbed into the cab of the old Ford F-700 truck. Shawn turned the ignition key to start and the big Ford V-8 engine roared to life. Shawn thought Mr. Thompson was right; the truck might be old, but the engine sounded like new. Shawn shifted the truck's five speed manual transmission into first gear, released the parking brake and the truck surged forward as he released the clutch pedal. ~~The truck was strong, tight and powerful, but it wasn't a Silverado. As the big Ford rolled forward toward the highway, Shawn looked out the side window to check the large mirrors to make sure they were properly positioned.~~

As Shawn looked in the truck's large rear view side mirror, he took his last look at his beloved Silverado, as he turned right toward the cabin. The trip back to the cabin was short, but busy. Shawn checks the truck's gauges, the oil pressure was excellent, over 60 lbs., and the fuel gauge showed full, a definite bonus. The truck had power steering, power brakes, air conditioning and an am-fm radio, but the interior was as plain as a rock.

He thought about the thousands of people that had rented this very truck to transport their only possessions cross-country to follow their dream of a better life. He hoped this journey would turn out good.

The young couple planned every detail concerning how they would load the truck. Dani wanted to bring the old antique bathtub, if they had room. From the moment they arrived at the cabin, the young couple went to work loading gold bars into ~~the backhoe's~~ front bucket and then ~~Shawn would back up from the hole and park behind the van truck's back door and stack the bars in the front of~~ the trucks van body next to the cab. Dani took time to bathe little Elizabeth and put her to bed. The child was tired and went to sleep quickly.

All night long the young couple loaded gold bars, coins, and hundreds of pieces of jewelry into the trucks van body. As the early morning sunlight began to glimmer over the mountain ridge, the job was nearing completion. Shawn used the backhoe front bucket to pile dirt and rocks back into the hole, ~~and then packed it tight by driving the large tractor back and forth over the hol~~e. He tried to think of something that might slow the pipeline crew's progress in order to give them more time to reach Canada. Shawn saw a one-gallon plastic jug of water sitting on the front porch. He grabbed the gallon of water, then jumped back on the backhoe and drove down the winding mountain road ~~to the highway. He parked the backhoe and walked down the hill about a hundred yar~~ds till he found the machine. Shawn quickly ~~removed the diesel fuel tank cap and~~ poured the gallon of water into the water tank. Shawn imagined that the machine would run fine for a few minutes, until the fuel injection pump picked up the water, and then it would shut off, dead in its tracks. He was hoping when it failed the crew would take the day off while a mechanic was called to find the problem ~~with the trencher machine. Shawn realized when the crew got to the hole they might find more gold bars and treasure, but it would take a couple of days.~~

~~They thoroughly checked the ground to be sure they hadn't left anything for the crew to find. He figured that every day they had,~~ before the pipeline crew found the treasure, ~~would put them that much closer to Canad~~a. When he returned to the cabin, Dani had begun to fill the cab and van body of the truck with everything she could manage to carry. Shawn quickly joined in and completed the job, including loading the antique bathtub.

They realized they needed to leave before the pipeline crew arrived, so they would not see them driving the big red and white moving van. Shawn looked at his ~~Georgia~~ road map and figured the best route would be to follow Highway 52 all the way to Dalton and then get on I-75 going north toward Chattanooga, TN. He could then stop for fuel at a truck stop and buy a road atlas to plan the trip to Canada.

As little Elizabeth continued to sleep, Shawn and Dani packed up the few remaining personal items from the cabin. Shawn realized he had a dilemma; he had to return the backhoe to Mr. Hamrick before they took off on their journey.

~~When he borrowed the backhoe~~ from Mr. Hamrick, ~~Dani followed him driving the Chevrolet pickup, but could she drive the big Ford van with its manual transmission? He knew it would take a couple of hours to drive the backhoe back to Mr. Hamrick and then walk back to the cabin. By then the pipeline crew would be at work and see them driving the van.~~

Shawn asked, "Dani, can you drive the Ford truck to Mr. Hamrick's."

She said, "No, but I could drive the backhoe, if you show me, what made it go and stop."

Dani was truly a tomboy; she had driven her father's farm tractor which operated very similar to the backhoe.

So Shawn showed Dani how to operate the forward-reverse lever, and of course, where the brake pedals were. He started the backhoe engine and let her operate the big machine moving forward and backwards steering and stopping to be sure she could handle the big machine. Shawn explained that he would lead the way down the mountain in the big truck and let her follow close behind on the backhoe operating in the lowest gear, but when they reached the highway, he would stop and help her shift the tractor into a faster gear for the short trip on the highway to Mr. Hamrick's hardware store.

Finally, they were ready to go, so Dani picked up little Elizabeth and gently carried her to Shawn who put her on the seat beside him in the Ford van. Then Shawn drove slowly down the winding mountain road with Dani driving the big yellow backhoe and stopped at the highway below. He then changed the slow gear in the backhoe to a faster road gear and turned on all of the tractor's lights and flashers. Then Shawn followed the backhoe, to be sure no one could run into the backhoe from the rear. In just a few minutes they arrived at Mr. Hamrick's hardware store. They pulled off of the road, parked the backhoe next to the front door and left a thank-you note and the keys in a drop box by the door. They didn't want anyone to see them in the Ford moving van, so Dani gently picked up little Elizabeth and held her in her lap as they turned west on to Georgia Highway #52 and the journey began.

Chapter 9

The sun was creeping up as it neared 7 a.m. The pipeline crew would be arriving soon and Shawn, Dani, and little Elizabeth were on their way!

"Canada or Burst!" Shawn said, as he ran through the gears in the old Ford truck. The young family who had endured so much hardship was now on the way to a new start. Dani closed her eyes and prayed for a safe trip. Just before 9 a.m. they arrived in Dalton, Georgia. Dani, who had been sleeping for about the last hour, was now awake and wondering where they were. Shawn had been navigating along the beautiful, but somewhat treacherous mountain roads with the early morning sun reflecting off the side mirrors in his tired red eyes. As the old Ford truck rolled into Dalton, the thought of food entered Shawn's mind.

They stopped at one of those hamburger joints that sell burgers about the size of a postage stamp and have the best breakfast for the least money. ~~Shawn decided to park on the far side of the parking lot, so he could keep an eye on the rear doors of the old moving van.~~

They enjoyed a delicious breakfast and had two cups of coffee trying to stay awake. They were very sleepy after being up all night loading the truck. Dani took Elizabeth to the rest room and Shawn asked some of the patrons where the next truck stop was traveling north. He was told that a truck stop would only be a few miles up the road at the next exit. When they exited the little restaurant they couldn't believe their eyes. An armored car had parked right beside their old Ford moving van.

Dani waved at the two occupants and yelled, "Want to Trade?" while pointing to the old red and white Ford van.

The iron-faced occupants of the armored car just shook their heads back and forth indicating, no.

~~As Shawn helped Dani up the steps of the Ford truck and handed Elizabeth to her~~, they were snickering about the fact that the contents of their old Ford was probably worth 100 times the value of the armored car and its contents. ~~As Shawn got in on the driver's side he said, "I wonder what they would say, if they knew this old truck contained tons of gold bars and coins, plus two trash cans full of diamonds and jewelry?"~~

Dani laughed and said. "Well, we offered to trade!"

Shawn and Dani were still laughing as they drove away.

As the fuel gauge worked its way toward empty, the truck stop appeared over the horizon. Shawn filled the gas tank with nearly 36 gallons costing over $120.00; the oil companies were on a rampage as fuel prices soared. Shawn walked inside and paid for the gas and bought a road atlas and a padlock for the rear door of the van.

~~When he returned to the truck, he and Dani set a course for a little town in~~

Manitoba, just across the border from the Minnesota State line. They decided to go to Nashville, TN and then stop and decide which way to go from there. Then Shawn decided to check the air pressure in the old truck's tires, because the ones on the back looked like the air pressure was low. The air pressure was apparently all right; the heavy load just made them look like they were under inflated.

As Shawn pulled back on the big interstate highway, his eyes felt like raw meat and he had developed a mild headache from the lack of sleep and from the stress. As they crossed the state line and approached Chattanooga, the traffic volume picked up and Shawn had to be very careful not to side swipe one of the many cars zooming by them. As they traveled on, Shawn kept a close eye on the old truck's gauges. Apparently, Mr. Thompson had told them the truth about the condition of the old Ford truck.

Shawn's mind drifted back a couple of years to the morning he pulled into the Russellville High School parking lot when he first laid eyes on Dani. He looked over at Dani and the baby and they smiled back at him. Not a word was said for several miles.

Dani was thinking. Here we are traveling toward Canada in an old moving van full of gold. Dani turned her head to look at Shawn and he smiled back at her.

About 50 miles south of Nashville, the two large cups of coffee had convinced them to stop at a rest area. As Shawn turned into the parking lot, he noticed water rushing across the road. Apparently a water pipe had burst and was flooding one side of the parking lot. Shawn slowed down to cross the heavy stream of water. As he pulled through, he noticed steam coming from the truck's rear tires. He knew this could mean trouble, so he parked and placed his hand on the rear tires.

"Ouch!" He shouted as he quickly removed his hand.

The tire was so hot. He knew that the load on the truck was much too heavy and that some of the weight would have to be removed, if they had a chance of getting to Canada.

After the restroom break, Shawn explained to Dani about the problem with the tires. They tried to figure out what to do. A man walked over to them and asked if they needed help. Shawn explained that the truck was over loaded and the tires were getting hot.

The man said, "I could tell something was wrong, when I saw the steam cloud develop around them, when you rolled through the water."

Shawn asked the man, "How long would it take for the tires to cool?"

The man replied, "Just sitting still about an hour, but you can cool them down with a water hose in about ten minutes."

The water at the rest area had just been turned off to fix the leak, so Shawn asked the man, "Where could he get water?"

The man said, "Go to the next exit. It's only a couple of miles north of here. Turn right after you exit and park between the Country Boy Inn and Bad Bob's Burgers. You will see a water hose on the side of the inn."

Shawn asked, "How do you know about the water hose?"

The man smiled and said, "I own both of them."

Shawn said, "Thank you for being so helpful."

As Shawn drove to the next exit, he knew that cooling the tires with water was only a temporary fix, but he knew that he would have to unload some of the cargo to make the trip to Canada. When they arrived at the next exit, they found the water hose, exactly where the man had told them and Shawn sprayed the tires until they were cool.

After replacing the water hose on the rack, they decided to try some of Bad Bob's Burgers, just to show their appreciation. Apparently, Bad Bob's Burgers were delicious and while they ate Shawn explained that the cargo weight capacity on the old truck was only 6000 lbs., and he explained that the gold probably weighed about 8,000 lbs, therefore, they needed to find a place they could hide some of the gold. He explained that the additional weight on the tires caused the sidewalls to flex as they rolled on the pavement, and the flexing of the sidewalls of the tires caused them to get hot. He explained that unless some of the weight was removed, eventually some of the tires would blowout and it could cause an accident or for them to have a break down.

Shawn just said, "No, we need to keep going, but we need to find a place to hide some of the gold."

Dani asked Shawn, "How much of the gold would need to be unloaded?"

Shawn said, "I would say about one-third of the gold would be enough."

Dani asked, "Could we rent a storage unit?"

Shawn said, "I don't think that would be wise. I'm afraid someone might recognize us, if the story gets out!"

As Shawn and his family finished the meal, they decided to try to make it to Nashville and try to find another place to cool the tires or find a place to hide some of the gold bars.

As they got back on the interstate, Shawn decided to drive 60 miles per hour instead of 70, just in case they had a blowout. The thought of leaving millions of dollars of gold behind made him feel bad, but he knew if he didn't, they would never make it to Canada.

As they rolled into Nashville, they were impressed with the hillside mansions and the large buildings in the downtown area. They both loved country music and they joked about buying the Grand Ole Opry! ~~Dani and little Elizabeth were enjoying the trip. They had gone to~~ sleep.

They drove for about an hour and Shawn knew it was about time to cool the tires again, so ~~they pulled off the interstate and saw a car wash and~~ pulled up next to ~~the last stall. The cool water instantly~~ turned to ~~steam, as it hit the hot tires.~~ Shawn wondered how many times he would have to cool the tires before he made it to Canada. He needed to find a safe place to hide a ton of the gold bars. Even if they couldn't return to get them, he could tell someone where it was.

As he cooled the tires, he looked at the road atlas. They were near the Kentucky border and the next large town would be Paducah. Shawn looked over at Dani and asked, "Did we bring the shovel?"

Dani replied, "Yes, I saw you throw it in after we loaded the tub."

Shawn said, "I may have to bury some of the gold in order to hide it!"

The gas gauge was getting low, so Shawn drove across the street to fill the fuel tank at a service station. The gas tank was eating up the cash money they had!

Shawn and Dani discussed the possibility of pawning a pair of solid silver candles holders.

After they got back on the interstate near the Kentucky State line, they saw a sign, "Horton Hills State Park." They decided to pull off the interstate for a little rest. As they entered the main gate they saw a sign that said: "Quiet, peaceful, secluded cabins for rent-day or week!"

They stopped at the Ranger station and signed in for one night. ~~The Ranger station had a cafeteria on one side so that campers wouldn't have to leave the park to find food. The young family soup and sandwiches to go, and then they drove back to cabin #24~~. The cabin was perfect; it was off by itself away from the other cabins, had a separate driveway from the road, and joined the National Forest land on the rear. Shawn backed the Ford van up to the side of the cabin.

~~After eating~~, Dani and little Elizabeth decided to take a nice warm bath. Shawn told them he was going for a little walk in the park! Shawn opened the rear door and retrieved the shovel. Shawn only walked about 150 feet from the cabin before he found what he was looking for, a small open area with soft soil for easy digging.

Shawn worked for about half an hour, digging a hole about three feet deep. Then he started piling gold bars near the rear of the van body and carried four of them at a time to the hole. It took 50 trips to move 200 bars that weighed 20 lbs. each. He hid one ton of gold and then covered it with dirt and every rock he could find on top. It was after 10 p.m. before Shawn finished.

When he entered the cabin, he saw Dani and the baby asleep, so he closed the door gently and went to the shower. The hot water felt good, but his lack of sleep was beginning to catch up with him. He quietly opened the bedroom door and got on the empty bed and was fast asleep in minutes.

At seven o'clock the small telephone began to ring. Shawn raced for the phone. Instead of his normal 'hello' all he said was "what!"

"Sausage, biscuits, and coffee are ready at the Ranger's station" was the recorded message he received from the phone.

As they entered the cafeteria at the Ranger's station, they could smell the fresh baked biscuits and butter. They walked over to the serving table and helped themselves.

The Ranger, a slim man with gray hair and mustache, was busy bringing more food from the kitchen. Apparently, most of the park's guests had come and gone by the time the McLeod family arrived.

The Ranger got a child's high chair from the corner of the dining room for little Elizabeth and Dani smiled and said, "Thank you."

The Ranger asked, "Are ya'll moving?"

Shawn replied, "Yes, we are."

The Ranger asked, "North or South."

Shawn said, "West."

The Ranger said, "I figured you were moving, driving a moving van."

The Ranger's wife brought a glass of milk for little Elizabeth and sat it on the table between Dani and Elizabeth and said, "That's a pretty little girl."

Dani said, "Thank you."

The Ranger's wife had a big warm smile; her gray hair was the only proof of her years.

After finishing a delicious breakfast, the little family loaded up their old Ford van and got back on I-24 toward Paducah, Kentucky. A gentle rain started falling. Shawn knew the rain would help cool the trucks tires.

Dani asked, "How was your walk in the park last night?"

Shawn glanced over at Dani and said, "We won't know until we drive for about 30 miles and check the tires."

Dani said, "I was afraid a bear might get you!"

Shawn smiled and said, "I wasn't worried about bears, and I had a shovel."

Dani asked Shawn, "Do you think anyone will find it?"

Shawn replied, "I don't think so. I buried it about 150 feet from the cabin, and I think it will be safe."

Dani said, "I guess that could be a little rainy day savings account."

Shawn said, "We need to keep this little savings account a secret between the two of us!"

Litty →

Dani said, "Yes, I understand. If we spend all of this, I guess we could take a walk in the park!"

They both laughed and gave each other a high five.

Chapter 10

They continued through Paducah and over the Ohio River. Shawn and Dani saw large barges transporting freight down the river. When the young couple reached Interstate 57 near Marion, Kentucky, they turned north looking for Interstate 64.

Shawn and Dani passed the time talking about their enormous wealth. They could help family and friends and Shawn wanted to buy his Silverado back. They decided that the number one goal would be to see that Elizabeth had a good future and be financially secure.

Shawn turned the radio on. A commercial ended and the news and weather came on. So far, no news was good news. As the music played, the young couple tried to relax. For about an hour, they just rode along the interstate and enjoyed the scenery.

As they approached Exit 51, they decided to pull off the interstate and eat at a restaurant called Grandma's Kitchen. After enjoying a great meal, Shawn studied his road atlas. Shawn and Dani discussed the fact that the cash money was running out fast and they needed to pawn something to have the money needed to reach Canada.

The little family loaded up in their old Ford truck and circled the parking lot, when Dani spotted Marty's Bait, Tackle and Pawn ½ mile ahead.

Old Marty drove a hard bargain, but he eventually gave them $500.00 in cash for the candleholder.

As the couple drove away, they felt much better. They could make the trip to Canada with the additional five hundred dollars. As they reached the interstate and turned west, Shawn figured they were only about 60 miles from St. Louis. He wanted to find Interstate 70 heading west toward Kansas City and then turn north to Omaha, Nebraska.

Shawn turned on the truck's radio and found a strong radio signal from a station in St. Louis. It was a country and western station and they enjoyed the music.

As they entered St. Louis, they crossed the mighty Mississippi River and saw the gateway arch. This was a spectacular site for a couple of country kids from Georgia. Shawn made several turns to get on Interstate 70 west toward Kansas City. The news came on the radio and the biggest story was the price of oil headed to new highs, as pump prices escalated across America.

After surviving St. Louis, the young family decided to spend the night in Columbia, Missouri. They stopped and rented a room. They paid cash and registered under the name of Mr. and Mrs. Golden. They asked for a room on the back side of the motel and backed the big Ford moving van up next to room #24. They took long showers, changed clothes, dressed little Elizabeth, and decided to find something to eat. They walked to a place called "Paula's Pizza" and ordered pizza and salads.

After leaving the pizza place, they went for a walk and stopped at a convenience store to get shaving cream for Shawn and bubble bath for Dani. She was afraid they didn't sell bubble bath in Canada. They also bought some snack foods and bottled water. When they returned to the motel room, the young family settled down to watch the news on television.

Shawn said, "The pipeline crews should have passed our cabin by now."

Dani said, "If they find something, they will probably keep it for themselves and keep their mouths shut."

Shawn said, "That could very well happen."

"For all we know, they may not find a thing and we could be worrying about nothing," said Dani with a big smile.

The young couple decided to turn in early; with some luck they could be in Canada in about 48 yours. At 7 a.m. the phone rang, the normal "wake up call." Then they both raced around the room to load up their possessions and returned the motel key to the office.

They stopped at a fast food place for breakfast and then crossed the road to fill up the old Ford truck at a U-Fill-It station. When Shawn returned to the Ford truck, Dani told him she needed a pit stop before hitting the road. The extra-large cup of coffee she had with breakfast was letting her know who was boss. Dani finished her rest room trip and was looking for some breath mints as the station's sales clerk waited on the other customers.

The store had a large television playing the news channel, as it sat on top of the first row of counters. Something on the screen caught her attention. She saw a news reporter talking and pointing to the mountains behind her. Then, the scene changed to an aerial view from a helicopter. She couldn't believe her eyes, as she glanced around the store to see if anyone else was watching.

The news reporter said, "So to recap this breaking news from the mountains of north Georgia. Several employees of a gas pipeline crew have been arrested for fighting and shooting at each other after they apparently dug up some sort of treasure."

Dani realized the pictures were from Mountaindale near their cabin. Dani decided to skip the breath mints and headed for the door.

As Dani reached for the door handle, Shawn opened the door from the inside and reached for her hand to help her climb up the steps to the truck's seat. Shawn could tell Dani was excited about something.

Dani exclaimed, "The pipeline crew found it!"

Shawn asked, "Are you sure?"

Dani replied, "It's on the *World News Network!*"

Shawn asked, "What did they say?"

Dani replied, "I only caught the recap, but the reporter was pointing toward our cabin and she was saying that several members of a gas pipeline crew had been arrested after getting into a fight and shoot out after finding some mysterious treasure and that a news conference had been scheduled for 11 a.m. eastern time."

Shawn started the Ford truck's big V-8 engine and drove away.

Then Shawn asked, "Did it say anything about us?"

Dani responded, "No, no it just talked about the pipeline crew."

Shawn said, "We find one of the most elusive treasures on the face of the earth and a pipeline crew has to be barreling down on us!"

Dani's face turned pale as she said, "What's going to happen to Elizabeth, if they put us in prison?"

"Nobody's going to prison, darling. By the time they find out about us, if ever, we will be safe in Canada!" said Shawn.

As Shawn pulled onto the interstate, he heard a police siren behind him. His heart skipped a few beats, as the police car passed him like a bullet! A big sigh of relief came over him, as he realized the police car was after somebody else! Even though it had scared him, too, Shawn tried to act calm.

Shawn saw a sign "Highway 63" next exit, and said, "Let's take Highway 63 and by-pass Kansas City."

As they slowed down to turn on Highway 63, they both laughed as they saw another road sign that said Mexico 15 miles!

Dani exclaimed, "Heck, we don't have anything to worry about; we're almost to Mexico."

Shawn said, "Isn't that our luck? We're racing toward Canada and we wind up in Mexico."

They drove on for a few miles and the news came on the radio. The first news story was about the price of gas. A hurricane had hit the Gulf Coast of Mexico near New Orleans and the oil companies had doubled the price of gasoline in the matter of a few weeks.

Then the reporter said, "And out of the North Georgia Mountains we have a story about some people who found a way to handle the rapidly rising gas prices. Late yesterday a gas company pipeline crew uncovered a treasure of tremendous wealth including solid gold bars, jewelry, and diamonds and Confederate money! Local, state and federal authorities are trying to figure out, if this could truly be the lost Confederate gold shipment. For those of you who failed history, as the Civil War raged for several years, the Southerners made one last ditch effort to win the war and all of the remaining gold, diamonds, silver, even jewelry was collected to be shipped to Europe to buy goods and ammunition, but somewhere in the North Georgia Mountains, the wagon train was ambushed and all the Union soldiers found was rocks. The common belief is that the Confederate troops buried the treasure and reloaded the wagons with rocks after realizing they were being followed by the Union soldiers. Regardless of what happened, the treasure has never been found. If this were the lost Confederate treasure, this would be one of the greatest historical finds in the history of America.

According to authorities the pipeline crew discovered the treasure about 5 p.m. eastern time yesterday. Apparently these men decided to work all night to retrieve the bounty, but just before sun rise this morning an argument arose over how to share the find. A fist fight turned into a gun battle and one of the men had to be rushed to an area hospital for treatment.

The local Sheriff, after realizing he had found something very big, called state and federal authorities. We have received word the gunshot victim's injuries were not life threatening and all three men have been arrested. So, as the sun rose this morning, a big story developed about fortune, greed, and violence. More news will follow and now back to Beth with the weather!"

Click! Shawn turned the radio off and said, "I think we need to get to Canada as quickly as possible!"

Dani said, "I agree; the sooner the better!"

As the young family reached the Iowa state line around 10:30 a.m., they turned right on Highway 2, and then back left on US 63 at Bloomfield going north. They decided to stay off the interstate in order to avoid the heavier traffic and to keep a low profile.

As the young family approached Ames, Iowa, they were frightened when they saw several police cars, just ahead of them. The flashing lights on the police cars put instant fear in their hearts! They were relieved to see a small car sitting sideways in the road and a pickup with a smashed grill sitting beside it.

Shawn said, "It's just a fender bender!"

A few miles past a place called Boone, they reached Highway 169 and turned north toward Minnesota. They continued north and traveled through Fort Dodge. They stopped for gas at a small community just north of Fort Dodge. Shawn filled the gas tank and then entered the store and bought a cooler. He also bought milk, juice, bottled water, and soft drinks. He scratched his head and thought for a second and then rounded up sliced ham, sliced cheese, potato chips, beanie weenies and several cans of boiled peanuts.

The clerk looked a little shocked, as he saw the items sitting on the counter and asked "anything else?"

Shawn said, "Oh yes, a bag of ice."

The clerk started pressing the keys on the cash register and said, "Going camping?"

Shawn responded, "It's more like a picnic."

The clerk still ringing up the purchases said, "Well you better get some bug repellant; the mosquitoes will eat you alive this time of year."

Shawn thought the clerk was right, so he walked back to the counter where the clerk had pointed and added bug repellent to his purchases.

Finally the clerk said, "That will be $149.28, son."

Shawn paid the man and loaded up his purchases and said, "Thank you."

Shawn opened the bag of ice and poured it on top of the goodies. He looked around to be sure no one was watching, as he opened the rear door of the van and put the cooler inside. He closed and locked the rear door of the van and handed the other items to Dani, as he entered the big Ford truck.

Dani asked, "Did you buy the store?"

Shawn said, "We might get lost trying to find a back road into Canada, so I figured we might need some food."

Dani said, "Well, I can't think of anybody I would rather get lost with, than you!"

Shawn pulled back on the highway and proceeded on toward the Minnesota state line. A few miles down the road he made a left hand turn onto Highway 9, and proceeded northwest for about 15 miles to reach Highway 71. He turned right on Highway 71 going north. The sun had set and Dani and little Elizabeth had drifted off to sleep, as the faithful old Ford truck constantly made its way north crossing Interstate 90 at Jackson. Shawn was thinking they were only about 250 miles from the Canadian border. If everything goes right, we will be crossing the border sometime tomorrow.

Chapter 11

As the sun set, Shawn drove north through Windom, Minnesota and then on to Springfield. They decided to get a room for the night and stopped at a small motel.

The young lady handed Shawn a key to room #11. After checking out the motel room, Shawn turned the television on and Dani and the baby took a shower. Shawn decided to make a couple of sandwiches. When the girls came out, Shawn showed them the sandwiches and went to the shower. Shawn was really enjoying the shower when a wild knocking at the door broke his peace. Shawn shut the water off.

He could hear Dani saying, "Someone's at the door."

Shawn wrapped a towel around his waist and opened the door just a few inches. It was the girl from the office holding some extra towels.

She said, "Here are some extra towels."

Shawn and Dani were very relieved and fell back on the bed.

"Wow, that was a close one!" said Dani.

Shawn said, "Look, we need to stop worrying. The story on the news has only been about the pipeline crew."

Dani said, "You are right; we may never hear anything else about the whole escapade!"

They just relaxed and watched television while little Elizabeth played with her toys.

The next morning, when the wake-up call came, the young family got dressed and was on the road before 7:30 a.m. Shawn wanted to get as close to the border as possible and then try to find a nice quite country road to cross the border. He knew he couldn't drive through a checkpoint.

As the family rolled into Redwood Falls, they decided to stop at a little diner for breakfast. The early morning crowd of regulars was lined up at the bar and most of the tables were filled to capacity. An older lady was cooking eggs, bacon, sausage and hash browns and a younger woman was busy taking orders. A string hung above the cooking grill with the orders written on small sheets of paper attached with clothesline pins. A television was playing, but the patrons were much too busy laughing, talking and eating to notice.

The young waitress turned toward them, as they approached the counter near the cash register. Her red lipstick and big red earrings encompassed a big smile and she said, "Hello, can I help you?"

Shawn ordered two large coffees and two sausage and egg biscuits to go. Shawn looked around and saw two empty chairs near the television, so they make their way over to them. Shawn remembered the cooler needed ice, so he ran next door to a convenience store to get a bag. Shawn had just left, when Dani saw something on the television screen that got her attention. The World News Network was showing the north Georgia mountains again.

The reporter said, "Federal authorities are seeking two persons of interest concerning the spectacular find in the north Georgia mountains. A young couple, Shawn and Dani McLeod, the apparent owners of the property where the treasure was found, are being sought for questioning. No charges have been filed against them at this time."

They showed pictures of Shawn and Dani and then the network showed a picture of a red and white Chevrolet pickup.

The announcer said, "They were last seen driving a red and white Chevrolet pickup like this one."

Dani sat spellbound watching the television. Then a phone number appeared on the screen for the F.B.I.

Dani stood up in front of the set to prevent the other patrons from seeing her picture. She held little Elizabeth close to her chest, as the waitress said, "Your order is ready, Honey!"

Dani followed the waitress to the pay-out counter to get their order and hoped nobody saw their pictures on television.

Shawn dumped the bag of ice in the cooler and then entered the diner. He could tell something was wrong.

Dani just motioned for him to be quiet. After reaching the parking lot, Dani said, "I saw our pictures on television and a picture of your pick up. They want us for questioning!"

Shawn helped Dani up the steps of the truck and then handed her the food order. He then ran around the front of the truck and climbed in on the driver's side.

As Dani told Shawn everything she heard on the television, Shawn quickly put the old Ford truck on the road. Dani explained that the pictures were their graduation pictures from high school.

Shawn said, "I think we will be fine. If they are looking for a red and white Chevrolet pickup, and we are traveling in an old Ford moving van, we should be safe."

Dani said, "I hope so!"

Shawn said, "We can be in Canada in a few hours and we will be safe there."

Dani explained, " My aunt and uncle live about 20 miles from the border and they told me there is nothing around them, but farm land, and they say they cross the border almost daily without going through any type of check point."

Shawn said, "Good, we need to find one of those places!"

Dani said, "Our parents, I bet they must be in shock!"

Shawn said, "Don't worry. Once we are safe, we will get word to them that we are alright!"

Shawn just kept driving north. He was careful to obey all traffic laws, trying not to attract any attention. As Shawn drove along, he turned the radio on and found a country and western station. A song by Toby Keith came on; it was one of her favorites.

They crossed Interstate 94 as the news came on the radio. The lead story was, "We have an update on our story about the young couple wanted for questioning involving the mysterious treasure found in Georgia. Authorities have released new information that the young couple, the McLeod's, could be traveling in an old Ford U-Move-It, red and white moving van, and Georgia plates no. B22 919."

Shawn reached over and turned the radio off, not a word was said. Shawn's mind was on, "Why, we are so close?"

Several minutes went by.

Finally, Dani broke the silence and asked, "Do you think we should turn ourselves in and try to convince the authorities we thought this stuff was ours?"

Shawn said, "I'm afraid it's too late and I think we can make it to Canada!"

Dani said, "We are close!"

The mood in the cab of the big Ford truck had turned very somber!

Dani said, "Now that they know about this truck, do you think we need to find another one?"

Shawn said, "We don't need another truck; we just need to paint this one!"

Shawn saw a road sign for a Wal-Depot store, one of those large discount stores that sell everything. The sign said 2 miles on the left. Shawn turned left into the parking lot and drove around behind it and parked completely hidden from public view. Shawn explained to Dani that he was going to buy some paint, masking tape, a roller, and a couple of newspapers.

Shawn put on his shades and pulled his cap down low and said, "I won't be long."

As Shawn opened the door, Dani said, "Elizabeth and I are going to walk across the parking lot to a pharmacy and get something for pain."

Shawn said "Alright, but be careful."

Shawn entered the big store and found the paint section. He decided to paint the big truck black. Not only did black cover well with one coat, but it would be easier to hide at night. He loaded up a five-gallon bucket of paint and all the necessary items to paint the truck. Shawn pushed the shopping cart to the check-out line. As he stood in line, he heard two men talking about the mysterious treasure found in Georgia.

Another man said, "If I find them, I'm going to shoot them and take the truck load of goodies!"

It gave Shawn a cold chill to think that someone could do such a thing. Shawn lugged the five-gallons of paint and the other items back to the truck and set them on the loading dock next to the truck. He was relieved to see Dani coming across the parking lot with Elizabeth in one arm and a large shopping bag in the other.

As she approached, he asked, "What's in the bag?"

Dani responded, "Popcorn, pizza, hair dye and scissors!"

Hair dye?" asked Shawn

Dani said, "Yes, we may need to change our appearance!"

Shawn was looking at his road atlas.

Dani put the bag in the truck, but continued to hold Elizabeth. Dani noticed an old black Ford truck parked behind the warehouse and said, "Why don't we just swap for that old truck. It's already black!"

Shawn laid his map down and walked around behind the old truck Dani had mentioned. She was right it was and old Ford truck and it was black.

The signs on the doors read "Handy Man Services" in big white letters. The truck had a current Minnesota license plate. This gave Shawn an idea. He got a screwdriver and removed the license plate. He returned to his truck and removed the Georgia plate and installed the Minnesota plate.

"Isn't that illegal?" asked Dani

Shawn looked around to be sure no one saw him change the plate and said, "I'm just borrowing this plate!"

Chapter 12

Meanwhile back in Russellville, Shawn's family had just finished the noontime meal when the news came on the television. The lead story was about Shawn and Dani. Shawn's mom fainted and fell in the floor, and Shawn's father raced to her side to try to revive her then looked back at the set and said, "What in the hell!"

Shawn's father grabbed a glass of water from the table and splashed it in Shawn's mom's face; she looked at everyone with a shocked stare. Shawn's sisters stared at each other and the television set.

Mr. McLeod said, "There must be some mistake. Why would the F.B.I. want to talk to our son?" He helped Shawn's mom up from the floor and over to the sofa and mumbled "It's got to be a mistake!"

Dani's father had just left a restaurant in Knoxville, TN when he heard the story on the radio in his car. He ran off the road and destroyed several mailboxes before he collected his composure!

Meanwhile, the doorbell rings. The girls answered the door. Two men dressed in dark suits and dark sunglasses were standing on the porch asking to speak to their parents. Mr. McLeod, after making sure that Mrs. McLeod was all right, responded to his daughters' request to come to the door.

Mr. McLeod was still shocked, as he walked toward the front door. The two men showed him their identification. They were Federal Bureau of Investigation agents.

The younger and taller agent said, "I'm Jerry Joyner and this is my partner Paul Stein, are you Mr. McLeod?"

Mr. McLeod said, "Yes, I am."

The older agent said, "We need to talk to you."

Mr. McLeod asked, "What do you want to talk to me about?"

"It's your son, Shawn," said Agent Stein.

Mr. McLeod said, "My son is a fine young man!"

Agent Joyner said, "I'm sure he is, but we need to talk to him!"

Mr. McLeod asked, "What do you need to talk to him about?"

Agent Stein said, "Apparently, someone has found the lost Confederate gold shipment that has been missing since the 1860's."

Mr. McLeod asked, "Why do you think my son knows anything about that?"

Agent Joyner asked, "Have you heard the news about a pipeline crew discovering a buried treasure in the north Georgia Mountains?"

Mr. McLeod said, "Yes, we heard something last night about that."

Mr. McLeod turned and looked, as Mrs. McLeod joined him at the door.

Mrs. McLeod said, "What do you want?"

Agent Joyner said, "We need to talk to your son and his wife."

Shawn's mother said, "I'm sure our son and his wife would never touch anything that didn't belong to them!"

Agent Stein asked, "When was the last time you spoke with them?"

Mr. McLeod said, "It's been about two weeks ago."

Mrs. McLeod asked, "Are they alright?"

The younger agent said, "We don't know."

Agent Stein said, "That's why we need to find them."

Mr. McLeod said, "Our son and his wife are law abiding citizens."

Agent Stein said, "I'm sure they are!"

Agent Joyner asked, "May we come in?"

Mrs. McLeod said, "Yes, I guess it's alright."

Shawn's sisters are confused and Misty asked, "What's going on?"

As Mrs. McLeod walked over toward a chair next to the fireplace, she said, "I'm not sure!"

The older agent, Mr. Stein, sat in a chair next to Mrs. McLeod and said, "All we know is a considerable treasure was removed from a hole only a few feet from the cabin your son and his wife were staying in and the treasure appears to be a tremendous historical find!"

Agent Joyner said, "We have strong reasons to believe your son borrowed a large tractor backhoe to level up around the cabin and must have accidentally discovered the treasure over the weekend."

Mr. McLeod stood and said, "We heard a pipeline crew found it!"

Agent Stein said, "A pipeline crew was working in the area and reached what was left of the treasure after you son and his wife left the cabin."

Mrs. McLeod said, "I just can't believe that our son would be involved in such a thing!"

Agent Stein said, "Crazier things have happened, a young couple that just lost their home and your son just lost his job, could cause perfectly normal people to react irrationally."

Mr. McLeod said, "My son knows right from wrong!"

Agent Joyner asked, "Do you have any idea where they could be at this time?"

Mr. McLeod said, "No, no we don't!"

Agent Stein asked, "Have you received any phone calls from them since they left?"

Mr. McLeod said, "No, not a word!"

Agent Joyner asked, "Who are your son's best friends?"

Mr. McLeod said, "I guess Donald Anderson, the banker's son, and Jerry from work."

Agent Joyner wrote on a pad and asked, "Jerry who?"

Mr. McLeod said, "I'm not sure; he only referred to somebody named Jerry that worked with him at the Barton Manufacturing Company."

Agent Stein said, "I can't overstress the importance of finding your son before the wrong people find him!"

Agent Joyner said, "You must give us any information you can about his possible location."

Mr. McLeod said, "We don't have any idea where they are."

Agent Joyner said, "If you're trying to hide them and are lying to us and they are eventually charged with a federal crime, the two of you could serve time in a federal prison for aiding and abetting after the fact!"

Mr. McLeod was furious and stood and yelled, "We have told you the truth, we haven't seen or heard from them since they left over a week ago, and you two gentlemen just wore out your welcome!"

Mr. McLeod walked over to the front door, opened it and said, "Get out!"

The younger agent's lack of maturity, experience and diplomacy had just gotten them the boot.

The older agent laid his card on the coffee table in front of the sofa and said, "I'm sorry if we upset you, but if you see or hear from them, you need to call us immediately," said Agent Stein.

"It would be a lot better for them to just turn themselves in," said Agent Joyner.

Mr. McLeod, still holding the door open said, "Like I said, gentlemen, you have worn out your welcome!"

Mr. McLeod's face had turned red with anger.

As the agents stood and walked toward the door, Agent Stein said, "If they are in possession of millions of dollars worth of gold and jewelry, their lives could be in danger."

The two agents walked out the front door and got in their Government issued tan Oldsmobile and drove away.

Agent Stein said, "I don't think you should have threatened them as you did. My feeling was that they would be cooperative."

Agent Joyner as he is driving out the gate said, "The wiretap should be finished by now and by making them mad, they may call them and warn them, if they know where they are."

Agent Stein replied, "I don't believe they know where they are and I believe they are honest and decent people."

The McLeods stood on the front porch and watched as the two agents drove out of sight. Mr. McLeod had his arm around his wife as they went inside.

A helicopter roared overhead and circled and came back over the house.

Mr. McLeod said, "Well, I guess they will be watching us, but if they want to waste their time, it's alright with me."

Mrs. McLeod, still looking pale, sat down on the sofa.

Mr. McLeod said, "I bet they have already tapped our phone and will be checking our mail!"

Mrs. McLeod asked, "Do you really think Shawn and Dani would run off with a bunch of gold?"

Mr. McLeod said, "I don't know, but who could blame them. They're just kids and they have been through hell!"

Mrs. McLeod just shook her head and said, "I just hope and pray they're alright!"

The helicopter circled several times back and forth moving slowly and occasionally stopping in mid-air.

Mr. McLeod sat down in his big brown recliner, looked up at the ceiling and said, "What can we do?"

The room was completely silent, except for the noise of the helicopter flying in the distance until the phone rang.

Mr. McLeod placed his hand over the phone and said, "This phone is probably tapped, so if they call, don't use any names, don't ask them where they are, and tell them up front the F.B.I. has been here!"

Mr. McLeod picked up the receiver and said, "Hello!"

It was Dani's father telling Mr. McLeod what he had heard on the radio.

Mr. McLeod said, "The F.B.I. have just left, there's helicopter flying over our farm, and our phone is probably tapped!"

Dani's father said, "I just can't believe this could be true. Our kids are good kids and I don't believe they could do something like this!"

Mr. McLeod agreed and the call ended shortly afterwards.

Mr. McLeod laid the phone down and motioned for everyone to follow him outside. On the way out Mr. McLeod turned the television on full volume. The girls held their hands over their ears, as they followed their parents outside. Mr. McLeod stopped about 50 feet from the house and pulled his wife and daughters really close and whispered, "They are probably using electronic surveillance equipment to bug our home, so be careful what you say."

Mr. McLeod raised his head and looked around, as if to see if someone is watching them.

He said in a whisper, "If you need to communicate anything that you wouldn't want the world to know, just write it down on a memo pad and show it to the rest of us!"

The phone started ringing, as the family entered the living room. Mr. McLeod motioned for everyone to be quiet, as he reached for the phone and said, "Hello."

A man on the phone said, "Hello, is this the McLeod residence?"

Mr. McLeod said, "Yes, it is."

The caller said, "I'm James Favor. I'm a reporter for the *World News Network*. Are you the father of Shawn McLeod?"

Mr. McLeod said, "Yes, yes I am!"

Mr. Favor asked, "Are you aware of the story running worldwide on our network concerning your son and his wife wanted for questioning by the F.B.I.?"

Mr. McLeod said, "Yes, we heard the story a few minutes ago."

The reporter asked, "Do you think your son and daughter-in-law would steal millions of dollars worth of gold?"

Mr. McLeod said, "Our son and his wife would never steal anything from anybody."

The reporter asked, "Have they contacted you or anybody in your family in the last week?"

Mr. McLeod said, "No, we haven't had any contact with them in nearly two weeks!"

The reporter said, "So they haven't been in contact with you and you don't have any idea where they could be?"

Then Mr. McLeod spoke in a very strong manner; "Our son and daughter-in-law are fine decent law abiding young people and would never get involved in anything wrong or illegal!"

The reporter asked, "Are you aware of a news release just coming out over the wire services that say your son's place of employment was destroyed by fire and a few days later his home burned to the ground and the state Fire Marshal is investigating both cases?"

Mr. McLeod yelled, "My son had nothing to do with either fire. One cost him his job and the other almost cost them their lives!"

The reporter said, "I'm sorry, Mr. McLeod, but we just wanted to get your comments before we put this story out on the air!"

Mr. McLeod said, "If you run such a story, my son will sue and if he doesn't, I will!"

The reporter replied, "The story doesn't accuse him of arson, it just reports that his place of employment and his personal home burned only a few days apart!"

Mr. McLeod yelled, "My son had nothing to do with either fire!"

The reporter said, "Two fires and now he is wanted for questioning concerning the disappearance of millions of dollars of gold and all of this is just a coincidence?"

Mrs. McLeod is trying to listen in on the phone call as Mr. McLeod yelled into the receiver, "You people are trying to slander our son. He's a fine decent person and so is his wife!"

The reporter said, "Sir, we are just reporting what's coming out over the other news networks. We are not accusing him of anything."

Mr. McLeod yelled, "You people need to wait and find out the truth before you release something that's not true.

Mr. McLeod slammed the phone down on the receiver so hard it bounced off the table onto the floor.

Mrs. McLeod asked, "What's wrong?"

Mr. McLeod replied, "The *World News Network* people are going to run a story about our son and the fire at the Barton Manufacturing Company and his home and say the fires are under investigation by the state Fire Marshal. I believe it is only a way of slandering our son!"

Mrs. McLeod asked her husband, "Where did those people get an idea like that?"

Mr. McLeod raised his voice, "Damn gossipers probably. Every gossiper within a hundred miles will come out of the woodwork to drag somebody decent through the dirt when something like this occurs!"

Shawn's mother and father had been so excited about the previous events in the past few minutes that they had not noticed their two young daughters standing and holding each other, trembling with fear. Mr. McLeod and his wife walked over to them and hugged them and tried to play down the events of the last few minutes and assured them that all of this was a big mistake. The girls wanted to know, if Elizabeth would be all right and Mrs. McLeod reassured her daughters that all would be fine after everything is cleared up.

Mr. McLeod told the girls, "You two young ladies go upstairs to your room and watch television or better still, read a book."

Mr. McLeod held his wife close and tried to calm her fears. He wondered, if any of what they have heard today could be true. Could Shawn and Dani have discovered millions of dollars of gold? He was very concerned as he thought about the criminal elements in society that would kill a man for twenty dollars, if the criminal was in need of drug money.

Chapter 13

Meanwhile, back in Minnesota, Shawn, Dani and little Elizabeth enjoyed the pizza and popcorn Dani had bought. Shawn realized he had to paint the truck as soon as possible! He thought to himself, "Probably every police officer in the United States would be looking for a red and white Ford moving van."

Shawn looked around the corner of the old warehouse to see how much traffic was on the street out front. He was shocked when he saw two police cars parked side by side in the parking lot only a few yards away. He wondered why the officers were parked just around the corner from them. He looked back at Dani and Elizabeth and wondered, "What was I thinking! I had to be crazy!"

His fears subsided, as he looked back around the corner to see the police cars leaving the parking lot. It occurred to Shawn that he could roll the van portion of the truck right where it was parked. Dani had placed a blanket on the ground for Elizabeth and gave her some toys to entertain her. Shawn explained to Dani that he had decided to paint the van body of the truck before leaving.

Dani helped Shawn tape up the truck and Shawn began to roll the black paint onto the truck's van body. In just a few minutes, the driver's side was black instead of red and white. As he rolled the satin black paint, he was impressed with the way it covered the old faded paint.

Shawn was suddenly startled by the appearance of two boys on bicycles who just seemed to appear out of nowhere. The boys watched Shawn apply the paint. They had rolled up so quietly that neither he nor Dani had heard them coming.

One of the boys said, "Wow! That looked like fun!"

Shawn's eyes weren't deceiving him, he was actually face to face with two kids. Shawn managed to say "Hi!" to the boys and asked, "Where did ya'll come from?"

The boy in the red shirt said, "We were taking a short cut to the bike trails down behind the shopping center."

Shawn continued to paint like nothing was wrong.

The kid in the green shirt asked, "Can we help paint?"

Shawn said, "Sure, why not?"

They quickly parked their bikes and walked over to Shawn ready to roll some of the paint.

Dani was a little fascinated at how well Shawn had recovered from the shock of the two boys' sudden arrival and his offer to let them paint.

As the first boy tried his hand at painting, Shawn asked, "Is there a road anywhere up the highway where I could find a quiet place in the country to work on the truck?"

The boy said, "Just outside the city limits, you will see Horse Head Mill Road. Just turn left and it will lead you to dozens of old abandoned farms and hunting clubs."

Shawn said "Thank you."

The boy rolling the paint stopped and let the other boy try his hand with the roller. Shawn waited patiently for the boys to have their fun.

Then, the second boy handed the roller back to Shawn and said, "Thank you. My dad never lets me help him paint."

As the boys were leaving, Shawn asked them," Please do not say anything to anyone about the painting."

The boys agreed and pedaled away.

Dani asked, "Do you think those boys will actually keep this paint job a secret?"

Shawn replied, "Sure. You let a kid paint something and they will be grateful forever."

Shawn just kept rolling the black paint and even got up on a loading dock to reach the far corners of the van's top. Shawn could see a path behind the Wal-Depot store that led to a back street and hopefully, a safer way out of town. He reasoned that even though the truck's van body was now black and had Minnesota license plates, it would be safer to take the back streets through town.

The young couple loaded up then drove down the side street. He drove until he came to a dead end. He then turned right and drove a short distance before he sees Horse Head Mill Road on his left. As he turned down the road, he saw abandoned farmhouse, after abandoned farmhouse.

Shawn drove until he saw an open gate on the left and headed down the path toward an old house and barn. The place looked deserted. It was exactly what they wanted. Shawn parked between the house and barn. An old shallow and an old- _well_ fashioned outhouse was just behind the barn. It was a beautiful old farmhouse, and it was the perfect place to finish the paint job on the truck.

Shawn went to work on the truck. It took about an hour for Shawn to paint the cab on the truck. As he stared at the new paint job, he thought, "Not bad for an old truck."

Dani decided to put together a meal out of the goodies Shawn had bought at the convenience store.

The peaceful afternoon was suddenly destroyed. From out of nowhere they heard a roaring noise, as a dozen bikers came roaring around the old house and stopped in a circle around them. Shawn grabbed an old crowbar he saw lying on the ground and held it in his right hand in a raised position.

The bikers were big and tough looking, but Shawn was prepared to fight till the death to defend his family. Then suddenly, the bikers killed the roaring engines. Shawn couldn't believe it; the bikers were laughing. The biggest, meanest looking biker looked around at the other bikers and said, "Well, boys, I think this is what they mean by catching a man with his guard down!"

They all laughed in agreement. Shawn was puzzled, as he stood there in front of Dani as she held Elizabeth.

Shawn swallowed hard and said, "Please don't harm my wife and child."

The big biker said, "Well, son, we didn't plan to harm anybody, but we did want to see what you folks were up to."

Dani and Shawn was still wrapped up in fear as the big biker said, "This is my grandparents' old home place and we saw your truck from the hillside over yonder and decided to investigate. So, let us introduce ourselves. We are "Heaven's Angels Bikers for the Lord!"

Dani looked at the bikers and all she saw was smiles.

Shawn said, "So, you're not killers?"

The big biker said, "No, sir, we are in the saving business!"

"Are you sure?" asked Shawn.

"I'm sure, son," said the biker.

Shawn still couldn't believe his ears. The big biker apologized for scaring them when they rode up.

"So this is your property?" asked Shawn.

The biker told him, "It had belonged to my grandparents, but they had passed away over twenty years ago."

Shawn apologized for trespassing and told the biker, "We will load up and leave."

The biker said, "You do not have to leave so quickly."

Then, the bikers fired up the big Harleys and sped away in a cloud of dust and thunder!

Shawn turned around and hugged Dani and said, "Heaven's Angels Bikers for the Lord." Wow! I thought we were dead!"

Dani confessed to Shawn, "I was absolutely terrified."

Shawn then told her, "We need to load up and hit the road."

They quickly loaded the truck and decided to eat on the road. The big Ford truck lumbered out onto the dirt road. As Shawn turned left, they said goodbye to the old farmhouse.

Shortly thereafter, they stopped at a stop sign and turned left on Highway 71. The old Ford truck picked up speed and the young family was on its way.

Chapter 14

It was getting dark and the young family was eager to get to Canada. It was too late to worry about how or why they made the decision to grab the gold and run. It was time to get serious about how to get safely to Canada. As the stars twinkled in the sky, both Dani and Elizabeth had fallen asleep. Shawn did his best to keep everything smooth and quiet.

The road had many curves and hills, so he wasn't able to drive very fast. Shawn glanced at the gauges; he realized the temperature gauge had moved almost to the red-hot position. The engine was running much hotter than it should under normal circumstances. A problem like overheating could jeopardize the border crossing. Shawn remembered a trick his father had taught him. If you notice your temperature gauge has risen, just turn on the heater. This would send about a quart of coolant into the radiator to help cool down the engine. He turned the heater control from cool to heat and moved the heater fan switch from off to high.

The temperature gauge slowly began to move back toward the normal range. He knew this would only temporarily bring the temperature down and that he still had a problem. The heat coming from the heater core quickly filled the truck's cab even with the windows down. Shawn needed to find a place to stop and look under the hood.

The sudden build-up of heat in the cab caused Dani to wake up and ask, "Shawn, why did you turn the heater up so high?"

Shawn explained, "The engine was running hot, so I turned the heater on to cool the engine until I could find a place to stop."

Shawn was driving only forty to forty-five miles per hour to help cool down the engine. He watched as the temperature gauge began to rise again.

Shawn saw a clear area just ahead on the right side of the road. It looked like an old parking lot. Shawn eased the big Ford truck off the road. Shawn saw a big semi pull over and follow him onto the gravel parking lot. Shawn let the truck's engine idle, set the parking brake, and reached for his flashlight under the seat. The flashlight's batteries apparently were dead and he just threw it back under the seat.

The truck driver walked up beside Shawn and asked, "Need some help, son?"

Shawn turned to see a tall thin man with black hair and mustache and asked, "Do you have a flashlight?"

The driver said, "Yes, I do."

Shawn informed the man, "I have an overheating problem."

The driver replied, "I know. I could smell the antifreeze when I was behind you."

As the driver spoke, he pulled a small flashlight from his pocket and handed it to Shawn.

Shawn opened the hood of the old Ford truck as steam was rising from a radiator hose.

The driver said, "Well, here's your problem, a bad hose."

As the driver spoke, he pushed the hose with his fingers and the steam became a stream of scalding hot coolant.

The driver said, "Just let it cool and wrap it with tape, then refill the radiator, and you can easily make it to the next town. I have some tape and a jug full of water just for emergencies."

Shawn said, "My name is Shawn McLeod."

The driver shook hands with Shawn and said, "My name is Roy Harrell."

Shawn told Roy, "I am glad that you stopped to help us."

Roy walked over to his big rig and opened the side pocket and removed a roll of black electrical tape and an old plastic gallon jug full of water. Roy walked back toward Shawn and said, "Let the engine cool down, wrap the entire roll of tape around the rupture in the hose, and let the engine idle while you pour the water in the radiator."

Shawn thanked Roy.

Roy said, "You're welcome and the next town is only a few miles up the road."

Roy turned and walked back to his rig and drove away.

As Roy changed gear after gear driving up the road, he thought to himself that the young couple resembled the couple he helped rescue from a burning house down in Georgia a couple of weeks before. "No," he said to himself. "It couldn't be them, because they had Minnesota license plates."

After the radiator cooled, Shawn wrapped the entire roll of tape around the radiator hose. He then started the engine and slowly poured the water in the radiator and now they were ready to go.

As they drove along, they saw a sign that said 'Justin, 9 miles." The little town of Justin was perfect; a small town with a garage and auto parts store, post office, a couple of other stores and, a little independent motel. Shawn parked in the motel parking lot. He went to the motel's office to rent a room for the night. The door was locked, but a sign in the window indicated a button to push for service after ten o'clock p.m. Shawn pushed the button and heard a ding-dong sound. He looked through the window in the door to see a young woman with blonde hair in a wheelchair coming toward the door. She unlocked the door and rolled back around the counter.

As Shawn entered the building, the young lady asked, "Can I help you?"

The lady had a big smile on her face, as Shawn approached the counter and said, "I'm sorry about being so late, but we need a room."

The young lady replied, "That's all right. That's what I'm here for."

She asked, "How many occupants for the room and how many nights?"

Shawn said, "Two adults, one child and one night only, please."

The young lady said, "The room would be forty-four dollars."

Shawn counted out the money and she handed him a key to room number 24.

Shawn asked, "Do you know what time the auto parts store opens?"

She said, "Seven o'clock."

She informed him, "Check out time is eleven o'clock a.m."

Shawn asked for a wake-up call at seven o'clock.

The motel was plain on the outside, but the inside was very nice and clean. Shawn turned the television on and located the *World News Channel*. Little Elizabeth played on the bed and Dani went to the bathroom for a shower.

Shawn watched the weather and sports. About twenty minutes later Dani came out of the bathroom and just stood there smiling and slowly turned around. Shawn glanced up at her and saw that she had cut her long blonde hair just below her earlobes.

"What have you done?" he said.

Dani said, "If the authorities are looking for a lady with long blonde hair, don't you think short black hair would be much better?"

Shawn said, "Let me guess. Now, you're going to dye it?"

Dani was up late dyeing her hair, but Elizabeth slept through the appearance makeover.

When the wake-up call came, Shawn was on it lightning fast, so it wouldn't wake up Dani and Elizabeth.

Shawn drove the Ford truck across the street to the auto parts store and garage. They changed the oil and replaced the bad radiator hose. He drove back to the motel parking lot in just over thirty minutes. When Shawn entered the room, he heard little Elizabeth crying.

The counterman walked behind the counter and retrieved a new replacement.

Shawn told the man, "I also need a gallon of antifreeze and a couple of hose clamps."

The counterman quipped, "You need at least two gallons on an F-700 or that thing will freeze like a Popsicle."

Shawn knew the counterman was right.

Shawn said, "Sure, why not?"

Dani said, "Shawn, Elizabeth seemed a little scared of me this morning."

Shawn said, "It's, because you look different."

Elizabeth was crying and reaching for Shawn.

He turned the television on and watched the news. The *World News Network* channel reporter asked people on the street what they thought about the young couple and the missing treasure. Every person the reporter interviewed said, "Let them have it; it's theirs anyway."

A young woman said, "If possession is nine tenths of the law, let them have all of it."

Another man said, "I wish them well and hope they get away- screw the damn government!"

Then the reporter showed news flashes from news services around the world in England, Russia, Brazil, France and Japan. The reporter said, "This story has captured the hearts and minds of people all over the world and they are one hundred percent in favor of the young couple keeping the treasure! That is, until the story came to Atlanta, Georgia where a congressman was condemning the actions of the young couple."

Congressman Bill O'Connor stated, "I'm sick and tired of people glorifying this McLeod couple. They are nothing, but thieves, and if I have anything to do with it, they will spend the next few decades in prison where they belong!"

The crowd boos and hisses their objections as the congressman's face turns red.

A tall lady with long black hair wearing blue jeans and a red University of Georgia jacket stood and said, "Could it be you politicians are jealous that a young couple managed to walk away with more treasure in a day than ya'll have been able to steal in a lifetime?"

The congressman boiled over and screamed, "That's an insult to my integrity! We are public servants and we are only trying to protect a treasure that belongs to all of us!"

The crowd cheered and applauded at the lady's comments so that the politician's comments are barely audible.

Then the reporter looked into the camera and said, "As you can tell, people in America, as well as the entire world, support the young couple who discovered a tremendous treasure on their own land and decided to run away with it. Personally, I would have a hard time condemning them myself. Now back to WNN from Atlanta, Georgia. I'm Steve Moore reporting."

Dani spoke excitedly, "Can you believe that people all over the world are on our side?"

Shawn smiled and said, "Unfortunately, it's the ones who have the ability to send us to the slammer that feel differently!"

Dani smiled and ran her fingers through her short black hair and said, "I hope the authorities are still looking for a blonde."

Shawn and Dani locked the motel room door and climbed aboard the old Ford truck.

Dani looked over at Shawn, as they pulled out of the motel parking lot and said, "Now that we have a black truck and black hair, do you think we could eat in a real restaurant today before we say goodbye to the USA?"

Shawn asked, "Do you feel so safe that you think two of the most wanted fugitives on earth cold stop at a restaurant and have lunch like normal people?"

Dani smiled and said, "Yes, I do."

Shawn pulled up to the gas pumps in front of Fast Freddie's convenience store and filled the truck's tank with regular before entering the store in pursuit of coffee, doughnuts and milk. Shawn noticed a very old lady walking by the front of the store, pushing an empty wheelchair.

The clerk said, "That will be $91.46, sir."

The clerk realized that Shawn's attention was on the old lady, so he said a little louder, "That will be $91.46, sir!"

Shawn turned toward the clerk and said, "I'm sorry, I wasn't paying attention."

Shawn handed the clerk one hundred dollars in twenty dollar bills and asked, "Why is that old lady pushing an empty wheelchair?"

The clerk just snickered and said, "That's Mrs. Birdie Mae. She takes her husband for a ride through town every morning, weather permitting."

Shawn looked back at the old lady now turning the corner and said, "But the chair is empty!"

The clerk said, "Oh, no, it's not! See her Herbert died last year after being wheelchair bound for over fifteen years, so she had him cremated, and if you look really close, you will see a brass urn that contains his ashes sitting in the seat."

Shawn just shook his head and said, "That's a heck of a love story!"

Shawn walked out of the store with two large coffees, a sack full of doughnuts, and a carton of milk for Elizabeth. He pulled out on the street and he turned right traveling north.

The smiles on their faces turned to frowns, as they saw a prison work detail on the side of the road. Shawn switched the radio on to change the somber mood. He turned the dial until he came to a talk show. The caller was complaining about the price of gasoline.

The woman said, "I can't fill up my car without financing it at the bank!"

The talk show host said, "Yes, it is much too high, but what can we do?"

Then the lady caller said, "Maybe we all need to dig up a bunch of gold like that young couple from Georgia!"

Dani looked back at Shawn and said, "Are they talking about us?"

Shawn said, "I'm afraid so!"

Then another caller came on the line and said, "There's a story on the Internet about the couple with the gold, and it said that they have made it to Mexico!"

The talk show host said, "I had heard that story earlier this morning and believed the leadoff story was "Goldilocks and Her Gold Bars Does Tijuana."

The caller remarked, "Yes, that was it, so I guess they made it!"

The talk show host said, "Personally, I don't believe much of what I see on the internet. They could have put that story on the internet to throw the authorities off their tracks!"

The caller replied, "You're right."

Dani said, "Goldilocks and Her Gold Bars!"

The next caller on the radio said, "The politicians will probably murder them and split the gold, if they catch them!"

Shawn turned the radio off. He looked at Dani and saw a wave of fear come across her face as she said, "How could people talk like that? I sure hope my dad and your parents don't hear anything like that!"

Shawn said, "Regardless of how this turns out, I will always love you!"

A tear ran down Dani's face, as she held little Elizabeth in her arms.

Chapter 15

Meanwhile, back in Atlanta, Georgia, a meeting was taking place between state and federal authorities. Clyde Bostrum, head of the Atlanta branch of the FBI, had called together a group of his agents, plus members of the U.S. Marshals, and agents of the Georgia Bureau of Investigation to better organize the search for the McLeods and the missing treasure. The meeting was being held in a conference room of the Federal Building. As Clyde entered the conference room, you could tell he wasn't exactly the happiest man in Georgia.

Clyde was approaching sixty-five years of age and had more than enough time in to retire, but had bypassed retirement to stay on with the bureau. Clyde was tall, had black hair and admitted to being a little bit on the mean side. Clyde had a space between his two upper front teeth that he utilized for enormously loud whistling when he wanted everyone's attention.

As he entered the large room with white walls and wood floors, he threw his brown leather briefcase on the forty-foot long wood conference table and turned around to speak to some of the other agents in the room. Clyde raised his voice and said, "Didn't I say noon? Where is everybody?"

Agent Ripford L. Thomas, better known as Rip by his co-workers, said, "I think they tried to sneak in some lunch, sir."

Clyde yelled, "Lunch, hell, we got a young family from Stickville making the most sophisticated law enforcement officers in the world look like dummies. And they are having lunch, when they should be here!"

Clyde rubbed his eyes and said, "I tell you, Rip, I haven't slept for two nights. We have hunted down some the world's most notorious fugitives, but we got two kids making us look like a horse's ass!"

Agent Thomas squeezed in a "Yes, sir."

Clyde continued, "I'm telling you, we can't win. Did you see that poll that came out this morning? Over ninety-nine percent of the American people say, let them keep the gold." Clyde ranted on, "Hell, the press has tagged the young lady with golden blonde hair as Goldilocks. Heck, I got behind a pickup truck in traffic, on the way here this morning that had a Go-Go-Goldilocks Bumper sticker! Did you see the *World News Network* this morning? People in Moscow are cheering this couple on, and it's not just Moscow; it's Madrid, Rio, London, Paris, Montreal, and everywhere else including Pig's Snoot, Louisiana are rooting for them to get away!" yelled Clyde.

Rip was a little younger than Clyde, but had been with the bureau for nearly 30 years. His hair was turning gray which matched his suit and his eyes were red which matched his tie. He looked more like a high school principal than an F.B.I.

agent.

Clyde looked around the room and yelled, "Where's the coffee? Didn't I request coffee? After two nights without sleep, the least you people could do is have a pot of coffee!"

A young agent volunteered, "I'll run down to the coffee shop and get some."

Clyde turned and yelled, "Don't waste your time ogling at the young lady's knockers that runs the coffee shop, they're fake!"

The young agent suddenly turned back towards Clyde and asked, "How do you know they are fake?"

Clyde said, "Because I paid for them; she's my granddaughter."

Clyde turned back toward Rip and said, "I tell you, if we don't catch this couple soon, we are going to be meter maids by the time the press gets through with us. Now explain to me why we can't find a red and white moving van with a young family traveling somewhere. There must be somebody who has seen them!"

Rip replied, "Well, there have been reports on the internet that they have made it to Mexico!"

Clyde's face soured as he yelled, "The internet. Hell! The internet has stories that President Bush is an alien from Mars; I don't give two cents what the internet says!"

Agent Thomas grinned and said, "I'm sorry sir, I just threw that one in there as an ice breaker!"

Clyde recoiled like a rattler after a missed strike and yelled, "I'm going to break something besides ice, if I don't get some results soon!"

Clyde sat down at the end of the long table, looked around and yelled, "Where's my map, didn't I request a map!"

Agent Thomas said, "It's over here, behind the plants."

Agent Thomas rolled a map stand out and parked it near Clyde.

As the law enforcement officers started taking their seats, Clyde rose to his feet, but didn't say a word. He walked around the room like an old ill rooster ready to spur.

Clyde stopped and faced the officers, and said, "I want to thank the U.S. Marshals and Georgia Bureau of Investigation Officers for attending. As you know we have become the laughing stock of the world over this young couple, the McLeods, who made off with an estimated three tons of gold bars, coins and a barrel full of diamonds, pearls, and only God knows what else!"

Clyde's eyes gazed off into space as he continued, "Now we know with such a heavy load, they couldn't travel far or fast in that old U-Move-It truck; it's over 20 years old and according to the previous owner, it has nearly 200,000 miles on the odometer." He looked back toward the assembled crowd and said, "We have searched every square inch within twenty-five miles of the cabin at Mountaindale and found absolutely nothing. Now that old truck and this little couple didn't just disappear from the face of the earth."

Clyde stared at the ceiling, then looked toward Rip and said, "Rip, can you hit the lights and turn on the projector? Now, this is a picture of an identical U-Move-It truck, it's red and white, and would stand out like a fire in a cave." He turned back toward the assembled crowd and said, "We have asked for the public's help in locating this truck and the young family, but we don't have one solid lead. My question is, how have they eluded us? Now according to statistics there are over 2000 of these old moving vans still on the road. Now this old truck has a gasoline engine and it gets approximately eight miles per gallon and they will have to stop a couple of times a day to fill up. We need to canvas service stations and pass out pictures of this old truck and our young couple."

Clyde walked over to pull the large map down from its rolled up position on the tripod stand. Instantly everybody in the room broke out in laughter. Clyde looked around the room. He looked about as shocked as someone who just found a possum in their mailbox. Finally Clyde turned to see a Go-Go-Goldilocks sticker right in the middle of the map of the United States. As he turned his head to look at the officers, you could see the fires of hell in his blood shot eyes.

He ripped the sticker from the map and yelled, "I want to know what smart butt put this sticker on this map!"

Clyde said, "Now gentlemen, if there is anybody here who thinks stealing millions of dollars of gold and treasure of national historical importance is funny, the exit is over here!"

The look on Clyde's face let everybody know he was as serious as an earthquake. The room got so quiet even though it was on the third floor; you could hear people walking on the sidewalk down below.

Clyde continued, "Now the general consensus is, they are attempting to flee the US of A, so they would most likely go to Canada or Mexico or they could try to ship it out by boat, but I don't think so." He looked around the room, as if he is buried in deep thought and then he said, "Now it's a possibility that they could just be hiding out somewhere, but we have checked this boy's family farm by air and on foot and found nothing."

Then Clyde's demeanor changed to concern as he said, "If this young man drove that truck load of gold to Mexico; that would be suicide. I hope for their own safety they have better sense than that!"

Clyde seemed to be thinking really hard, as he turned and asked the other agents, "What thoughts do you have?"

A U.S. Marshal stood and said, "Another possibility is they could have reburied the gold at another location and then burned the truck."

Clyde gave serious consideration to the Marshal's suggestion and then said, "That's a possibility and that could answer the question of why we don't have a positive sighting."

An agent stood and said, "What they have accomplished, so far, is pretty amazing, if you ask me!"

Clyde rolled his eyes and responded, "They had surprise on their side and I guess determination and willpower, but this isn't the greatest criminal act of the century."

A young Marshal stood and said, "Sir, I believe it is the biggest, because the true value of the gold and treasure could be several hundred million dollars!"

A moan could be heard from the officers in the room, but Clyde's expression didn't change as he said, "The bigger the crime, the harder the fall!"

Another U.S. Marshal, a young man wearing his camouflaged uniform, stood and asked, "Have you checked the families and friends to see if they have been receiving help from them?"

Clyde said, "Yes, we have a tap on the McLeod's phone and we are tracking their movements, as well as the young lady's father, but so far we have nothing."

Another U.S. Marshal stood and asked, "Have you checked on the results of the fire Marshal's investigation into the fire at his work place and at the personal home of the McLeods."

Clyde looked over at Rip and said, "I believe Agent Thomas has that information for us."

Then Agent Rip Thomas stood and said, "The state Fire Marshal's office has informed us that the fire at the Barton Manufacturing plant was arson. But the Fire Marshal said that apparently Shawn had nothing to do with it. They believe it was the disgruntled son-in-law of the owners. Also, they said the fire at the McLeod's home was caused by an old gas line that apparently was stress cracked and no charges will be filed against the McLeods in either case."

Clyde asked, "Do we have a character report on Shawn McLeod?"

Agent Thomas rose and said, "Shawn McLeod has no criminal record and made good grades in school, even helped his father on their farm and worked part time at a local grocery store. Dani McLeod, Shawn's wife, made good grades in school. No criminal record. She had moved to Russellville her senior year in high school to live with her grandparents after losing her mother who was killed in an automobile accident by a drunk driver."

Clyde said, "So this young man made good grades in school, and neither have a criminal record."

As Clyde pondered his own words, Rip stood and asked, "What made them do it, Sir?"

Clyde looked back at Rip and said, "I don't know. Young people in desperate straits might have felt they had nothing to lose."

Rip said, "We need to find this young couple for their own good, before someone recognizes them and murders them for the gold!"

Clyde looking very serious as he faced Rip and said, "You are 100 percent correct. If we don't find them soon, their bodies may be found floating in a river somewhere. Not only them, but, apparently, they also have a baby."

Then Rip said, "We've got to find them and soon!"

A young woman suddenly entered the conference room, rushed up to Clyde, with a piece of paper, handed it to Clyde and said, "I apologize for the interruption, but I thought you might need this information."

Clyde looked at the paper, and then said, "Gentlemen, the State of Georgia has just issued a one million dollar reward for the capture of the McLeods and the recovery of the missing treasure!"

Rip stood again and said, "I bet that will get the phones to ringing!"

Then Clyde read on, "Law enforcement officers will be eligible to receive this reward."

Everybody in the room cheered and applauded.

As the room exploded into excited discussion among the officers, Clyde walked over to Rip with a concerned look on his face and said, "I'm not sure this is a good idea; this could cause more confusion than a rat snake in a hen house!"

Clyde finally had to restore order with the most earsplitting whistle you can imagine. Then he said, "This could cause a disaster. We have to shut the exit doors tighter than the plastic wrapper on a Chinese made toilet plunger and we have to do it now!"

Clyde looked around the room and then continued, "This young couple did something very stupid, but unless we get to them first, this young family may pay with their lives for what they have done." He walked back to the center of the room and said, "We will be blamed and hounded by the press. And the press glorifies them. The American people have turned them into folk heroes, but it is anarchy. We must find them!"

Rip Thomas stood and spoke, "We have contacted Home Land Security and they will be watching the seaports and airports, so we need to concentrate on the borders with Mexico and Canada!"

Clyde pointed to the big map beside him and said, "If they didn't hide it, then they are somewhere trying to cross the border and that is where we need to concentrate our search."

Then the door opened again the same young lady who brought the first message gave Clyde another piece of paper and then walked away. As Clyde read the note, his face lighted up like a hundred watt bulb.

Clyde said, "We have good news, Dani McLeod has relatives in Manitoba, Canada. Now that leads me to believe they are going north!"

Rip Thomas stood and said, "Remember, we need to concentrate our attention on gas stations."

Clyde said, "The eyes of the nation and the world are on us. If we let them get away, then terrorist elements around the world will think they can walk right in and that's something we don't want. We must not fail."

Clyde thanked everyone for coming and then he headed for the door.

Chapter16

Shawn turned the big Ford van around and pulled back on the road. Shawn drove and listened to Dani talking about the relatives they were going to visit. She told Shawn they lived near White Mouth Lake. She explained it was only about twenty miles across the border.

The couple came around a sharp curve and saw a traffic jam. Shawn was concerned, until he saw a bunch of cows wondering around on the shoulder of the road. Then things changed, as he slowly made his way around the curve. He saw two Minnesota State Police cars just ahead of them.

Shawn was concerned. Slowly, the traffic moved on toward the police cars, as the police officers motioned for the drivers to proceed. Finally, they moved by the police officers. Shawn and Dani were wearing their darkest pair of shades and trying to act normal. As Shawn began to slowly accelerate, he heard a loud whistle. As he looked back in the truck's large rear view mirror, he saw first one, then both, police officers waving for him to stop. Shawn's heart was beating so fast and hard, he was afraid the officers could hear it. He stopped and waited for the officer to approach.

When the officer got to the truck Shawn asked, "Is something wrong, Officer?"

The young officer said, "I could smell smoke, when you came by me. I think something is wrong with your truck!"

Shawn was relieved, but concerned. Mechanical problems could mean trouble, as well. Shawn locked the parking brake, opened his door, and stepped out of the truck. The officer was looking under the van body of the truck near the rear wheels.

The officer said, "I don't see anything on fire, but I could see and smell smoke as you drove by!"

Shawn hoped the officer wouldn't recognize him wearing a cap and shades.

The officer said, "I can smell it, but I can't figure out what it is."

Shawn said, "I had a radiator hose burst last night and that might be the antifreeze we lost burning on the muffler and giving a strange smell."

The young officer said, "That could be it; I could have mistaken steam, for smoke."

Shawn thanked the officer for his concern and said he would keep an eye on the situation and he thanked the officer as he climbed back in the cab of the truck and drove away. A wave of relief came over them, but they knew they still had about eighty miles to go before they could relax.

As the big truck reached highway speed Dani said, "I thought we were toast!"

Shawn said, "I was a little scared myself!"

Dani said, "Our paint job and disguises must be working."

Shawn said, "I must admit your idea to cut and dye your hair was a brilliant one; you're not only beautiful, but you are also very smart, my dear."

Dani smiled at Shawn and said, "Let's stop at a real restaurant where we can sit down, relax, and enjoy a meal together."

Shawn replied, "Alright, I'm tired of junk food too."

They drove for nearly an hour before they came to a little town with a Happy House Restaurant. Shawn looked at Dani seeking approval and Dani smiled and said, "It's fine."

Shawn turned into the parking lot and drove around back and parked behind the building. The small diner was one of those you see made from a singlewide mobile home. They have a table at each end and a counter and chairs that ran from one end to the other. All of the seats were taken, except the table at the right end of the little diner, so they sat down at the table. The smell of delicious food cooking filled the air and the chatter of the other patrons bounced off the glass windows that ran the length of the building. One lady was busy cooking up a storm of food and another lady was busy taking orders and serving the food.

In a few minutes a mid-forties lady with a name tag that said 'Jenny' came down to their table and apologized for the wait. Jenny was a nice looking lady about 5'5" tall with dark brown hair and eyes. She had a big smile and was busy chewing bubble gum. Jenny retrieved a pencil from behind her right ear and pulled the order pad from her pocket, smiled and said, "Can I help you?"

Shawn and Dani had been studying the small menu on the table and they ordered deluxe club sandwich meals with cola and a big bottle of milk for little Elizabeth.

Jenny asked, "Is the order "for here" or "to go?""

Dani quickly responded, "For here."

The patrons on the other end of the diner paid at the counter and left. Two men dressed in camouflaged uniforms entered and took the table on the other end. Jenny's eyes followed the two men, when they entered and sat down. The two men acted a little arrogant toward the other patrons.

The older one, a middle aged man with red hair, yelled at Jenny, "Hey toots, we are in a hurry!"

Jenny finally walked down to their table and took their order.

Jenny suddenly appeared at Shawn and Dani's table and they realized the "for here" order was in carry out trays and paper bags.

Shawn and Dani were shocked, but the concerned look on Jenny's face told them something was wrong.

Jenny handed the food to Shawn and Dani. Then, she leaned down and whispered, "The two men that just came in and are seated at the table at the other end of the diner are U.S. Marshals. They have been looking for you for a couple of days, so wait until I distract them and make a break for the door!"

Shawn and Dani were horrified and just couldn't believe she was going to help them escape.

Shawn reached for his wallet to pay for the food, but Jenny said, "No, this is on the house!"

Dani was very impressed by her actions and said, "Thank you, but how could you tell who we were? Did our disguises fail?"

Jenny leaned down and whispered, "Honey, with a face that pretty, I could identify you, if you were bald headed!" Then Jenny said, "Now you wait until you hear a bunch of screaming and hollering, then you get out the front door and follow that old gravel road out the rear of the parking lot about a mile down the road where you will cross an old wooden bridge. Then, you will see a big red barn on the left. That's my house. Just park behind the barn, eat your food and I'll be there in about forty-five minutes and I will help you."

Shawn could only manage a "Thank you."

Dani said, "Thank you so much, but why are you helping us?"

Jenny just smiled and said, "Heck, Honey, people are rooting for you to get away and besides one of those jerks pinched my behind this morning! Now when you hear the screaming, you get that pretty little wife and baby out of here and go to my house."

As Jenny turned and walked away, Shawn and Dani just stared at each other for a split second trying to digest what had just taken place. Dani turned her head just in time to see Jenny pick up a glass pitcher full of scalding hot coffee. Jenny winked at her, as she turned and walked toward the table at the other end of the diner. The two men who apparently, had no idea about what was about to happen were looking out the front window and talking about the weather.

Shawn and Dani waited for the mayhem. Almost instantly, screams of pain and anguish are mixed with an explosion of cursing that would have embarrassed a sailor. Jenny had supposedly, accidentally, let an entire pitcher of scalding hot coffee slip from her hands, as she approached the table and its entire contents of boiling coffee had splattered into the two men's laps!

Shawn and Dani grabbed the baby and the food and raced toward the door as every eye and ear in the little restaurant was focused on the two men in pain. As Shawn pushed the glass door open he heard Jenny exclaim, "Oh, I'm so sorry, fellows; it just slipped out of my hand!"

Shawn and Dani wasted no time getting into the Ford truck. Shaw turned around and proceeded down the gravel road Jenny had told them about. In just a couple of minutes they crossed an old wooden bridge. Then, they saw a big red barn on the left side of the road. Shawn quickly entered the driveway and parked behind the big red barn. The barn and surroundings were beautiful. Shawn shut the engine off and looked over at Dani. She looked like she was in shock.

Shawn asked, "Are you alright?"

Dani slowly turned her head to face Shawn and said, "I think so!"

Shawn exclaimed, "Can you believe that wonderful woman?"

Dani said, "She's an angel. Can you imagine how painful it would be to have an entire pot of scalding coffee dumped in your lap?"

Shawn said, "You know, I almost felt sorry for them."

Dani replied, "Those fools really paid for pinching her behind, didn't they?"

"They sure did," Shawn said.

The young couple saw a picnic table just ahead of the truck and decided to borrow it and enjoy the food. After their meal, Shawn and Dani studied the road atlas trying to figure out where they were and how to get to the border as inconspicuously as possible. In a few minutes a red S-10 Chevrolet Blazer came around the building and parked beside the Ford van. To the young couple's relief, it was Jenny.

She stepped out of the Blazer and yelled, "Did I fix those smart butts or what!"

Dani raced over to Jenny while holding little Elizabeth and gave her a big hug. "Thank you so much. What you did was absolutely incredible!" Said Dani, as tears ran down her face.

Jenny smiled and responded, "All in a day's work. Nothing to it; actually, I have wanted to do just that for nearly twenty years, but today I finally got the nerve!"

Shawn asked, "How did you know they were U.S. Marshals?"

Jenny replied, "My cousin is a State Police officer and he told me who they were and what they were doing!"

Shawn said, "I'm sorry. I hope we don't get you into any trouble with your cousin."

Jenny said, "Nonsense, my cousin's opinion of those two is a lot worse than mine!"

Dani said, "You must be an angel; you just showed up at the right time and place to save us!"

Jenny said, "You know, I don't think anybody ever accused me of being an angel before, but it feels good."

In all the excitement, little Elizabeth leaned over in Dani's arms and reached for Jenny. Jenny happily reached out for little Elizabeth and said, "What a beautiful little girl!"

Dani said, "Well, thank you."

Jenny held little Elizabeth and said, "She's so precious."

Little Elizabeth seemed to be perfectly happy and content in Jenny's arms.

Dani said, "Your place is so pretty. I really love it."

Jenny smiled and said, "Well, thank you. My husband and I bought this place ten years ago and it had a barn, but no house. So we turned this barn into a house."

Dani smiled and said, "I like it."

Jenny said, "Come on inside and I'll show you around."

Shawn and Dani followed Jenny into the barn-home. Jenny led them into the large living room. The vaulted ceiling was over twenty feet high and had a sky light on one side and hanging plants on the other. They could see an over-hanging balcony where the stairs ended to the rear of the room above.

Dani said, "I guess your son and husband will be shocked, when they get home and find us here."

Jenny replied, "Our son is in the Army and is stationed in Iraq and my husband is a long haul truck driver. He came home last night and left again this morning for Florida."

Dani said, "I guess you must be lonely with your son and husband away."

Jenny responded, "Yes, but I've been putting in so many hours at that darn diner that I don't have time to get really lonely."

Little Elizabeth had fallen asleep in Jenny's arms, so they laid her on a bed in a bedroom that is next to the living room. The three returned to the large living room.

Jenny said, "I can lead you to the border, but it would probably be best to wait until sundown."

Dani saw a picture on the wall of a much younger Jenny and a man and asked, "Is this your husband?"

Jenny walked over to where Dani was standing and said, "Yes, that's my Roy."

Dani said, "He looked familiar."

Then Jenny led Dani to another picture. "This is my son, Eric," said Jenny.

Dani said, "Oh, he's handsome!"

A very concerned look came to Jenny's face as she said, "I just pray he comes home safe."

As the women walked around the room, Dani confided in Jenny how they made a crazy, rash decision to load up the treasure and run and she explained to Jenny all of the bad things that happened to them before they found the treasure. Dani's face showed a ton of concern, as she explained to Jenny what led them to make such a decision.

Jenny said, "I was a little wild and compulsive when I was young myself."

Then Jenny said, "Let's turn the news channel on and see what the latest is on your story."

Within a minute of the television coming on, a newscaster ended one story and then said, "We have a report on the Goldilocks story from a small town in mid-state Minnesota. Paul Jones has the story."

"Hi John, I'm here in Wadena, Minnesota with a Mrs. Roush whose son and his friend came home with paint on them. Can you tell us what you found out please, Mrs. Roush?"

"Yes, sir, my Jimmy came home with paint on his hands and clothes and he wouldn't tell me at first, so I had to call the mother of his pal Junior. Junior finally broke down and told us that they had helped a young couple paint an old red and white truck that was parked behind an old vacant warehouse next door to the Wal-Depot store."

The reporter asked, "And what color was the paint?"

Mrs. Roush said, "Black, it was black. Will I qualify for part of the million dollar reward?"

Dani stood and yelled, "A million dollar reward!"

Shawn said, "It must be a mistake!"

Jenny said, "The story about the reward came out this morning. Didn't you hear about it on the news?"

They all looked back toward the television screen as the reporter continued, "We have been informed that the police are now viewing the Wal-Depot stores surveillance tapes to see, if they can find the McLeods purchasing the paint and yet another twist in the Goldilocks story unfolding here in the state of Minnesota. I'm Paul Jones for the *World News Network* in Wadena, Minnesota. Now back to you, John."

As John picked up the story again he recapped, "The truck authorities are looking for what will be black now, instead of red and white. So stay tuned and we will keep you informed 24-7 on WNN."

Then suddenly the News channel went to commercials. Shawn continued to hold Dani in his arms as she said, "Oh my, a million dollars reward!"

Jenny said, "Don't worry, honey, you're going to be across the border in a little while and besides most people don't believe the government will actually pay the reward."

Dani sobbed in Shawn's arms, "Now that they have reported the truck is black, we don't have a chance!"

Shawn continued to console Dani as she cried, but he also realized they are in real danger. He even considered painting the truck again.

Dani said, "It's hopeless!"

Shawn said, "Please don't cry, darling!"

Dani suddenly turned toward Jenny and said, "You tried to help us. Why don't you turn us in so you can get the money?"

Jenny stood and said, "I'm not going to turn you in and you're going to make it. Now, just calm down!"

Little Elizabeth woke up in a strange room and started crying and Dani rushed to check on her.

Jenny said to Shawn, "We need to get on the road; it's going to be dark soon."

Chapter 17

Meanwhile, back in Atlanta, Clyde Bostrum was being inundated with copy cats; hundreds of sightings were being reported from Miami to Seattle. Everybody in America who owns one of those old used U-Move-It vans have put them up for sale. Over one hundred people had confessed to stealing the treasure. Clyde had been rushed by helicopter to several sites where a red and white truck driven by couples, usually wearing blonde wigs, were stopped and demanded to be arrested. One old lady wearing a blonde wig was over ninety years old. After the state of Georgia put out the million-dollar reward, people were turning in neighbors, friends, relatives and even each other. Clyde stood by his desk and drank half a bottle of Pepto Bismal and looked out the window wondering why he just didn't retire last year and not become the laughing stock of law enforcement.

A young lady raced into the room and said, "Mr. Bostrum, you need to answer line four."

Clyde just stood there by the window and looked out over the streets of Atlanta. He didn't realize she was in the room, as he stood there while the phone on his desk rang constantly. Clyde wondered, if he jumped from the third floor window would it kill him or would he just wind up crippled and humiliated.

The young lady yelled, "Sir! You need to answer line four!"

Clyde finally turned to face her and said, "Let me guess! Two orangutans driving a red and white ice cream truck wearing blonde wigs have been stopped on I-285 and have confessed."

She said, "No, it's important, the Minneapolis, Minnesota office is on the phone with urgent news for you!"

Clyde turns and walks toward his phone, but just before he answered, he looked back toward the young agent and said, "If this is another smartass call like the one I got from our Houston office who offered to loan me an old blood hound named 'Tater', your butt's going to have teeth marks all over it."

Finally Clyde picked up the phone and said, "Hello, Clyde Bostrum here."

Then as he listened to the call. His face lit up like a florescent light bulb.

Agent Henry Downs said, "Clyde, this is Henry Downs in Minnesota. We have just received word from Wadena, Minnesota police that two kids helped a young couple paint an old red and white truck parked behind a Wal-Depot store."

Clyde interrupted and said, "Let me guess; she wants to know if she can turn her kids in for some of the reward money for aiding and abetting after the fact. Right, Henry?"

Agent Downs said, "No, Clyde, just listen. We have agents on the scene and the surveillance tape from store proved it was him. It was Shawn McLeod!"

Clyde yelled, "Are they sure, absolutely sure!"

Agent Down said, "Yes, we are absolutely positive it was him."

Clyde's face lit up like the Las Vegas Strip as he asked, "What color was the paint?"

Agent Downs said, "Black, gloss black, five gallons of gloss black."

Clyde yelled, "I'm on my way!"

Clyde slammed the phone down on the receiver and yelled at the young lady, "Get me a charter jet. I'm going to Minnesota!"

The young lady said, "Yes, sir!" and walked out the door.

Clyde packed his brief case and then pushed the intercom button on his phone and yelled, "Have a car waiting for me at the front door!"

Meanwhile, a man in Justin, Minnesota had just closed his garage and auto parts business and walked across the street to a motel to help his wife fix dinner. He had closed a little early, because his wife had been confined to a wheel chair after having hip surgery. As he walked into the motel office, and then around behind the counter to their living area in the rear, the local news came on the big screen television on the wall in front of him and his wife.

"This is a Channel 24 news bulletin. Reports are that the McLeods, the young couple from Georgia who have eluded a nationwide dragnet for days, have apparently painted their old red and white truck black sometime yesterday in the small town of Wadena, Minnesota. Authorities believe they are trying to slip into Canada. A one million dollar reward has been offered by the state of Georgia for their capture. People with information about the couple could share in the reward, but they must have had personal contact with them!"

The couple at the motel looked at each other for a split second and then raced for the telephone. The lady in the wheel chair cut her husband off, as he tried to race by her. He tripped and fell head first into a large trash can, as his legs dangled and kicked and his muffled screams for help went unanswered. His wife dialed the 800 number on the television screen.

Meanwhile, two Minnesota State police officers had just loaded up their food tray at a restaurant when the news story flashed on the screen of a television playing just above them. When the story came on, they raced for the door.

A convenience store operator in Justin, Minnesota was busy ringing up customer's orders, when he saw the story on the television; he just grinned and said, "Now, that's a hell of a love story!"

A truck driver just outside of Nashville, Tennessee heard the news report and thought of the young couple he helped the night before, but he thought, "No, they had a Minnesota license plate."

Chapter 18

Meanwhile, back at Jenny's house, Shawn and Jenny planned a route from Jenny's house to the Canadian border. The route would lead them on country roads that are mostly traveled by the farm families in the area. Shawn realized that they have only a 50/50 chance of making it across the border.

Dani sat in a big soft comfortable chair holding little Elizabeth to her chest as Shawn knelt down next to her and in a whispered voice he said, "Why don't you and the baby stay here with Jenny and I'll try to get the truck across the border. If I make it, Jenny could drive you across tomorrow?"

Dani said, "No, we started this crazy journey together and regardless of how it turns out, we will stay together."

Shawn leaned over the side of the chair and hugged Dani and said, "If anything goes wrong, I will tell them it was all my fault, and I will take the blame."

Shawn looked at Jenny and said, "I don't want to risk getting you into any trouble. If we get caught, we won't say anything about you."

Jenny walked over to a cabinet on the wall and removed a portable citizens band radio and walked back over to Shawn and gave it to him and said, "I have one of these in my car and you can plug this one in your cigarette lighter, so we can communicate with each other."

Shawn looked at Dani and said, "I'm ready, if you are."

Jenny said, "I need to be at least a quarter of a mile ahead of you, so I can warn you, if I see danger."

Jenny tried to assure them the back roads should be safe and that northern Minnesota people are fiercely independent and don't particularly care for the federal government.

Shawn went to install the CB radio and to check out the old truck. It was full of engine oil, coolant, and the gas gauge showed over half a tank of gas. Shawn patted the hood of the old Ford truck and said, "Just a few more miles and we will be safe, old friend."

Little Elizabeth was still a little cranky after her short nap, but Jenny gave her a bottle of chocolate milk to make her happy.

Dani handed little Elizabeth to Shawn and climbed up the steps of the truck.

Jenny came out the door of her home and said, "If I see something suspicious, you will need to hide, or come back here."

Jenny got into her Chevrolet Blazer, backed up, and pulled out of the driveway.

Shawn entered the driver's side of the truck and said, "I can't believe we tried to do something so crazy."

Shawn turned toward Dani and said, "I'm sorry for dragging you into this insane caper."

Dani said, "You didn't drag me, darling. It was both of us that came up with this crazy quest and I don't want you to feel like it was all your fault."

Shawn gave Dani a wink and they were on their way. Shawn waited at the end of the driveway for about thirty seconds. He looked at the map again as he gave Jenny time to put some distance between them. Shawn turned left and proceeded north. The lump in his throat was getting bigger and he had to keep his eyes opened every minute of the next few miles.

After driving about three miles, Jenny's voice came over the CB radio as she said, "I just met a large green combine and you will probably see it just over the next hill.

Just as they reached the hill, the big green combine passed on by. The driver, a big heavyset man with a full beard, just smiled and waved. Then Shawn pulled back on the gravel-covered dirt road and drove a little faster in order to catch up with Jenny. As Shawn drove along the road, he thought about how peaceful and beautiful the countryside was. They saw an occasional farmhouse, barns, fences, and a barking dog or two.

The farms reminded Shawn of his family's farm and Shawn felt a little homesick. The thought occurred to him that he might never see his family's farm again and he felt very sad. Shawn wished he had never found the gold and treasure. He had something worth more than all of the treasures on earth: Dani, the baby, his parents, his little sisters, and the beautiful farm he was raised on, was more than anyone could ever ask for in one lifetime. Shawn thought about his parents; they must be worried sick about them. Shawn had been daydreaming so much that he had forgotten which way to turn, so he called Jenny on the CB radio.

Jenny said, "Come on straight through the intersection. I will stop and wait for you."

In a couple of minutes, they pulled up beside Jenny's red Blazer and stopped. Jenny was standing at the rear of her car and Shawn could see that something was wrong. As darkness fell, Jenny said, "I guess in all the excitement, I forgot I was low on gas."

Shawn asked, "Do you have enough to get home?"

Jenny said, "Yes, but I can't lead you all the way to the border.

Shawn said, "It's alright. We will be fine. Just turn around and go home."

Jenny said, "I hate to leave you."

It was getting darker by the minute and everyone knew they needed to get going, so Dani gave Jenny a big hug and said, "Thank you, you've been so kind. I will never forget you!"

Then Shawn walked over and gave Jenny a hug and said, "Thank you so much!"

Jenny said, "I'm sure you will be alright, just follow this road until you cross an old wooden bridge, that's how you will know you're across the border." Jenny continued, "After crossing the wooden bridge, continue to follow this road until you come to a small town. Then call your family."

Jenny waved good-bye, as Shawn and Dani climbed back into the big Ford truck's cab and drove away.

Chapter 19

Jenny turned around and drove back toward her home and thought, "Roy is always coming home with all those sensational stories like the one on a recent trip where he helped a young couple out of a burning house in the middle of the night down in Georgia. Now I'll have a story for him!"

Shawn drove slowly along when suddenly, out of nowhere something strange appeared in front of them. Shawn's foot hit the brake pedal so fast and hard, he stalled the engine. Dani screamed as the truck stopped just inches from the object ahead of them. Instantly, Shawn and Dani looked at each other and both yelled, "A moose!"

Little Elizabeth, frightened by the sudden stop, started crying as Dani removed her from her child safety seat. Standing in front of the truck is a full-grown male moose. With antlers about four feet wide and its eyes staring back at them.

Shawn blew the truck's horn repeatedly, but the big animal just ignored them and stayed put. Shawn grabbed the truck's parking brake handle and opened his door.

Dani yelled, "Be careful, it might be dangerous!"

Shawn walked up to the big animal and yelled, "Get out of the way!"

The moose just looked at Shawn and then turned its head, as if to ignore him.

Dani still trying to calm little Elizabeth down, held her in her arms and watched as Shawn continued to yell at the moose.

Shawn waved his arms and yelled again and again, but the moose just stood there like he was a statue. Shawn then tried to talk to the moose. He said, "Now let's be reasonable. You can stand anywhere you want to in the United States, Canada, or Mexico; if you will just M-o-o-o-o-ve and let us get by!"

The moose didn't move.

Shawn screamed and yelled and screamed, but the moose didn't move.

Dani, after calming little Elizabeth, put her back in her child seat and got out of the truck and walked around to the front and said, "Shawn, you shouldn't yell at a dumb animal!"

Shawn turned toward Dani and snapped, "If he doesn't move, I'm going to run over the ugly beast!"

Then suddenly the moose looked back toward the young couple and let out a big 'ooooooooo' sound.

Shawn screamed at the moose, "Mooooooove!

The moose once again bellowed 'ooooooooo."

Dani yelled, "That's it! I'm not going to stand out here in the night air and watch a moose and a jackass yell at each other," and she got back in the truck.

Shawn looked back toward the moose and said, "Now are you happy? You have caused my little sweet wife to yell at me!"

Then suddenly the big moose broke wind and walked away.

Shawn yelled, "Thanks a lot," as he held his hand over his nose.

Finally, Shawn returned to the big truck and started the engine.

Dani asked, "What happened? How did you get it to move?"

Shawn just said, "It's something you wouldn't want to share."

Shawn revved up the big Ford truck's V-8 engine and with a gallon of adrenalin said, "Nothing is going to stop me now. If I see another moose in the road tonight, we will provide moose burgers for everybody in Northern Minnesota. So break out the barbeque sauce."

Shawn became a man on a mission, more determined than ever to get across the border. But as he let out on the clutch peda,l the truck didn't move an inch. Shawn looked at Dani, as the truck made a screeching sound. Shawn figured he had failed to get the truck in gear, so he revved the engine again and shifted the gearshift lever to neutral, and then back to first gear. But, again the truck didn't move. It just made the same screeching sound. Shawn tried again and again, but the once faithful and reliable old truck just sat still and made the screeching sound.

Shawn was so frustrated he didn't know what to do. As he sat there and realized something had apparently broken in the truck's power train, and he wasn't going anywhere. Suddenly, he opened the door and jumped out and screamed in the direction where the moose had left and yelled, "Are you happy now you big stupid, ugly flea bitten hat rack!"

Shawn then just fell on the ground in front of the truck and yelled, "Why me, Lord, what did I do, what did I do?"

Dani got out of the truck and walked over to Shawn, as he laid face down on the ground and knelt down and patted him on his back, as he lay on the ground like a bear rug. Dani whispered, "I love you!"

Shawn didn't speak, but after a few minutes of drowning in self-pity he said, "Please, kill me!"

Dani knelt down again and hugged the lifeless figure on the ground and said, "No, I'm not going to kill you. You are just having a bad day!"

Then Shawn whispered, "It's been a month of pure hell!"

As Shawn laid on the ground in front of the truck, Dani saw a set of headlights approaching behind the truck and said, "Shawn, get up. Someone is coming."

Shawn mumbled, "Good, maybe they will kill me."

Dani was still trying to get Shawn up off the ground when the approaching vehicle slowly drove around the Ford van and stopped near the front of the truck. The black four door Dodge Durango sat idling beside Shawn and Dani as the driver, a big tall middle age black man got out of the driver's seat and ran around the front of his vehicle and yelled, "What happened, did you have an accident?"

Shawn still lying face down on the ground murmured, "My whole life has been an accident."

Dani looked up and said, "No, we almost hit a moose and then the truck wouldn't move."

The passenger in the Durango, a middle-aged black lady opened her door and asked, "Is he alright?"

Dani said, "I think so."

The man asked, "What can we do to help?"

Dani said, "I guess we need a tow truck."

The man scratched his head and said, "A tow truck out here and at night would cost a small fortune."

The lady asked, "Why is he lying on the ground?"

Dani explained, "We stopped suddenly for a moose, and then the truck wouldn't move, and so he just fell on the ground in frustration."

The man said, "So, he's had a bad day."

Dani just shook her head yes and said, "And now he wants someone to kill him."

The man and his wife walked over to Shawn, as he laid face down on the ground and the man said, "I'm Otis Green and this is my wife, Winfred. We will help you get your truck fixed and back on the road, but first you will have to get up, dust yourself off, and shake my hand."

Shawn rolled over and used the truck's bumper to help pull himself up on his feet and said, "I would be most grateful, sir."

Mr. Green looked at his wife and said, "Look, honey, he looks much better already!"

Shawn introduced himself as Patrick, his middle name, and Dani as Elaine, her middle name and shook Mr. Green's hand and thanked them for offering help.

Mrs. Green said, "We are glad to make your acquaintance."

Little Elizabeth started crying. As Dani walked around the truck to check on her, Mrs. Green said, "We need to get this family out of the cold night air and take them to our house for some hot chocolate and doughnuts."

Mr. Green said, "While you women warm up the chocolate, we can tow this truck to our house with my tractor.

Dani said, "That would be wonderful, thank you so much!"

Mrs. Green said, "It's our pleasure to help."

Mr. Green spoke to Shawn, "Just leave the parking lights on. We can be back in a few minutes."

They all got into the Durango and drove away.

Mr. Green told Shawn he had an old salvage Ford truck in the woods behind his house and he was pretty sure the parts would interchange and he went on to explain that when he stopped so suddenly it probably broke an axle. Shawn was impressed with Mr. Green's knowledge involving the problem with his truck.

As they topped the hill, they saw a big white house on the left. As they entered the driveway, they saw a board fence on both sides and a big barn just to the left of the house. Mr. Green parked the Durango in the barn and said, "Well, folks, we're home."

Walking toward the house, they saw a big front porch with several rocking chairs on each side. The first thing they saw, as they entered the big living room was a large picture of a much younger version of Mr. and Mrs. Green. Mr. Green was wearing a U.S. Marine uniform.

Mr. Green said, "Well, guests, make yourselves at home. I need to change my clothes. We were on our way home from prayer service."

Mrs. Green showed Dani the way to the bathroom and Shawn played with little Elizabeth until Mr. Green returned.

As Mr. Green and Shawn walked out the front door he shouted, "Get that hot chocolate ready.

As they entered the barn, Mr. Green grabbed a chain hanging over a wooden gate and climbed up on a 100 + horsepower John Deere tractor. Shawn stepped on the tractors steps and held on as Mr. Green started the big tractor's engine, and then backed out of the barn. In just a couple of minutes, they were back at the Ford truck. Mr. Green turned the tractor around and backed up in front of the truck. He got off the tractor and attached the chain to the truck's front bumper bracket and the other end to the tractor's draw bar frame. Mr. Green, then told Shawn to start the truck's engine, so the power steering and brakes would work and release the parking brake.

Mr. Green said, "It is uphill all the way to the house, but you need to gently apply the brakes when we get to the barn, to prevent the truck from rolling into the tractor."

Shawn said, "I understand."

In only a few minutes, the tractor had pulled the truck to Mr. Green's barn. Shawn was relieved to know the truck was out of the road and now parked under one of the large trees in the Green's yard.

Mr. Green parked the tractor, and then walked out of the barn and told Shawn to put the truck in gear and let off the clutch. The strange noise was more of a grinding sound. Mr. Green walked to the rear of the truck and put his hand on the center hub on the driver's side and then walked around the truck to the passenger side and then shouted, "Shut it off!"

Mr. Green said, "It's the axle on the passenger side, but don't worry I have an old salvage truck that has a complete rear end in it."

Shawn asked, "How hard is it to replace?"

Otis explained, "Oh, it's not too bad; with a little luck, we can change it and have you on the road before noon tomorrow."

Shawn was relieved to hear Mr. Green say he could fix the truck.

Mr. Green must have been reading Shawn's mind as he said, "Don't worry. I'll donate the parts, if you help me with the work."

Shawn couldn't believe his ears.

Mr. Green placed his hand on Shawn's shoulder and asked, "Are you moving?"

Shawn said, "Yes, we are on the way to see some of my wife's family. I lost my job and we are looking for a new start."

As Shawn and Mr. Green entered the house, Shawn could smell food. Mrs. Green had apparently figured out the young family had not eaten and warmed up some ham slices and made them a couple of killer sandwiches. The food was delicious and they had a good time picking at Shawn about the misguided moose. The two families talked for about an hour after eating the sandwiches and enjoying an extra round of hot chocolate with Mrs. Green's touch of cinnamon. Mrs. Green saw that little Elizabeth had fallen asleep in Dani's arms, so she led her to a guest bedroom across the hall. The room had wood paneling on the walls and ceiling, and a big bed with a red quilted top, plus a child's bed in the corner. Mrs. Green explained this was the room used by their children and grandchildren when they came to visit. She showed Dani the adjoining bathroom with a tub and shower and the linen closet full of towels and bath cloths.

Mr. Green said, "We'll need to get up early, so I will knock on your door at 6 a.m."

Shawn and Dani thanked the Green's for their hospitality and Shawn walked out to the truck to get a change of clothes while Dani made good use of the shower. That night as Shawn laid in the bed beside Dani, he realized he needed to tell the Green's the truth. He just had to hope and pray they wouldn't turn them in.

The magnitude of what they had done was beginning to wear on Shawn. In the darkness of the room, Shawn prayed that God would forgive him for such a foolish act and hoped something good would come of the whole mess.

At 6 a.m. they were awakened by the loud knock on the door and Mr. Green announcing, "Breakfast is served in the dining room."

As the young couple got dressed, they decided to let little Elizabeth sleep and walked across the hall to the wonderful smells of breakfast.

Mrs. Green said, "Good morning," as she stood in front of a table piled high with eggs, sausage, hot cakes and a large bottle of maple syrup. The fresh brewed coffee is what struck Dani's fancy, as she poured up a large cup.

Mr. Green said, "Have a seat," and as the families sat down together, the Green's reached out to Dani and Shawn to hold hands as Mr. Green said the blessing. "Heavenly Father, we ask you to forgive our sins, bless our families and especially our guests and protect us this day, as we thank you for food and blessings, amen!"

After enjoying the delicious breakfast, Shawn stood and said, "I need to tell you something. We gave you our middle names, but actually we are - -."

Mr. Green interrupted Shawn and said, "Don't say anymore, son. We have a pretty good idea who you are, but don't tell us. We are helping a stranded family on their way, but don't give us any additional information. Do you understand?"

Mrs. Green spoke, "My husband and I were young just like you and we made many foolish mistakes, but we survived, and so will you, so don't worry. You are safe with us."

Mr. Green said, "Well, young man, we have work to do."

Mrs. Green said, "Honey, would you help me wash the dishes?"

While the women washed the dishes, Mr. Green led Shawn out to the barn where they got on a golf cart and zoomed out of the barn, and in just a couple of minutes, they arrived at an old salvage Ford truck. The cab had burned to a cinder, but the rear end looked fine. Mr. Green walked around the truck and declared, "It's the same; you're in luck son!"

Mr. Green walked back to the rear of the golf cart and picked up a toolbox and in a few minutes, he had unbolted and removed the axle from the center of the truck's hub. Shawn was impressed when Mr. Green handed him the axle, grabbed the toolbox and said, "Let's go."

Shawn held the axle and Mr. Green laid the toolbox on the back and away they went.

As they approached the house, Shawn was amazed to see how big the trees around the house and barn were.

Mr. Green looked over at Shawn and said, "The splines have to match and your truck will be as good as new."

Shawn knew what Mr. Green meant; the splines were grooves cut into the small end of the axle. Some axles have a different number of splines. Shawn was hoping his would match. Shawn could hear something in the distance and then suddenly a helicopter zoomed overhead from east to west.

Mr. Green raced inside the barn and returned with a big camouflaged tarpaulin and yelled, "Take one end and climb up on the hood of your truck, so we can cover it."

In less than two minutes the camouflaged canvas covered all of the truck, except the wheels. Mr. Green went back into the barn and returned with a handful of rubber straps with metal hooks on the ends and they fastened the canvas to the truck.

Mr. Green looked at Shawn and said, "If anyone should ask, this cover is to prevent bird dropping from getting on your truck."

Chapter 20

Meanwhile, Clyde Bostrum had spent the night in Wadena, Minnesota at a motel and he was in a bad mood. He had trouble getting to sleep the night before thinking about the possibility that the McLeod's might outrun him to Canada.

Clyde had boarded a National Guard helicopter just before sun up and they were patrolling along the Canadian border. As the sun came up over the horizon, Clyde's tired red eyes felt like raw meat. Clyde had a trash can size cup of coffee for breakfast and a couple of Standback powders for dessert. Clyde's kidneys didn't like the helicopters sudden moves and gyrations. He had held it as long as he could stand it and he yelled at the pilot, "I need you to set this thing down somewhere."

The pilot was confused and said, "I can't set it down in these fields, because it will destroy the crops and cause cattle to stampede."

Clyde was in no mood for an argument. He yelled, "You either set this thing down or I'm going to pee out the damn side of this flying egg beater!"

Shawn and Mr. Green were busy trying to remove the bad axle from Shawn's truck when the helicopter flew slowly overhead, started circling, and then landed in an open field about three hundred yards west of the Green's home. Shawn's heartbeat doubled and Mrs. Green and Dani walked out on the front porch to see what was going on.

Mr. Green ran back into his barn and returned with a pair of binoculars. He quickly focused on the helicopter.

After the helicopter landed, Clyde removed his seat belt and walked about one hundred feet east of the aircraft, as he unzipped his pants. He had the strangest feeling he was being watched. Even though his back was turned to the helicopter, as he relieved himself, he still had an uneasy feeling.

Mr. Green started laughing and handed the binoculars to Shawn and said, "Here take a look."

Shawn focused first on the helicopter and then on Clyde.

Shawn laughed and said, "I guess we caught him at a bad time!"

Mr. Green said, "Yes we did."

Shawn asked, "Couldn't he be arrested for exposing himself in public?"

Mr. Green just laughed and said, "I don't know."

They both laughed and Mr. Green put the binoculars away as the helicopter lifted off, and then proceeded to the west.

Shawn and Dani were relieved to see the helicopter fly away.

Dani ran to give Shawn a hug. Dani started and said, "I thought we were caught!"

Shawn said, "Don't worry, it's alright!"

Dani continued to cry and said, "Let's just give up and beg for mercy!"

As Shawn held Dani in his arms and tried to calm her fears, Mr. Green walked over and placed his hand on her shoulder and said, "I fought in Vietnam and in Granada and in Panama and I will get your family and that truck across the border, if it's the last thing I do on this planet!"

Dani raised her head from Shawn's shoulder and looked at Mr. Green. Mr. Green said, "Now, stop crying and show me a smile."

Dani stopped crying and tried to put a real smile together, but a kind stare was all she could produce.

Mr. Green went back to work and in a few minutes he pulled the axle out of Shawn's truck, and yelled, "Bingo, It's the same type axle!"

In a few minutes Mr. Green had bolted the replacement axle in and said, "Shawn, crank her up and let's see what happens."

Shawn started the engine, placed the truck in gear and pulled forward. Then, he put it in reverse and it moved backwards. The repair had been a complete success.

Shawn asked Mr. Green, as he reached for his wallet, "How much do I owe you?"

When they returned to the house, Dani came to the door and said, "Lunch will be ready in a few minutes. Mrs. Green said for you men to wash up!"

Mrs. Green had prepared a big pot full of beef, potatoes, and carrot stew and a platter of biscuits. After enjoying the delicious meal and thanking the ladies, Mr. Green leaned over toward Shawn and whispered, "We need to go for a ride."

The two men got into Mr. Green's one ton, four door red Dodge dually truck and drove out the driveway and turned left going north.

Mr. Green explained, "We need to check the road to be sure it's clear and safe."

They had driven two miles, when they came over a hill and Shawn saw an old wooden bridge. He remembered that Jenny had told him when you cross an old wooden bridge you would be in Canada.

Shawn thought, "If only that stupid moose had been somewhere else, we would be safe now!"

As they approached the bridge, two men in camouflage uniforms seemed to appear from nowhere. The men were holding M-16's.

One of the men motioned for them to stop. Mr. Green brought his truck to a smooth stop. Shawn couldn't tell, if the men were police or military, so he pulled his cap down until it rested on top of his dark shades.

Mr. Green let the driver side window down and asked, "What's up, gentlemen?"

As the two men approached the driver's side window, their U.S. Marshal badges were very visible. The older of the two men was tall and thin and had gray hair and a mustache. He motioned for the younger Marshal to relax and said, "We are watching roads crossing the border and I need to see your driver's license."

Mr. Green reached for his wallet and noticed the Marine Corps tattoo on the arm of the Marshal.

As he handed the license to the Marshal he asked, "You're a Marine?"

The man's attitude changed completely, as he said, "Yes, yes I am."

Mr. Green said, "I'm a Corps man myself, did you serve in Nam?"

The Marshal answered "1967-'69 and 1971."

Mr. Green said, "Well, heck were you in Da Nang in '69?"

The Marshal said, "Yes, I was in and out of Da Nang dozens of times!"

Mr. Green said, "I was stuck there for nearly eight months as a supply clerk."

The Marshal reached out to shake hands with Mr. Green and said, "Well, I'll be darned, I probably came to you for supplies."

As Mr. Green talked, he got out of the pickup.

Shawn thought, "If the Marshal asked for my identification, I would be toast."

Mr. Green asked the Marshal, "How old are you?"

The Marshal replied, "I'm 59."

Mr. Green said, "I'm 59, also."

As the two men laughed and talked, Mr. Green kept his back against the driver side window trying to block the man's view of Shawn. The younger Marshal had retreated to an area under the bridge where they had a tent.

Shawn thought, "If the axle in the truck had not broken last night, we could have been arrested or even shot."

A cold chill came over him, as he thought of Dani and little Elizabeth being shot at and he realized he should leave them somewhere and try to cross the border alone.

Mr. Green and the Marshal talked for nearly an hour before they shook hands again and Mr. Green and Shawn finally drove across the bridge. Mr. Green was whistling the Marine Corps hymn, as he drove away from the bridge. Then, Mr. Green looked over at Shawn and said, "Now, do you see why I wanted to check the route?"

Shawn said, "Yes sir, I can see why. I was thinking, if the axle had not failed last night, they would have arrested or maybe even shot us!"

Mr. Green looked back in his rear view mirror and said, "Well, we will have to come up with another plan, but we are going across the border tonight!"

Shawn asked, "Did you say we?"

Mr. Green said, "Yes, we are going to cross the border tonight. You can't make it without me!"

Shawn said, "I don't want to get you into trouble, you have been too kind already."

Mr. Green said, "You need me. I know a place we can cross that is on a farm; part of it is in the U.S. and part of it is in Canada."

Shawn asked, "How can you get the owner to cooperate?"

Mr. Green said, "The farm's owner is my cousin and he's gone to Florida to visit family."

Shawn asked, "Are you sure this will work?"

Mr. Green asked, "Do you have a better plan?"

Shawn looked over at Mr. Green and said, "No, no I don't!"

Mr. Green said, "We are on the way to the Canadian side and then drive back through to be sure that it is all clear."

Shawn was impressed with this fine man. He reminded him of his father, the way he always figured some way around a problem. They drove for several miles before Mr. Green stopped in front of a metal gate with a big letter "G" in the middle.

Mr. Green got out and opened the gate and yelled at Shawn, "Come on, son. Drive on through."

Then Mr. Green closed the gate and Shawn moved back to the passenger seat. As Mr. Green drove, it was apparent to Shawn that this was a cattle farm with large open pastures and a big pond.

When they reached the gate on the south side of the farm Mr. Green said, "Now we are back in the U.S.A., the border runs across this property almost perfectly dead center!"

Mr. Green stopped at a similar gate and got out and opened it and again. Shawn drove the Dodge through the opened gate. As Mr. Green got back in the truck and drove away he explained, "We can drive about a mile down this old dirt road and then we can follow an old logging road all the way back to my house."

As they drove along Mr. Green explained why he talked to the Marshal for such a long time. He explained it was to get as much information from him as he could without making the officer suspicious. Mr. Green said, "An F.B.I. agent from Georgia had arrived the night before and was taking the search personally. He told me the search will continue until you are captured or they have proof you have already made it to Canada."

Shawn asked, "Why would he take this so personal?"

Mr. Green just grinned and said, "I guess, because he's head of the Georgia office and he feels embarrassed that two kids in an old truck just drove away with probably the biggest treasure in the history of America!"

Shawn just bowed his head and said, "I'm sorry; I did it!"

Mr. Green just smiled and said, "Don't worry son. I don't believe there is a soul on the earth who wouldn't have tried the same thing under the circumstances, even me!"

Shawn was relieved to see Mr. Green laugh and said, "I just don't know what to do."

Mr. Green said, "Well, it's too late to go back and I'm going to see that you make it!"

Shawn confessed, "I feel terrible about the fact that I have endangered my wife and child!"

Mr. Green said, "Relax, I'll help you get across the border, but you can't tell anybody I helped you. Do you understand?"

Shawn said, "Don't worry. If I get caught; I'll take all the blame!"

Mr. Green said, "Corporations are endangering our sovereignty by buying off our elected officials. Most of the farms here are owned by rich folks and they are operated by a caretaker who couldn't care less."

Shawn asked, "Why don't they care?"

Mr. Green replied, "Most of them are just losers and some are alcoholics or worst."

As they arrive back at Mr. Green's farmhouse, they park his truck in the barn. Mr. Green shut the engine down and explained, "We need to build a water cooler for your truck's engine and muffler."

Shawn asked, "Why does it need a water cooler?"

Mr. Green said, "The Marshal I talked with at the bridge said they were using a heat sensor system on the helicopters to try and catch anyone crossing the border at night."

Shawn asked, "How does that work?"

Mr. Green replied, "It's some of the new technology that can detect anything hotter than the normal surroundings like an engine, muffler or for that matter a person or animal."

Shawn said, "So, we are going to cool down a muffler."

Mr. Green said, "Yes, we are and we need to insulate under the hood and over the exhaust system, so we can hide as much heat as possible."

Shawn helped Mr. Green as he mounted a ten-gallon metal tank horizontally across the front of the van body, just over the truck's cab. They then ran a plastic line to the engine compartment and another one under the truck and positioned it, just above the muffler. Mr. Green connected a small spray fitting on the ends and a shut off valve just outside the holding tank. Next, the two men cut the camouflaged tarpaulin to fit the trucks van body and fastened it with the rubber straps. Mr. Green then cut pieces of the tarpaulin to fit the roof of the truck and the top of the hood over the engine compartment.

Then, Mr. Green walked into his barn and he came back with a gallon bucket of adhesive. Shawn just watched, as Mr. Green used a wide putty knife to smear a film of the sticky adhesive across the hood and top of the truck. Then, Mr. Green walked in the barn and got a four foot wide roll of silver looking fabric.

Mr. Green made a few measurements. Then, he started cutting the shiny silver material. In a few minutes he had smeared the adhesive, so it would stick to the underside of the truck's hood that covered the engine.

Mr. Green explained, "This shiny material is a heat shield and this will hide the heat from the helicopter's heat sensors."

Mr. Green cut a piece of the material about four feet by six feet and coated it with the adhesive and then stuck it to the floor of the van body above the muffler.

As the two men worked, about every thirty minutes, a helicopter flew overhead. After they finished the work on the truck, Mr. Green helped Shawn figure out how to get to the Davenport's ranch.

Mr. Green explained, "The most important part of this trip is to cross the border!"

Shawn shook his head in agreement and said, "Yes, you are right."

Mr. Green said, "And we need to cross it tonight, every day we wait, the harder it will be."

Shawn said, "I'm sorry for all the trouble I caused you and Mrs. Green."

Mr. Green said, "Heck, we have enjoyed having you here. It is not every day that a young family walked off with a truck load of gold and broke down in front of our house."

Chapter 21

Meanwhile, the WNN (*World News Network*) had been running stories 24-7 about the young family. So many sightings had been reported to the police that many calls are going unanswered. Clyde Bostrum had dug in his heels along the Minnesota - Canadian border and the local authorities had become a little irritated by the man's fiery attitude! He screamed orders at everybody; he seemed to have forgotten that he is a guest of a local Sheriff's department.

After getting to know Clyde, the local officers are beginning to join the millions of Americans who are hoping that the McLeods can safely escape to Canada.

Clyde walked through the lobby of the Sheriff's office and before he sat down at a desk in one of those little cubicles, he yelled at one of the young female deputies, "Hey, young lady, get me a cup of coffee while you are resting!"

The young female deputy had her fill, she walked across the room and got an empty coffee pot and then proceeded back to Clyde's cubicle, where Clyde had parked his butt in a reclining chair behind a desk. As Clyde read some notes in his pad, the young deputy walked in and threw the coffee pot on his desk so hard, it bounced off and hit the wall.

She yelled, "Here's your damn coffee pot, big boy. If you want coffee, you can get it yourself, but if you yell at me one more time, I'm going to cram it up your butt. Do you understand?"

Clyde looked up in shock, as he dropped his note book. The young lady slammed the door to his cubicle and walked away. Instantly everybody in the precinct rushed to place chairs, tables and every possible object available in front of his door. In less than a minute, a truck load of furniture, file cabinets and snack food machines blocked his door tighter than a bank vault.

Clyde's muffled screams could be heard a block away.

He yelled, "This isn't funny, I'm a federal officer. Impeding my movements is a violation of federal law. Do you understand?" He shouted, as he began to kick at the door and curse at the top of his lung's capacity.

As Clyde continued to scream and beat on the door, everybody else went back to their normal duties.

Meanwhile, back at Shawn's parents' home, Mr. and Mrs. McLeod had been up for nearly three days. It was hard to sleep when you know that thousands of law enforcement officers and only God knows who else are looking for your son, daughter-in-law and only grandchild. The McLeods had prayed night and day since the shocking news came on the television on Tuesday. Mr. McLeod looked out the window at about one hundred news people camped out just outside the gate that led to their home. He just shook his head in disbelief, as he tried to figure out why Shawn had attempted such a crazy endeavor. Shawn had always been a fine son and did well in school. Mr. Peterman, his teachers and relatives couldn't say enough good things about him. Mr. McLeod wondered what in the world came over him to pull such a stunt.

At the same moment, ~~nearly~~ → *ouelt* ← one thousand miles away Shawn was thinking about his father and mother and he wanted more than anything to call them and just let them know they were alright, but he knew the call would be traced by the authorities.

Dani's father was sitting at a bar in a restaurant in Birmingham, Alabama, watching television news on a big screen and has already had three doubles. The bartender walked by and stopped right in front of him to watch the latest news update about Goldilocks. Dani's father leaned over the counter and, in a whispered voice said, "Goldilocks is my daughter."

The bartender looked over at him and said, "So what, I'm really Batman."

Then the bartender walked off to serve another customer.

Dani's father looked back toward the bartender and thought, "I wouldn't have believed him, if he had told me something like that."

After completing the work on the truck, Shawn and Mr. Green walked back to the house and entered the living room. Little Elizabeth was playing on the floor and Dani was sitting beside her. Shawn could tell Dani had been crying, so he knelt down beside her to comfort her.

Mrs. Green entered the room and announced that the food was ready. She said, "Fried chicken, mashed potatoes with gravy and biscuits are hot and ready."

Mr. Green said, "I didn't ask for this, but ask or not, I'm involved and I want to help you get across the border to your relatives."

Mrs. Green walked over to the chair beside Mr. Green and sat down beside him.

Mr. Green took another breath and said, "If you stay here, you'll get caught and we will all be in trouble. We must get you safely across the border, so you need to eat, shower and get ready."

Dani rose to her feet and all of them proceeded to the dining room.

The smell of the delicious food was like a welcoming force, as they sat down at the table. Mr. Green asked for everyone to hold hands around the table, as he bowed his head and prayed, "Heavenly Father, please bless this food for the nourishment of our bodies, as we prepare for a short trip to complete a long journey. We beg you to help this situation have a peaceful and safe conclusion. Amen!"

After the meal Mr. Green and Shawn tried to get Dani to stay with Mrs. Green and make the trip the next day, but Dani was persistent.

She said, "We started this trip together and regardless of how it ends, we will complete it together."

Everyone knew that she was determined to go, so everyone worked together to make it happen.

While Dani and Shawn are showering, Mr. Green borrowed his wife's Dodge Durango and raced south to a little crossroads where a country store and a gas station sat on opposite corners. Mr. Green parked near the rear corner of the country store and walked around the side to a pay phone. He pulled his cap down over his eyes, just in case the place had security cameras. He glanced around to be sure no one was watching him, as he opened the phone book and located the phone number for the state police. He glanced around again, as he dialed the number and waited for an answer.

The voice on the other end of the phone said, "State police, can I help you?"

Mr. Green asked, 'Is the reward still available for the Goldilocks case?"

The police dispatcher said, "Yes, it is."

Mr. Green asked, "Can I remain anonymous, but still get the reward?"

The radio operator from the state police said, "Yes, I will give you a code number. Just a minute please – pause – yes, I have it (E486-a). Just write this number down and you can call back after they are captured to collect your reward."

Mr. Green tried to talk like he was drunk as he said, "Da couple are broke down near I-29. Da couple miles east on Highway 75. Da pulled off da road and piled limbs on top ov da truck?"

The operator said, "Thank you very much. When we arrest them, just call any law enforcement agency and the reward will be placed in escrow for you."

Mr. Green hung up and looked around again to make sure no one saw him and then returned to the Durango for a quick trip home.

The operator quickly relayed the tip to state police officers in the area.

Clyde was riding with a young officer when the call came in.

Clyde screamed, "Hot dog! I knew I would get them."

The young officer stopped to turn around when Clyde yelled, "Take me to that location faster than a teenager in a borrowed hot rod."

If Clyde had been a dog, his tail would have been wagging; his tongue would be hanging out, and he would be panting!

The reported location was over 60 miles away, so Clyde grabbed the police radio microphone and demanded the radio dispatcher find him a helicopter to rapidly take him to the location. The operator told Clyde the only available helicopter was on the way back to Grand Forks to refuel, but he would contact him after returning to the search.

Clyde was frustrated. He wanted a helicopter and he wanted it now.

Clyde yelled, "Well, tell them to hurry. 10-4!"

The young deputy had turned the flashing lights on and was pushing the Ford Crown Victoria to nearly 80 miles per hour on a two lane road.

Mr. Green drove home without attracting attention. After arriving, he helped Shawn check out the old truck. Mr. Green explained that he would stay at his cousin's house overnight and drive an old Jeep home the next morning.

As the men worked on the escape plan, Mrs. Green helped Dani bathe and dress Elizabeth for the trip. Mrs. Green did everything she could to ease Dani's fears and help her feel better.

Mr. Green remembered one place where he was afraid the Ford van might have a problem. The place was known as Wildman Creek. It was about twenty feet wide and up to two feet deep. Mr. Green decided, just to be sure, to drive his tractor up the dirt road and then park in the woods near that area, just in case the truck gets stuck.

Shawn could drive through the fields and woods and be safely hidden from the road.

Mr. Green could be ready to pull the heavy loaded truck out of the creek, if needed. Mr. Green didn't want the truck and tractor traveling together toward the border. He hoped the authorities had fallen for his fake call, but couldn't be sure. Mr. Green knew from his military days that even the best laid plans can run into a snag, but he figured if something went wrong, he would help Shawn and his family across the border in his tractor. He figured that, even if they had to abandon the truck, their freedom was the most important thing.

Mr. Green asked Shawn, "Are you sure you remember the route that we had taken earlier in the Dodge?" and said, "Just stop at Wildman Creek. I'll meet you there and drive the Ford van the rest of the way to my cousin's farm."

After Mr. Green was sure Shawn understood the plans, they walked back to the house. Mrs. Green was rocking little Elizabeth in a rocker recliner and Dani was trying to relax in a recliner next to Mrs. Green. When they entered the room, Shawn could see that Elizabeth had fallen asleep in Mrs. Green's arms.

Shawn reached for Elizabeth and Dani hugged Mrs. Green and said, "Thank you so much. I hope someday we can visit again."

Mrs. Green replied, "I'll pray for you to have a safe trip."

Mr. Green whispered to Shawn, "Don't forget to turn the water mister on at the first gate."

The young family loaded up in the Ford van and Mr. Green backed his John Deere tractor from the barn. Mr. Green gave Shawn a 'thumbs up' signal and Mr.

Green drove down the driveway toward the road and Shawn drove west across a field toward the rear of the Green's farm. Mr. Green was only idling the big diesel tractor engine, as he drove north on the farm road.

As Shawn reached the first gate, he remembered to turn the water mister on to help reduce the heat from the engine and the muffler. Shawn drove slowly along the route Mr. Green had showed him earlier in the day. The trail was a little bumpy, but it was safer than the road.

Meanwhile, as Mr. Green drove his tractor up the road, he saw a pair of headlights coming toward him. He was concerned; you almost never see anyone on this road late at night. As the vehicle approached, Mr. Green pulled the tractor over to the right side of the dirt road to let the oncoming vehicle pass by safely. The vehicle slowed down and then stopped. Two men stepped out as the blue lights on top started flashing. Mr. Green's thought of sending Shawn across the back trail was correct. Mr. Green tried to act normal as the officer asked for his identification and where he was going.

Mr. Green said, "I'm on the way to my cousin's place; he's out of town and he wanted me to go check on his stock."

One of the officers asked, "Why are you going to check on them at night?"

Mr. Green responded, "His helper is old and a little senile and called me to make sure everything's alright."

The other officer asked, "Why are you driving a tractor over there?"

Mr. Green said, "I'm going to spend the night and early tomorrow morning, I'm going to move the large wheeled feeders closer to the barn, for easier feeding during the winter."

The officers were pleased with his answers and returned his identification and drove away. Mr. Green was concerned. The route he had planned would only put them on public roads for about a mile, but he knew he had to be careful.

As Shawn drove through the field, he realized he was now on one of Mr. Green's neighbor's land, so he needed to be careful and quiet.

Chapter 22

Meanwhile, Clyde had acquired his helicopter and was on the way to the location of the reported sighting. Clyde was in radio contact with units on the ground, as they directed them to the location.

As Shawn drove along, he was worried about the helicopters. He didn't know that Mr. Green had sent the authorities on a false call to buy them time. Mr. Green was also concerned about the helicopters and was driving with the tractor's cab doors open, so he could hear better.

The moon was almost full and Mr. Green hoped that would help hide the lights of Shawn's truck. Then suddenly, out of nowhere, a helicopter appeared just east of him. It circled right over his big green tractor and then hovered almost directly overhead. A high powered search light suddenly illuminated his tractor like it was daytime. Mr. Green just continued to drive on like normal. The helicopter crew was in radio communications with the two officers that had just spoke with Mr. Green. The officers relayed information to the helicopter crew that they had already stopped and questioned the farmer in the tractor. The helicopter then circled and proceeded on out of sight. Mr. Green was relieved to see them fly away, and hoped they didn't see the lights from Shawn's truck. He figured that they probably missed seeing Shawn, when they circled south before turning west.

The information Mr. Green had received from the Marshal earlier in the day was very valuable. The Marshal had told him that only one of the helicopters in the area had the heat detecting equipment. Mr. Green hoped the false report he made would cause them to rush that particular helicopter toward the west side of the state. Mr. Green realized the heat shield and water misting system would only reduce the amount of heat emitting from the truck, but he hoped it would be enough to help them escape.

The fact that the tractor had become a decoy gave Mr. Green the thought to park it in an old abandoned barn near a farm house just up the road and to walk over the hill to the place he was to meet Shawn. So, Mr. Green drove on by the farm trail he had planned to use and parked his tractor in the barn just a short distance away. Mr. Green figured, if the helicopter came back it would be better for the tractor to be parked in the barn and not in the vicinity of the truck. He knew he would be late after walking through the woods, but he had told Shawn to wait for him at Wildman Creek. Mr. Green had a lot of experience crossing creeks, and if he got stuck, he would send Shawn back to the barn to get the tractor.

Meanwhile, Shawn had reached the last gate where he is supposed to stop and wait for Mr. Green. Shawn decided to open the gate and pull through and stop just short of the creek. As Shawn exited the truck and opened the gate, he thought he heard something behind him, but he turned around and didn't see anything. Shawn then drove the truck through the open gate and parked it just a few feet from the creek. He went back to close the gate behind the truck, so they would be ready to go when Mr. Green arrived. He closed the gate and then turned around to walk back to the truck when suddenly he heard a "click" sound. He stopped and looked in the direction of the noise. As he looked to his left nothing could have prepared him for what he saw. A very obese lunatic with a beard wearing pin stripped overalls and holding a double barrel shot gun with his left hand and lighting a cigarette with his right hand. Shawn froze in his tracks.

"Well, lookie here what I done gone and found. You must be that couple trying to sneak across der border with da truck full of gold, ain't you?" said the lunatic.

Shawn's voice escaped him for a split second, then he managed to say, "Please don't shoot. The reward is yours!" All Shawn could think about was what would happen to Dani and little Elizabeth, if this scoundrel shot him!

As the truck's big V-8 engine idled, Dani began to wonder why it was taking Shawn so long to close a gate. She looked in the rear view mirror on her side and saw the gate was closed, so she looked across the front seat to the driver side mirror. She saw Shawn just standing, still facing the other way. Little Elizabeth had fallen asleep, so she put her in her safety seat and then opened the door to check on Shawn.

Shawn was terrified at the sight of the big dumb looking guy and was trying to assure him they would let him turn them in for the reward without any trouble.

The big ugly lunatic removed his cigarette and said, "Hell, I hear what's in that truck is worth a sight more than a million dollars."

Dani suddenly appeared and the bum turned toward her. "You must be none other than Goldilocks!"

Dani screamed and Shawn grabbed her and pulled her behind him.

The bum said, "I guess this must be my lucky day!"

Shawn thought about trying to charge the bum, but he was afraid the bum might shoot Dani. His mind was racing, as he tried to come up with something!

The lunatic yelled, "Now move to the front of the truck, so I can see you better!"

Shawn held Dani as they slowly walked toward the front of the truck as ordered. Now the truck's headlights were glaring in their faces and a lunatic with a shotgun was standing in the shadows. Shawn thought what on earth could be worse!

The man asked, "So how much gold you got in that truck?"

Dani answered, "I don't know, but we will give you all of it, if you will just let us go!"

He then said, "Well, that's awful neighborly of you, little girl, but this shotgun gives me the power to take whatever the hell I want!"

For just a brief second, there was silence, as the three just stared at each other.

The lunatic was staring at Dani and said, "My, my, my, you are as pretty as the picture on TV, ain't you, honey?"

Shawn pleaded, "Please just let us go; you can have the gold and the truck. Just don't hurt my family!"

The lunatic spat and then said, "Well, young fellow, while I decide your fate just sit down on the ground and prop your legs Ingun style."

Shawn said, "Just take the truck and go!"

The lunatic screamed, "Sit down or I'll blow your damn head off!"

Shawn was terrified, but he sat down and crossed his legs like the lunatic had ordered! Shawn was trying to think of some way to distract the lunatic; he had to think of something fast.

Dani started crying and sat down beside Shawn, but the lunatic yelled, "Hey, little girl, I didn't tell you to sit down, now did I!"

The lunatic spat and laughed and said, "Now stand up here in front of the truck!"

Dani struggled to her feet, stood up and walked slowly to the front of the truck. The bright glare of the trucks headlights kept her from seeing the lunatic with the gun.

The lunatic yelled, "Now, little girl, take off that shirt you're wearing, so I can be sure you ain't hiding nothing!"

Dani was horrified and she was trembling, as she slowly unbuttoned the shirt and dropped it on the ground.

Shawn thought, maybe I can charge him while he's distracted, obviously this man would kill them both and probably throw Elizabeth in the creek, if he failed.

As Dani sobbed and trembled, the lunatic took another drink from his whiskey bottle and yelled, "The brassiere too, honey!"

Dani continued to tremble and sob, but this scoundrel was enjoying her suffering and humiliation.

Her hands were shaking so hard, she was having trouble unlatching her bra, as she looked up hoping for mercy from the lunatic and saw something in the shadows. Then suddenly, she saw a lightning fast movement and heard a Kaa-swatt! sound and the obnoxious lunatic hit the ground so hard, you could hear his joints crack!

Out of nowhere Mr. Green had slipped up behind the lunatic and delivered a lightning fast karate chop to the lunatic's neck, and as he fell, Mr. Green grabbed the shot gun in midair. Never in the world had two people been happier to see a marine arrive on the scene than Shawn and Dani.

Dani quickly covered her breasts with her arms and Shawn raced to her and they hugged each other so hard they were like one person for a few minutes. Shawn tried to calm her down, but she continued to tremble and cry.

Shawn looked over at Mr. Green and asked, "Is he dead?"

Mr. Green in such a cool and calm fashion while unloading the shot gun said, "No, no he just taking a little nap!"

As Dani finally began to calm down, Mr. Green laid the shot gun across the hood of the truck and picked up Dani's shirt, and as he handed it to Shawn he calmly said, "I can't leave ya'll alone for five minutes without you getting into some kind of trouble!"

This Marine still had it. His graying hair didn't mean he couldn't take control in a heartbeat.

Mr. Green said, "I'm sorry Dani, but we need to get out of here!"

Shawn asked, "Where did you learn that?"

Mr. Green calmly replied, "Marine Corps, son, we had to be good at hand to hand combat in Vietnam."

Shawn helped Dani up the stairs of the truck and she sat in his lap on the passenger side. Mr. Green opened the driver's door and fumbled around looking for something he remembered seeing under the seat of the truck earlier in the day.

Dani had quieted down, but was still trembling as Shawn held her in his arms.

Shawn said to Mr. Green. "I'm just glad you got here!"

Then Mr. Green found an old piece of nylon rope rolled up in a ball under the seat.

Mr. Green said, "There's something I need to take care of, but it will only take a minute."

Mr. Green closed the door and walked away from the truck.

The peaceful hum of the idling V-8 engine was a soothing background noise as Shawn whispered, "I love you" into Dani's ear as he held her.

Several minutes went by before Mr. Green returned to the truck. He opened the driver's door very gently and laid the lunatic's shot gun under the truck seat and climbed into the driver's seat.

Shawn whispered to Mr. Green, "What should we do about the jerk that threatened us?"

Mr. Green just grinned and said, "I don't think he will cause any more trouble tonight!"

As Mr. Green put the truck in first gear and rolled slowly toward Wildman Creek, he thought about the hell he had gone through in Vietnam. Not since then had he struck another human being.

The truck tilted from side to side, as the rushing water slammed into the truck's wheels, but slowly and surely, the old Ford pulled on through the creek and climbed the bank on the other side.

A sigh of relief came over Mr. Green, as he followed the two rut path. He realized they were only a few miles from the border. The lunatic had caused them to lose some valuable time, but he just hoped the false report he had made would give them time to escape.

Shawn still holding Dani in his arms, leaned over and whispered to Mr. Green, "I want to thank you for saving our lives!"

Mr. Green continued to watch the path and whispered back, "It was nothing; any old retired Marine could have done it!"

Shawn whispered, "You are still a Marine!"

Mr. Green didn't show any emotion, but was deeply touched by Shawn's compliment.

The path had become more challenging, as they encountered heavy brush and tree limbs that dragged along the sides of the old Ford van, but the determined Marine kept going.

Mr. Green saw something in the side mount mirror that got his attention. He saw lights in the sky approaching fast from the rear. Mr. Green saw an old wooden bridge ahead that passed over a shallow creek and steered the truck for the creek.

Shawn realized something was wrong.

Mr. Green shifted the truck into a lower gear as he said. "A helicopter is closing in on us from the rear!"

The concerned look on Mr. Green's face put fear in Shawn's heart, as the truck splashed into the creek. Mr. Green drove the truck down the stream and under the wooden bridge, and then stopped the truck with the parking brake. By using the parking brake to stop the truck, the bright red brake lights on the back of the truck didn't come on. The big van barely squeezed under the bridge, but Mr. Green figured he had to give it a try. They had to hide the truck.

The helicopter passed over them and kept going.

Mr. Green said, "That was close!"

Shawn said, "That was close! Do you think they saw us?"

Mr. Green replied, "I'm not sure, but they kept going!"

Mr. Green said, "We need to wait for just a few minutes to be sure that helicopter doesn't return before leaving the protective cover of the bridge.

Shawn pointed out how close the bridge was to the roof of the truck and asked Mr. Green, "How did you know this truck would fit under the bridge?"

Mr. Green replied, "I didn't. We e are only about a mile from my cousin's farm and it should only take a few minutes to get there, if the truck will pull out of the creek."

Mr. Green put the truck's transmission in first gear and eased out on the clutch pedal and the faithful old Ford truck eased forward, and slowly, but surely climbed the creek bank and onto the path.

Suddenly, Mr. Green stopped the truck and lifted the parking brake handle.

Shawn looked over at Mr. Green and asked, "What's up?"

Mr. Green looked over at Shawn and said, "Sacks!"

Puzzled, Shawn said, "Sacks!"

Mr. Green explained that before they left, he put some croaker sacks and pieces of wire behind the seat. He told Shawn they needed to put some sand in them and wired them to the mud flap brackets, so they will drag behind the truck and cover their tire tracks on the dirt road ahead.

Shawn asked Mr. Green, "Is this some more of your Marine training?"

Mr. Green opened his door and said, "No, Indian trick!"

Mr. Green removed the sacks and they put several handfuls of sand in them and tied them behind the wheels. They got back in the truck and Mr. Green turned left onto the dirt road. In just a couple of minutes, they were in front of the gate that entered Mr. Green's cousin's farm. Mr. Green jumped out of the truck and opened the gate and drove the truck through the opening. Shawn offered to get out and shut the gate, but Mr. Green told him he had his hands full. He was referring to the fact that Dani was still sitting in his lap.

Mr. Green drove slowly along as he passed a barn, his cousin's farm house, and then the fish pond. From there, he drove on until he came to the gate on the north side of the property. He pulled up close to the gate, stopped and looked over at Shawn and Dani and said, "Congratulations! You are now in Canada!"

A giant sigh of relief came over Shawn and Dani as Dani said, "Oh, thank God!"

Shawn reached over to give Mr. Green a high five, but Mr. Green handed him a map instead.

Mr. Green told Shawn that he needed to follow the map to the big red X that led to Dani's family's farm.

Shawn asked Mr. Green, "What can we do to repay you for rescuing us?"

Mr. Green replied, "You don't owe me a thing!"

Then a real serious look came over Mr. Green's face, as he looked out of the windshield, toward the northern sky and said, "It was a fall night like this nearly one hundred fifty years ago that a young couple like yourselves helped my great, great, grandfather and great, great grandmother and their baby boy cross this same border to escape the bonds of slavery. That young couple risked their lives and freedom to help them, and now I have repaid that debt!"

Then as Shawn and Dani sat motionless for just a few seconds, Mr. Green opened the driver's door and got out and opened the big gate. He then walked back around to the driver's door and removed the shotgun taken from the lunatic and laid it up against the side of the truck and said, "I better take this shotgun with me. If the Canadians stop you they would be more upset about it than all of the gold on earth."

Shawn and Dani opened the passenger's door and climbed down the steps and then walked around the truck to where Mr. Green was. Dani walked over to Mr. Green and gave him a big hug and began to sob, "Thank you, you saved us!"

Shawn walked over and wrapped his arms around Dani and Mr. Green and said, "We will never forget you!"

Mr. Green looked up and said, "I don't know what caused two fine young people like you to pull such a caper, but Mrs. Green and I will be praying for a safe and happy conclusion."

Then Mr. Green turned and walked over to the truck, picked up the old shot gun, threw it over his shoulder, and marched off into the darkness of the night whistling the Marine Corps hymn.

As Dani and Shawn held each other, little Elizabeth woke up and started crying. Dani climbed into the passenger side of the truck, and Shawn drove through the open gate. After closing the gate and taking a fast look at the map, the young family's journey was underway again.

As Shawn drove away from the gate Dani said, "I don't know, if we will ever see Jenny or the Greens again, but I will always keep their memories in a safe place in my heart!"

After reaching the border there was no big rejoicing or celebrating. The magnitude of what they had done had finally set in. As Shawn drove along being careful to make the correct turns, Shawn thought regardless of how this turns out, he wanted Dani and Elizabeth to be safe! Shawn thought about his parents and how worried they must be after the events of the last week. He also thought about Dani's father, her grandparents, Mr. Peterman, Mrs. Barton, his former co-worker Jerry and his friend, 'The Donald' Anderson, and wondered what they would think of him after committing such a crazy act.

Meanwhile, Dani had turned sideways in the seat holding little Elizabeth in her arms and even though her eyes were open, she was gazing back in time about her childhood when she and her mother baked cookies and when her father took her for a pony ride at the county fair and how her grandparents showered her with love and attention.

A tear ran down her beautiful face, as she remembered the day her mother was killed and how she refused to believe it until she saw her mother's body at the funeral home. Dani wondered what would happen to them and why they so foolishly risked their future for a fortune that really didn't mean anything to her now. In the darkness of that old truck's cab she had come to realize the most valuable treasure on earth is pure, sweet, simple love! The love she had for Shawn and Elizabeth, her father, grandparents, Reverend and Mrs. Stone and Shawn's family was the most valuable treasure anyone could possess. Dani thought regardless of the treasure in the back of that old truck; she knew that she was one of the richest people on earth. She realized that more than anything she wanted her family to stay together and she would give anything to turn back the calendar and undo the events that now threatened the future of her little young family. She wondered how many people make a rushed decision and afterwards would give anything to turn back the clock, but as the sands of our lives pass through the hour glass of eternity we have to live with the decisions we make. She looked at Shawn, as he drove along trying to follow the map in the near darkness of the truck's cab and saw how considerate he was. He could have just turned the interior light on, but he didn't want to disturb her or the baby. She prayed that God would send a blessing to them, so they could stay together for the rest of their lives.

Chapter 23

Meanwhile, Clyde Bostrum was having another bad day- er- night. He had pulled dozens of law enforcement people off of the search for the McLeods in the eastern part of the state to check out the false call on the west side of the state. He was in a terrible mood and his feet and back were having a contest to see which one could ache the most. As his helicopter lifted off from the ill-fated search area, he told the pilot to proceed east along the border.

Clyde might not have won any contest for being charming, but he was in fact one of the best lawmen in the nation. He figured that call he had received must have been made to throw him and the search team a curve ball. He correctly figured that it had been placed to give them time to escape on the east side of the state. Clyde had been trying to acquire information from Canada about the location of Dani's relatives and a message was finally relayed to him at midnight. The report showed Dani had a phone call with her aunt and uncle, the Davenports, who lived only a few miles from the Ontario and Minnesota borders in the Manitoba Province.

Just what he thought; he had been tricked. He told the pilot to step on it, as he rushed eastward along the Minnesota-Canadian border. He called for any new information the rest of the search team had obtained in the last few hours. He was told about a farm tractor moving north along a dirt road, but ruled that out as unrelated.

As Clyde studied a map of the area, he drew a straight line from the Wal-Depot store, which was the last positive sighting to the area where Dani's relatives live and showed it to the pilot.

Clyde yelled, "I want all the search teams to concentrate on this area."

Clyde was on target. The line he had drawn was almost exactly where the McLeods were crossing at that time. He relayed a message to helicopter with the heat detecting equipment to concentrate their search in this particular area along the border.

He said, "I want to know of any source of heat, even people on a boat. Just rule out the damn dogs and rabbits, but check anything larger." When Clyde laid the microphone down he mumbled, "Somebody has got to be helping them; I just know it!"

The pilot responded, "I wouldn't be shocked, sir. The press has made them the biggest folk heroes of our lifetime and I wouldn't be shocked, if the Queen of England was to grant them political asylum."

Clyde's butt flinched at the thought and yelled, "I hope she will tend to her own business. Hell, she can't keep the royal family out of trouble."

Then suddenly, a report came in from the heat detecting helicopter. They had detected the heat of one or more persons near a creek just south of the border. Clyde ordered his chopper to the scene. When they arrived, the search helicopter had its extremely powerful search light fixed on something on the ground, as it hovered above. It had picked up a heat source near an old cattle feeder.

Clyde yelled, 'Hell, that's just a cow, but check it out to be sure!"

Now both helicopters were hovering overhead; they were shocked. Whatever it was, it didn't run away. As the helicopters circled overhead, a ground unit raced to the scene. The helicopters couldn't land at night until a ground crew directed them in to be sure the area was free of power or telephone lines. The crew on the helicopter with the heat detecting equipment radioed Clyde to tell him that the heat source on the screen was too large for a single person, so they figured it was two people huddled together. The ground crew was nearing the location and reported finding a fresh set of tire tracks from a six wheel truck consistent with the type truck that they were pursuing. he said

When Clyde heard this report over the police radio, "We got 'em cornered like birds in a net!"

His smile turned to a frown, when his pilot informed him they only had fifteen minutes of fuel left, and if the ground crew didn't get to the location soon, they would have to go back to an airport about 25 miles away to refuel.

Clyde was screaming at the top of his lungs, "It's a damn cow pasture in the middle of nowhere. Now sit this flying windmill down or the next thing you will be flying will be a kite!"

Fortunately for Clyde, the ground crew arrived just in time and gave them the all clear signal for them to land. The instant the helicopter landed, Clyde and the other officers raced toward the cattle feeder with their guns drawn and flash lights beaming. As they approached the feeder, Clyde figured it was probably the McLeods, but what they found, turned his already sour stomach. Instead of two young people huddling together, they suddenly focused on the naked back side of a jumbo sized man. Clyde's face wrinkled up in a knot, as he realized he had been mooned by a man's butt, the size of a wash tub.

All of the other officers laughed at the sight, but Clyde wasn't laughing.

Clyde just looked up at the sky and said, "I don't beat my wife. Heck, I don't even chew tobacco!"

As the crowd laughed at the fat man hogtied to the cattle feeder, he was cursing and yelling, 'What's so damn funny? Untie me, you hear me?"

Clyde just turned away from the ugly sight and said, "It just can't get worse!"

Another officer pointed out, "It could get worse," because Clyde was standing in a fresh pile of cow manure.

As Clyde looked down at his brand new western wear boots, he started screaming, "One laugh out of you guys and I'll personally strangle every damn one of you!"

As the other officers tried to untie Lance Corporal Green's fancy knots, they questioned the man about how he wound up in such an embarrassing and compromising situation.

He said, "My name is Oliver Hodge," and he claimed, "The McLeods had got the drop on me, tied me up, and left me to die of exposure."

Mr. Green had apparently decided to show this piece of trash, how it felt to be humiliated, after what he had done to Dani. The officers all looked at each other in disbelief as the buffalo sized cussing man finally got to pull up his britches.

One of the ground search crews took old Oliver in for questioning and the other search team followed the tire tracks that had passed through the gate right beside the cow feeder.

The helicopter crew with the heat sensors lifted off to continue the search, but because Clyde's helicopter was so low on fuel, they decided to wait on the scene for information from the other teams. Clyde was feeling lower than the foot valve at the bottom of a deep well, his surroundings were depressing, and he wanted some good news for a change. The ground crew radioed that they had followed the tire tracks to an old wooden bridge. They reported that the vehicle had pulled off of the path and drove under the bridge. Then the helicopter called and said they were pursuing a heat source in that same area about thirty minutes earlier, but they had lost it.

The police radio in the helicopter just kept spitting out more compelling information that they had just missed the McLeods. The ground crew radioed back that they must have driven into the creek and under the bridge to cool the hot mufflers and hide from view.

Clyde was angry and stated, "Damn it, somebody must be helping them, how could two teenagers think of that!" Clyde looked up at the sky and said, "Why me, I'm a good man, except for an occasional belt of Jack Daniels, for my bad back."

As he looked back toward the pilot, the pilot just turned away from Clyde and tried not to laugh.

In a few minutes another call came in from the ground crew following the set of truck tire tracks and the news wasn't good. Apparently, the tracks had ended on a country dirt road that wandered back and forth across the border. The team's assessment was that the vehicle had made it to Canada.

Clyde's chin dropped at the thought of the McLeods making it across the border only minutes ahead of him. Clyde ordered the pilot to take him across the border and continue the search, but the pilot refused and said the helicopter barely had enough fuel to get back to the airport to refuel. Clyde was as disappointed as a starving buzzard that finds a rubber chicken.

Clyde's flight back to the airport was quiet and his ride back to his motel room was even quieter. In his room, he settled down in a big stiff chair and rumbled through his suitcase for a pint of Jack Daniels. As he sipped on the bottle, he wondered how he would live down the fact that two teenagers had stolen a multi-million dollar treasure right under his nose and outran him to Canada.

Finally after about an hour, the tired lawman from Georgia fell asleep in his clothes in a motel room in Minnesota. He snored so loudly, the people in the adjoining room thought they heard a chainsaw idling.

Meanwhile, Shawn kept driving down one quiet country road after another until he came to a large wooden house with an even bigger barn and a small cottage that sat between the two. An old fashioned zig-zag fence ran the length of the property along the road. It perfectly matched the description of the farm house he was hunting. He hated to wake Dani, but they needed to get off the road as quickly as possible.

As the big Ford V-8 engine idled, Shawn saw the front porch light come on and a big man with a beard walked out on the porch. Then a lightning flash illuminated the area enough for Shawn to see a sign on the fence near the driveway that said 'Davenport Farm.' The thunder that came with the lightning awakened Dani.

She stretched and twisted and asked Shawn, "Where are we?"

Shawn just pointed toward the big farm house and said, "Eight ball, side pocket".

Dani rubbed her eyes and said, "The what?"

Finally, she saw what Shawn was referring to.

Dani yelled, "That's my Uncle Hugh! You did it; you found them!"

Shawn put the truck in first gear and slowly accelerated forward toward the house. As Shawn stopped in front of the house, Dani opened the door and climbed down the step and she raced toward the man on the porch and yelled, "Uncle Hugh!"

As Shawn shut the engine down, little Elizabeth woke up and Shawn reached over and picked her up from her seat.

As Dani hugged her Uncle Hugh, the front door opened and out stepped her Aunt Sue and Dani hugged her and Uncle Hugh in one big family hug.

As Shawn and the baby exited the old faithful Ford truck, Dani raced over to grab Shawn by the arm and pulled him over toward her aunt and uncle.

Dani excitedly yelled, "This is my wonderful husband, Shawn, and our baby Elizabeth!"

Dani's Aunt Sue walked over to hug Shawn and said, "Let me hold that beautiful little girl."

Uncle Hugh walked over to Shawn and shook hands and said, "Good to meet you, Shawn."

Aunt Sue said, "Come on in, I'll fix some hot chocolate and warm up sweet rolls."

As Shawn, Danny and the baby entered the big cypress sided house, they were welcomed by a nice warm fire in a large stone fireplace. The large room had bare beams overhead and the natural wood paneled walls gave the home a warm country look. Hugh and Shawn stood in front of the fireplace and talked while Dani and Sue made hot chocolate in the kitchen.

Hugh explained to Shawn that they had been expecting them and that Dani's father had called him and told him what was going on.

Shawn asked Hugh, "Do you think we will be safe in Canada.

Hugh responded, "I don't know, but according to the news, the public is for you nearly one hundred percent."

Shawn said, "I just don't want to get you or your family in any trouble."

Shawn asked, "Do you think the Canadian government will pursue us?"

Uncle Hugh said, "I'm not sure."

The women in the kitchen were discussing a similar subject, but managed to make hot chocolate and warm the sweet rolls. Sue entered the room holding a large serving tray with the rolls and a pitcher of hot chocolate. Dani followed with cups and napkins, while little Elizabeth toddled along holding a toy bunny rabbit by its ears.

For over an hour they talked about the treasure, the trip, and about family and friends. Little Elizabeth fell asleep in Dani's lap; the excitement wasn't enough to keep her awake. Just before sunrise, Dani's Aunt and Uncle led the young family to a guest house. It was just a small cottage between the house and the barn. They had been expecting them, so the guesthouse was nice and warm. They told them to get some rest and they would try to help them figure out what to do tomorrow.

Aunt Sue showed them where the towels and blankets were, and then Dani's Aunt and Uncle left them, so they could get some sleep. Shawn, Dani and the baby were so tired, they all got in the large bed and pulled the covers up tight. Dani kissed Shawn and little Elizabeth and within a few minutes they drifted off to sleep. In the peace and quiet of the guest house, the young family found peace and rest from a long and tense journey.

Chapter 24

As the sun came up that morning, Shawn's family was watching the *World News Network* as unconfirmed reports came in that the family being pursued by American authorities had slipped across the Canadian border. Shawn's mom still wearing her house coat, sipping on a cup of hot black coffee, looked over at Shawn's father and said, "I just hope they're alright, wherever they are!"

Shawn's father, still in his pin striped pajamas, agreed by rocking his head back and forth as he stared at the television set.

Shawn's mother asked, "Do you think they will ever be able to come home?"

Mr. McLeod just shook his head and said, "I don't know!"

Mrs. McLeod asked, "Why don't we talk to a lawyer?"

Mr. McLeod looked over at her and said, "That is a good idea."

Mrs. McLeod added, "Then, when they call us, we will know what to tell them."

Mr. McLeod reached for the television remote control to turn the volume up. They saw familiar people on the screen. Mrs. Barton, Sheriff Giles, and Shawn's former co-worker, Jerry, are being interviewed.

As the volume came up, Mrs. Barton said, "Shawn and his little family are wonderful people and I love them dearly."

Then the interviewer asked, "Did Shawn have anything to do with the fire at your business?"

"Mrs. Barton responded, "Absolutely not, my son-in-law has just admitted he accidentally started the blaze while filling his boat with gas and then left in a panic!"

The reporter said, "So this young man, Shawn McLeod, had nothing to do with the fire at your plant."

Mrs. Barton responded, "That's correct. Shawn would never do anything wrong, he is a fine young man and the accusations that he might have had something to do with the fire are ridiculous!"

Then the reporter walked over to Sheriff Giles and asked, "Sheriff Giles, did Shawn McLeod have anything to do with the explosion and fire at his house?"

Sheriff Giles answered, "No, the fire was apparently caused by a cracked natural gas line that led to the home's water heater, and Shawn, his wife, and child barely escaped the fire. If not for a passing truck driver helping them out of the window, they probably wouldn't have survived."

The reporter asked, "So, Shawn McLeod had no involvement in either fire, or are there any charges pending against him for anything?"

Sheriff Giles responded, "Shawn McLeod and his little family have been a blessing and an asset to our community and I just hope when all of this nonsense is over, they can come home and live in peace!"

Then the reporter walked over to Jerry, one of Shawn's former co-workers at the plant, and asked, "What kind of person is Shawn McLeod?"

Jerry leaned over a little closer to the microphone and said, "I would trust Shawn with anything I own and would say he was one of the hardest working, most honest decent people I ever met in my life!"

The reporter pulled the microphone back and said, "So you say he is a man of honesty and integrity and would you be willing to work with him again?"

Jerry once again leaned closer to the microphone and said, "Absolutely, I don't know what happened up in the mountains, but I'm sure Shawn wouldn't do anything wrong."

Then the reporter turned around to face the camera and said, "So, Shawn's former boss, co-worker and local Sheriff all proclaim this most sought after fugitive, to be a model of honesty and integrity and they wish him and his family well. Everybody else we talked to in this small town just west of Macon, Georgia said that this young man had impressed them with his spotless character."

The reporter turned back around to Mrs. Barton and asked, "Mrs. Barton would like to say something to Shawn?"

Mrs. Barton smiled and said, "Shawn, we love you and miss you and your family!"

The reporter turns back toward the camera and said, "Well, now you have the story from Russellville, Georgia. I'm John Farr for the *World News Network*."

Then the news network host reporter came back on, "In a related story, a very large, intoxicated man was found tied to a cattle feeder with his backside exposed by a search team. The search team apparently looking for the elusive McLeods, along the U.S. and Canadian border during the night, said the man claimed to have been held at gun point and tied up by Goldilocks and her husband, Shawn. So for this story, we will go to Sherry Lee reporting live from a small town in Minnesota."

The camera then zoomed in on a young lady standing in front of a small town courthouse in Waylon, Minnesota.

The reporter said, "Hi, I'm Sherry Lee reporting live where a strange story that has unfolded in the Goldilocks drama. A local man known to be a heavy drinker and somewhat of a trouble maker is being held for questioning by state and federal authorities. He claimed the young couple, the McLeods, pulled a shot gun on him, robbed him, tied him up and pulled his pants down, leaving his backside exposed to the elements, while tied to a cattle feeder.

Sources who spoke to me, who wish to remain anonymous, said federal and state officers using heat detecting sensors on board a helicopter found the man in, let's say an embarrassing situation, while searching for the young couple along the Canadian border. While authorities don't believe his story is completely accurate, they do believe that he had some contact with the McLeods. Tire tracks in the vicinity show a truck similar to the one the McLeods have been traveling in were visible in the area. The person I spoke with believed it was the McLeods and that they have made it across the border, but officially the search continues. I'm Sherry Lee reporting for the *World News Network*."

Shawn's parents just looked at each other in shock. Mr. McLeod just shook his head and said, "I can't believe all of this is happening; I just can't believe it."

Local authorities are continuing to question the man found during the night by the federal and state authorities.

A Minnesota State Police Officer asked Oliver Hodge, "How did a young couple driving a two ton truck slip up on him in the dark."

Oliver replied, "I guess I was a bit drunk, but I got rights just like anybody else."

The officer replied, "A little drunk, you blew a two point four on our breath analyzer machine. Do you call that a little bit drunk?"

Oliver said, "Well, it doesn't matter, I was threatened at gun point and I want them brought to justice!"

The local Sheriff spoke up, "Personally, I would be more likely to believe you, if you told me aliens ate your brain!"

Oliver yelled, "I'm going to sue them for my mistreatment, unless I get part of da reward money!"

Chapter 25

Clyde Bostrum awoke in his motel room after sleeping in a chair. He could now add headache to his back and aching feet. He managed to stand up and headed for the shower. The water spraying on his hurting head was so bad, he could hardly stand it. After surviving the pain and noise of the shower, he called for a state police car to pick him up at the motel.

When the call came in at the state police office, the receptionist said, "I'll have someone pick you up as soon as possible."

She then punched the button on the PA system and said, "I need a volunteer to pick Clyde up at his motel."

She turned around to see if anyone volunteered, but the room was suddenly silent and strangely empty. Paper documents were still floating in mid-air and the place was so quiet, she could hear the dust settle.

Eventually, a new officer entered the station and was assigned the dirty job no one else wanted. Then like magic, the room was full of active and busy people.

Meanwhile, Dani's father watched the current updates on the news channel and wondered where they were. He just prayed they were all right. He had been so lonely after losing his wife in a tragic car wreck and his daughter moved away. At least until now, he could call her, when he felt sad and lonely. He just hoped and prayed that they were all right and that someday they could be together again.

As Clyde entered the State police headquarters, everybody was about as happy to see him, as a rock in a bowl of soup, but Clyde didn't care. He figured he wasn't in a popularity contest. He had a job to do and even he had realized the McLeods had won the race to Canada. Clyde went straight to work trying to contact the Canadian Mounted Police in Winnipeg, Manitoba. He called and asked to speak to the head Mounties. You can just imagine how happy they were to get a call on Saturday morning from somebody about as irritating as old Clyde calling for the 'Head Mounties.'

He was told to call back Monday morning and they hung up on him. Ole Clyde would have exploded, but his head hurt too badly, so he called the director of the F.B.I. on his special line, only to receive a recording reminding him to call back on Monday.

His anger gauge was pegging, as he called the State Department and then the Attorney General. Both had answering machines that told him to call back on Monday. He was absolutely frustrated; he couldn't get anybody on the phone.

Then it occurred to him, he had forgotten to call Mrs. Bostrum, his wife, before he left for Minnesota. He realized he needed to call her and smooth things over, but instead she screamed over the phone and told him he would spend eternity on their couch and slammed the phone down so hard, Clyde could feel his brain vibrate.

He sat back in his chair and tried to decide what to do. By Monday, the McLeods could be in China. Clyde tried to requisition a state police car to drive to Canada and look for the McLeods, but he was told he would have to talk to the section chief on Monday. He slammed the phone down so hard, it probably was recorded on seismograph equipment in Seattle and yelled, "Damn Saturdays, I can't find a single car or person to help me!"

Clyde realized he had to calm down; his head was hurting so badly, he might not live till Monday!

After giving up on a loan-er, he called a taxi to take him to a car rental agency, nearly twenty-five miles away. If he couldn't get any help, he decided to rent a car and look for the McLeods on his own.

At the car rental agency, he refused to pay the two hundred dollars to insure the car while in Canada yelling, "I've never put one scratch on a rental car in over thirty years!"

When they brought his car around front, it was one of those little cars about the size of a footlocker. Clyde protested, but he was told that was all he could get, unless he wanted to wait till Monday.

Clyde broke out in a rage and yelled, "If one more person tells me I've got to wait till Monday, I'm going to kill somebody."

Clyde barely squeezed into the tiny car and drove away.

After an hour of bouncing around on back roads, he finally reached the border crossing on U.S. Highway 71. He waited in line as the Mounties checked the people ahead of him. He had his Georgia driver's license and F.B.I. badge in hand, as he arrived at the checkpoint. Clyde is questioned about his trip and he told the officers he's after Goldilocks and they remind him he has no legal powers in Canada and they demand his hand gun.

Clyde argued about giving up his gun and demanded to speak to their supervisor, but he is told he won't be available until Monday. Clyde finally gave up his gun, as he is warned again, that he has no legal authority in Canada.

As Clyde finally drove through the checkpoint, he was about as agitated, as a tadpole in a cup of coffee.

Talks are underway at the State Department level with their counterparts in Canada for the recovery of the treasure and return of the McLeods, as Clyde negotiated the back roads of South Eastern Monitoba.

Back at the Davenport farm as Shawn, Dani and the baby slept late. Dani's Uncle Hugh drove the old Ford moving van into his barn to hide it from view. Hugh wondered, if he could be in trouble, because he gave them shelter. Sue Davenport was busy cooking a meal worthy of royalty, but she also worried about the legal questions. They were very happy to see Dani and her family, but she wished it could have been under normal circumstances.

People all over the world have adopted the young family as their own. 'Go! Go! Goldilocks!' stickers are everywhere. It's the number one topic of discussion everywhere! A sign in front of a motel in Indiana read, 'Welcome Goldilocks!" Signs in parking lots spring up, 'Reserved for Goldilocks!' Late night talk shows ask Goldilocks to call them so she can tell them her side of the story. A truck dealer in Nevada offers to give Goldilocks a new truck for stopping by. A restaurant in Baltimore offers Goldilocks burgers for people on the Go! Go! People report finding messages left in ladies rooms across America written on the mirrors in lip stick, 'Goldilocks was here!'

A church in Arkansas had a sign that said, 'Pray for the McLeods!' A sixty minute laundry in Dallas had a sign that said, 'We accept, cash, checks, credit cards, or Gold!' A kid in Utah wore a shirt that said, 'Attention Goldilocks please adopt me!' A bumper sticker on a car in Miami said, 'If you're Goldilocks, I'm single!' A bank in Memphis had a sign "Welcome Goldilocks, we have a large vault!' A sign in front of a bar in Montana read 'Goldilocks welcome –no cover charge!' A truck wash on I-75 in Georgia read 'Attention Goldilocks stop for free truck wash, PS: we accept tips!'

A sign spray-painted on an underpass in Dayton said, 'When Goldilocks talks, E.F. Hutton listens.' A country music song is rushed into production; 'Goldilocks, Goldilocks, I love you, you and your lovely gold bars, I mean hair!' The Wal-Depot store in Wadena, Minnesota bragged, 'Goldilocks shopped here!' A sign in Atlanta read, 'Goldilocks, Goldilocks, where did you go!' Internet sites praised the McLeods and wished them well!

As the politicians tried to condemn the McLeods, they saw their ratings drop to the single digits. A sign in Sacramento read, 'Midas had the golden touch, but Goldilocks had the golden tons!' A weather man in Detroit turned his back to the TV camera while giving the weather report to show a sign that said, 'It will be golden wherever Goldilocks is!' Even the president of the United States is asked during a news conference, if he thought he could get Goldilocks vote and he responded, "If I can't get her vote, I would at least like to get a donation."

The entire press corps stood, and applauded and cheered!

A well-known night talk show host told the audience, "I just want to let Goldilocks know my wife has given us permission to fool around," then he looked back and forth to be sure no one else heard and said, "And if you lean that way, she's available to fool around!" The audience went wild with applause!

A sign in front of a bank in New York said, "Welcome Goldilocks, we can help you prepare for your golden years!" An investment firm on Wall Street had a sign, "Attention Goldilocks, we offer golden opportunities."

The radio talk shows are going wild. People are saying, "Let them go!" Some are saying they are sick and tired of the government taking so much of what we work for, so they support the McLeods and cheer them on. The state of Georgia Welcome Sign has been altered by pranksters to read, "We have golden opportunities for everyone!" And finally a bumper sticker in Montgomery, Alabama said, "Goldilocks for President!"

Back at the Davenport farm, Shawn, Dani, and little Elizabeth sleep late. The large Davenport home was full of busy excitement, as Sue prepared a large noontime meal. The Davenport children, son David and daughter Marsha, were busy helping with the laundry and house cleaning chores. It's as if everybody expected something special to happen, but nobody knows what.

As talks progressed between the U.S. State Department and the Canadian government, the Royal Mounted Police dispatched officers to the area around the Davenport farm. The officers are only to observe the situation at this time. American C.I.A. satellite surveillance tapes have proven that the McLeods have crossed the border and tracked them to the Davenport farm. The State of Georgia didn't have to put a lot of pressure on the Federal Government to help recover the treasure; national leaders are just too eager to get their hands on all that gold.

Chapter 26

Clyde Bostrum had stopped along a mountainside road to study his map. The information given to him by the Canadian government was vague at best. They didn't expect him to actually cross the border to look for Dani's relatives, but Clyde worked by his own rules. As Clyde studied the map, he felt the call of nature. His extra-large cup of coffee had begun to give his bladder trouble. So, he got out of the tiny little red car and walked around the side of the cliff and then followed a trail up around the hillside until he was a good sixty to seventy five feet above the road. Then finally, in private he unzipped his pants and commenced to relieve himself. That was when a bird flew over and dropped something on Clyde's head.

Clyde flew into a rage, bent over, and threw a rock about the size of a baseball, high into the air trying to hit the bird, missing its intended target by yards. The rock hit a rock about the size of a football which rolled down the hillside, until it hit a rock about the size of a bread box.

As Clyde wiped the bird poop off his forehead, he was unaware of the chain of events surrounding the misguided rock. The rock the size of a breadbox rolled down the hill and dislodged a rock the size of a refrigerator, which rolled down the hill and over the cliff and landed dead center of the little red rental car.

The crash sounded like an explosion in a junkyard. Clyde thought, "What in the hell was that?" as he zipped up his pants, turned around, and walked back down around the cliff.

When he first laid eyes on the car, his eyes bulged like a frog. The only part of the car still recognizable was the license plate. The little car was so flat you could use it for a throw rug. Clyde just couldn't believe it, as he stood there looking at what was a new car just a few minutes before. He rubbed his eyes hoping they were deceiving him, but as he looked back, he saw engine oil and coolant trailing out from under the car like a dying monster. Then, Clyde remembered refusing to buy the additional insurance to cover the car in Canada. The words rolled back through his mind, "I have never put a scratch on a rental car in over thirty years!"

Now, he was stranded in the middle of nowhere, without transportation. Suddenly, he heard a bird chirp and was convinced it was the same one. He wondered was it chirping or laughing. Clyde reached for his pistol, but it wasn't in the holster. He remembered the border guards took it. In over thirty years of law enforcement, he never reached for his gun until now, and it wasn't there. Clyde just stood there and wondered what he was going to do now. Then suddenly, Clyde heard music; heavy metal music coming from the road behind him.

An old pickup truck appeared around the curve and Clyde started waving his arms and yelling, "Help!"

As the truck came to a stop, Clyde came face to face with two teenage boys; one with green hair and the other had a ring in his nose and an orange Mohawk haircut. They had all kinds of earrings, tattoos, and piercings. It was enough to turn Clyde's stomach. The driver turned the music off and they just looked at Clyde.

Clyde thought these two guys would frighten Dracula! Clyde was glad that he didn't have his pistol, because the first thought he had when he saw them was to put them out of their misery, but Clyde was desperate.

Clyde finally spoke, "Howdy fellows, I seem to have had a little car trouble. Can you give me a lift into town?"

The two teen's eyes are glued to the big rock sitting on top of what use to be a new car. Then, they looked back at Clyde.

Clyde just grinned and said, "Just a little accident."

The driver turned the music back on and started rolling forward.

Clyde out of desperation yelled, "I have cash; I'll pay!"

The driver stopped and waited for Clyde to produce the money.

Clyde pulled out a five dollar bill.

The driver started moving, again.

Clyde yelled, "Alright," and pulled out a twenty dollar bill, but the teenagers are not impressed.

So they start rolling again, then Clyde pulled out a fifty dollar bill. The truck stopped and the passenger reached for the money.

Then the passenger yelled, "Thanks man. Now we can get stoned like your car."

As Clyde tried to open the door the teen said, "No way man, in the back!"

Clyde yelled, "For fifty bucks, you should ride in the back and let me in the cab!"

The passenger closed the door and said, "In the back."

Clyde is frustrated, but he walked to the rear of the old pickup. As he put his foot on the rear bumper, the teens laughed and speed away. Clyde fell on the pavement behind the truck and again reached for his pistol.

As he rose to his feet he yelled, "If I catch you, I'm going to pull every damn one of those rings out with a pair of pliers!"

Now he was stranded and fifty dollars lighter, so he started walking. He walked along the deserted road grumbling like an old porcupine disturbed from his daytime nap. He walked about a mile before he heard someone coming; it was an old flatbed truck. Clyde ran out into the road to wave his arms and yelled for help. The ragged old truck's red paint had long faded out and blended with the surface rust and the windshield had more cracks than three miles of sidewalk, but Clyde wasn't choosey.

As the truck came to a stop, he saw a big cage on the back full of geese. The older man driving and female passenger were both overweight and half drunk. The two occupants were so large they filled the entire cab of the junky old truck and they just stared at Clyde as he spoke, "I had some car trouble and I need a ride."

The driver scratched his three day old beard with his left hand and motioned toward the rear of the truck with his right hand and said, "Jest step on da rear bumper and hold on to da cage. But make it snappy buddy, I'm in a hurry!"

Clyde wasn't exactly crazy about the idea of standing on the rear bumper and holding on to a cage, but he was desperate. He made a quick attempt at a smile and said, "Thank you, pal," as he ran to the back of the truck and stepped up on the rear bumper.

The second he climbed up on the bumper and grabbed the cage, the old truck jerked forward and Clyde was on his way. Clyde looked into the cage. He was face to face or maybe face to beak with about forty geese, and they didn't look very friendly. I guess considering the fact that they were on the way to a slaughter house probably would have been enough reason to be a little bit mean. As the old truck picked up speed, feathers started blowing out of the cage and into Clyde's face. A big goose lunged forward and pecked his clinched fingers that were wrapped around the metal rods of the cage. Clyde yelled, "Ouch, dammit," as he removed his left hand from the cage, then suddenly another goose pecked his right hand. Clyde kept swapping hands and yelled more profanity than a drunken sailor kicked out of a New Orleans whorehouse.

As Clyde fought to hold onto the cage and dodge the feathers, the old truck passed through a country crossroad intersection. Canadian Mounties parked at the intersection broke out in laughter as they saw Clyde holding on to the truck as he passed. One of the Mounties said, "Did you ever see such a well-dressed man in such a predicament?"

The Mounties were part of a team sent to the area to monitor the situation involving the McLeods and the Davenport farm.

After fifteen minutes of complete misery, the old flatbed truck finally arrived in a small town. Clyde stepped off the back of the old truck and tried to remove as many feathers as possible. Clyde finally mustered a "Thank you."

As the old truck rolled away, you could hear the driver and passenger laughing.

Unfortunately for Clyde this small town didn't have a car rental agency, but it did have an old general store that on top of everything else, sold a few clunkers.

When the store clerk saw a well-dressed man looking at the clunkers, he realized this man probably had money and the prices double. The two vehicles on display are an old 1988 Chevrolet Cavalier with over two-hundred-fifty-thousand miles and rusted holes so big, you could use it for a basketball hoop and an old Ford van, wrecked on the passenger's side that was barely drivable.

The store clerk approached Clyde and said, "I can tell you are a man who knows a quality used vehicle when you see one."

Clyde just looked at the clerk. He is six foot tall and so skinny he could walk home during a cloud burst and stay dry, and said, "All I see is junk!"

The clerk who realized Clyde is not the fool he thought he was said, "Alright, maybe they need a little paint."

Clyde asked, "How much?"

The clerk said, "Fifteen hundred cash, each."

Clyde yelled, "Fifteen hundred cash, I wouldn't give fifteen hundred for both of these rolling junk yards.

The clerk said, "Well, Clinton is only thirty-five kilometers; maybe you can catch another ride!"

Clyde realized, he's desperate and said, "Look buddy, I'm in a jam, do you have anything," and he mumbled as he counted the cash he had left, "for $378.45."

The clerk realized the fat cat wasn't as well off as he first thought said, "Well, I do have something out back."

He motioned for Clyde to follow him, as he walked around behind the general store and pointed to the most homely looking vehicle on earth. It was an old Yugo, rust bucket. The driver's door and windshield were missing and the fudge color was lighter and darker in places. It looked like something chewed it up and puked it out! The right front fender was missing and the bumper was tied on with a rope. Just looking at it made Clyde feel nauseated, but he realized how desperate he was and asked, "Will you throw in a tank of gas and a rag for the missing gas cap?"

Chapter 27

Meanwhile, a beautiful table of food was set and ready at the Davenport home and Uncle Hugh decided to wake up their guests while it was still hot. Hugh walked over and gently knocked on the door of the guest house. The knock at the door caused Shawn to wake up in a panic mood. Then, Hugh knocked again and Dani woke up and Shawn jumped out of bed and said, "Yes!"

Uncle Hugh called, "The food's hot and waiting!"

Dani and Shawn are relieved to know that everything is alright. They quickly get dressed and walked over to the main house.

Uncle Hugh is standing on the front porch and said, "I was afraid you would sleep all day and I would have to eat all the food."

As Uncle Hugh talked, he grinned and rubbed his stomach.

As they entered the house, Hugh and Sue's son, David, and their daughter, Marsha said, "Good Morning," to their guest. The two families enjoyed the big delicious meal, which included baked ham, mashed potatoes, biscuits, and blue berry pie. David and Marsha entertain little Elizabeth while the adults retreat to the living room to enjoy a cup of fresh brewed coffee.

Uncle Hugh said, "I think we need to get word to your families and let them know you are alright."

Shawn and Dani nodded their heads in agreement and Shawn said, "Should we just call them?"

Uncle Hugh said, "I'm not sure how to contact them. Dani, your father told us Shawn's family thought their phone was bugged."

Shawn said, "I could call my best friend, The Donald, or a former co-worker of mine named, Jerry."

Dani spoke, "I could send my Dad an e-mail at the home office where he works."

They all agreed they needed to get word to their parents, but they are not sure how to do it. They don't want to get anybody in trouble, so they will have to be very discreet. As the two couples discussed the problem, they realized the most important thing to do is just let them know they are alright, but to be sure not to tell them where they are. They realized they could put their families in legal jeopardy, if the F.B.I. found out that they had contacted them.

Then, Uncle Hugh remembered something Shawn said about working at a small town grocery store. Uncle Hugh offered to drive across the border and call a friend of his in Texas and get him to call Mr. Peterman. He could ask Mr. Peterman to call Shawn's parents to come pick up their order, hang up, and then take the phone off the hook. When they come to find out what the strange call was about, he could tell them you are alright.

Everyone agreed this is a good plan and Shawn knew his parents would go to Mr. Peterman's store to find out what the call was about. Hugh explained Dani's father told him that he was in daily contact with Shawn's parents, so they could discreetly convey the message to him.

Shawn said, "I love it; no one would be suspicious about my parents going to Mr. Peterman's grocery store."

Shawn wrote Mr. Peterman's phone number on a piece of paper and Uncle Hugh walked out the front door and went to the barn. He opened the barn door and backed his Jeep Cherokee out and drove away.

After Uncle Hugh left, the discussion turned to what to do with the truck and its valuable contents.

Aunt Sue asked, "Why don't you investigate the possibility of returning the gold, if the government will agree to drop all charges?"

Dani and Shawn liked the idea, but didn't know how to make contact without the authorities knowing where they were.

Aunt Sue suggested an attorney could be used for the negotiator.

Shawn spoke up, "My dad said the best attorney on earth is a man named Max B. Asbell. He's from Warner Robins, Georgia. Maybe we should call him."

The possibility of a negotiator sounded good to Dani.

Dani said, "I'm just ready for all of this mess to be over." Dani looked down and said, "I miss my father and I know he is very lonely after losing mom."

Shawn said, "I agree, I miss my family and I'm sure they have been worried sick!"

Aunt Sue asked, "What compelled you to do this in the first place?"

Shawn and Dani just looked at each other and Dani said, "It was a spur of the moment decision and with the pipeline crew barreling down on us we just panicked, loaded up the gold and took off!"

Shawn said, "You have to think about it, we had just lost our home and I had lost my job and a pipeline company had just sent us a letter demanding we move our house!"

Dani said, "I never could have dreamed that people all over the world would have made such a big deal out of it!"

Aunt Sue said, "The news said the treasure could be worth over one hundred million dollars. That is what made this the biggest story since Neil Armstrong landed on the moon."

Shawn said, "I don't think we got it all. The pipeline crew apparently found some of it."

Then Aunt Sue asked, "How was the trip?"

Dani responded, "It wasn't too bad at first. It was actually fun, but after the story broke and especially after they reported we had painted the truck black, we began to panic!"

Aunt Sue asked, "Would you like to see the latest news on the news channel?"

Dani just looked down at the floor and said, "You can, if you want to, but I think I would rather go for a walk."

She looked over at Shawn and put her hand on his. Shawn and Dani held hands and walked out the front door together.

As David and Marsha continue to entertain little Elizabeth and Shawn and Dani went for a walk. Aunt Sue decided to watch the news channel. It was about twenty minutes before a news update came on, but there was nothing about the Goldilocks story.

After a walk, Dani and Shawn returned to the guest cabin and decided to take the rare opportunity of being alone to take care of an important biological need. They made love and then, they drifted off to sleep in each other arms.

Chapter 28

Meanwhile, two Canadian Mounties found Clyde's flattened rental car. The officers stopped, got out, and walked around the car with a big rock on top of it, and one of them said, "I have the strangest feeling that this has something to do with that well-dressed man we saw riding on back of that old truck loaded with geese."

The Mounties called in the tag number and found out it was a rental car rented by one 'Clyde Bostrum,' an American F.B.I. agent.

The younger Mountie looked a little squeamish as he asked the older Mountie, "Do you think there is a body in there?"

The older Mountie said, "No, I see engine oil and antifreeze trailing from the ill-fated automobile, but there was no blood!"

The older officer then picked up his radio and called headquarters for a tow truck. When the tow truck arrived, the driver got out and laughed so hard he had to hold on to the truck to be able to stand up.

Then, the tow truck operator asked, "Should I tow the rock or what's left of the automobile?"

They all laugh.

Unfortunately for Clyde, all of this will be billed to him, because he didn't pay the $200.00 for insurance. Meanwhile, Clyde had returned to the area, driving his rolling junkyard and trying to find Dani's relatives.

Back at the Davenport farm, Aunt Sue had finally found a story on the news channel about the Goldilocks story.

The reporter said, "American authorities are convinced the McLeods have made it to Canada and may be staying with relatives. We have been told by reliable sources that negotiations are under way between the American and Canadian authorities to return the treasure and the McLeods to the U. S. It is believed that the Canadians are cooperating with the American authorities and a solution to the situation could come soon."

Sue turned the set off and wondered if she and Hugh would be in trouble. Her heart raced as she thought about what might happen.

In a few minutes Shawn and Dani returned to the big house holding hands and looking refreshed. They took one look at Aunt Sue and knew something was wrong.

Dani walked over to Aunt Sue and asked, "What's wrong?"

Aunt Sue was reluctant to break the bad news to the young couple. She realized they hoped they would be safe in Canada.

Aunt Sue said, "I guess it's the excitement getting to me."

Headlights could be seen coming down the driveway from the road. Shawn walked over to the window to get a better look and was relieved to see Uncle Hugh and the Jeep Cherokee circle in front of the house and park in the barn. Uncle Hugh walked across the yard and entered the big house. As the front door opened, he walked in and said, "WOW! That was a trip. I didn't think I would ever get back across the border!"

Dani asked, "Did the call go alright?"

Uncle Hugh answered, "Yes, it went fine. My friend in Texas is a private investigator and it took me a while to explain, but I didn't let him know exactly what this is about. I just told him I would explain later."

Then Uncle Hugh walked over to his big recliner and sat down.

Shawn asked, "Is the traffic normally that heavy at the border?"

Uncle Hugh replied, "Well, it can get pretty heavy on Saturday afternoons, but I have a feeling the border police are a little more sensitive than normal." Then Uncle Hugh said, "On the way down, I got behind the most beat up old junkie car driven by a well-dressed man and when I passed him, he gave me the dirtiest look you could imagine."

Dani said, "Maybe he was having a bad day."

Uncle Hugh said, "Maybe so, but you don't see a man wearing a $500.00 suit driving a $50.00 car every day."

Aunt Sue said, "Why don't you take your baths and I'll warm up the leftovers."

It sounded like a good idea to Shawn and Dani, so they took Elizabeth and went to the guest house.

On the way to the cabin Dani said, "I'm worried about Aunt Sue. She looked very pale when we came in."

Shawn said, "Having unexpected family arrive, and especially under such strange circumstances, could cause a lot of stress."

After Shawn and Dani leave Uncle Hugh moved over next to Aunt Sue and said, 'I've never seen so many Mounties in my life. At the border you can't walk for them and they are watching every intersection."

Aunt Sue said, "I'm concerned. I love them, but I'm afraid we could be arrested for helping them."

Uncle Hugh said, "I'm not sure, but we can't turn them in. They are family."

Aunt Sue replied, "You are right. They are so sweet. I couldn't turn them in or refuse to help them."

Uncle Hugh said, "Did you hear the latest news? The authorities are convinced they are in Canada and that talks are under way to return them and the gold to the U. S."

Aunt Sue said, "Yes, I saw it on the news channel. I thought I would be sick when I heard it."

Uncle Hugh said, "When I crossed the border, they asked me a bunch of questions and then, they searched my car."

Sue said, "We have to help them, but what can we do?"

Hugh said, "Let's just try not to talk about it tonight when they come over to eat, but first thing tomorrow morning, I'll wake them up early and try to help them figure out what to do. Maybe we can call a lawyer."

Aunt Sue said, 'You are right. Canadian authorities are generally quite liberal in these matters and might grant them political asylum, if they turn themselves in."

Meanwhile, in every bar and restaurant from New York to San Diego, the number one discussion is about Goldilocks. Nearly 100% of the American people are in favor of letting the McLeods have the treasure.

Clyde Bostrum had a different opinion, as he got lost and wound up back at the U.S.-Canadian border. After he realized where he was, and because it was getting late, he figured he would cross back into the U. S. and use his credit card for a motel room and a good meal.

As he approached the border, Canadian authorities' laughed at his car and when they saw his American identification and discovered he was an American F.B.I. agent, they howled with laughter. One of the Mounties said, "I heard the American government had money problems, but I didn't know it was this bad!"

The Mounties continued to laugh. It had been a long day and they needed a good laugh.

Then, the officers from the U.S. checkpoint only 50 feet away, walked over to see what's going on. They also laughed at Clyde's car.

Clyde got angry and stepped out of the Yugo and yelled, "Alright, boys, now you've had your laugh. I've had a bad day and I need a nice motel room and a good meal, so let's get things moving!"

The Canadian authorities run Clyde's I.D. while the Minnesota State Police inspected his car. The Minnesota Police informed Clyde that his car will have to be impounded; they won't allow it on the state roads.

Clyde exploded in anger, "I paid the last three hundred seventy eight dollars in cash I had for this car and I plan to get three hundred seventy eight dollars worth of use out of it!"

The Minnesota police still refused to let him in and Clyde demanded to talk to their superior officer. The officers called their captain and informed Clyde that he will have to move his car over to the shoulder of the road to wait for their captain to arrive.

Clyde grumbled, but he complied, when his Yugo finally cranked; all of the officers applauded. Clyde pulled the old Yugo onto the shoulder of the road and parked it only a couple of feet from a fifty foot cliff. Clyde walked back toward the officers who were in a huddle in the middle of the road and yelled, "Call that Captain of yours and tell him to step on it. I'm in a hurry!"

One of the Canadian officers asked Clyde, "Did you abandon a rental car earlier today, sir?"

Clyde's stomach turned as he said, "Well, yes. I seem to have had an unfortunate accident and I'm on the way back to the rental car company to report the mishap, but as you can tell, I've run into a little delay!"

The Canadian officer said, "You will have to satisfy the tow truck operator and recovery crew for the disposal of your rental car, before you can cross the border sir."

Clyde yelled, "I spent every dime I had on that damn car!"

The Canadian officer said, "A credit card would suffice."

That's when it occurred to Clyde that his credit cards were in his briefcase and his brief case was in the little red rental car, flattened by a large rock. Clyde's facial expression went from bad to worse, as he realized he was over one thousand miles from home, penniless and his credit cards were destroyed.

Clyde felt a little over-heated, so he walked over to the Yugo and threw his coat through the missing door and it landed on the gear shift. As he turned to walk away, he heard a strange sound. He stopped and looked back to see the Yugo rolling over the cliff. Apparently, when he threw his coat in the car, it knocked the car out of gear and started rolling and went over the cliff. Smash, crash, bang, boom, crash, blam, bong and the car wound up over fifty feet down a cliff on a pile of rock, shattered to pieces.

The officers all ran to the cliff and removed their hats and held them over their hearts to mourn the final trip for the old Yugo. The car laid scattered in pieces at the bottom of the cliff and Clyde stood there on the shoulder of the road in disbelief.

The Minnesota police officer picked up his portable radio, pressed the transmit button and said, "Eighty four to Captain, eighty four to Captain. No need to proceed to this location. The car you were to inspect" and he paused as did everybody, to take one last look over the cliff, "has been scrapped."

The Canadian officer spoke up and said, "I'm sorry sir, but you will have to pay to have that one recovered as well."

Clyde turned his horrified face toward the young Canadian officer and said, "Can I have my pistol back, I only need it for a moment."

The Canadian officer wrote another ticket for the recovery of the ill-fated Yugo and handed it to Clyde. The officer said, "A credit card would suffice."

Clyde just stared at the young Canadian officer and said, "My credit cards were in my rental car."

Now, Clyde was broke and couldn't post a bond for the recovery of not one, but two cars, and the Canadians wouldn't let him leave until he could settle the claims for the two destroyed cars.

The young Canadian officer said, "I am afraid, sir, I'll have to transport you to the nearest constable's station to arrange some sort of payment for the two recoveries."

"You can't treat me like this. I'm an American F.B.I. agent and a veteran," said Clyde.

The officer just said, "This way, sir," and he led Clyde to a Canadian police car.

As Clyde got into the police car, the officer said, "You will enjoy the trip; this car has doors."

All of the officers just laughed like a pack of hyenas at sunrise.

Chapter 29

Meanwhile, Shawn's parents have received the message from Mr. Peterman and were greatly relieved and called Dani's grandparents and her father from a pay phone next to the fire station. The message was, "We don't know where they are, but they are safe!"

After enjoying a fine meal and each other's company, the two families retreated to the large living room for coffee. Aunt Sue brought out a box of old family pictures and they had a wonderful time reminiscing about old times and Dani got to see some of her relatives that she never got to know, but when she saw a picture of her mom when she was a small child, it broke her heart. Dani just can't forgive herself for the events of the day of her mother's death.

Uncle Hugh got up and stretched and said, "It's after ten thirty, we better turn in, and tomorrow is a new day."

Shawn, Dani, and the baby headed back to the little guest house. As they walked out the door Uncle Hugh said, "I'll wake you up early tomorrow morning for coffee and Danish."

As usual little Elizabeth fell asleep in just a few minutes, but Shawn and Dani laid down on the big bed and just talked and held each other. The discussion as usual was what to do? Eventually they fell asleep in each other's arms. As the little family slept, a new day came, as the sun began to erase the darkness of the night.

A loud knock-knock-knock at the door awakened the young couple. Dani just pulled the covers over her head and hoped she could get a little more sleep.

As Shawn opened the door expecting to see Uncle Hugh, his eyes opened wide. Shawn's gazed at a sea of red. He just stood there and looked at dozens of Royal Canadian Mountie law enforcement officers in their bright red coats. Oddly enough they were all smiling, and the one at the door said, "Top of the morning to you sir, might we have a word with you?"

Dani threw the covers off and sat up in bed and said, "Oh no!"

As Shawn looked toward the main house, he saw Uncle Hugh talking to several of the Mounties.

So, as the early morning rays of light broke over the tree lined ridge behind the Davenport farm house, Shawn realized the possibility that the life he had once known could possibly be altered forever. Dani dressed only in one of Shawn's shirts, leapt from the bed and rushed to Shawn's side.

The Mountie at the door tipped his hat to Dani and said, "Good morning Ma'am, you must be the famous Goldilocks."

Shawn was speechless and in shock, as Dani wrapped her arms around his chest.

Dani started crying and said, "Please don't send us to prison; we were going to give it back!"

As Dani cried, Shawn just stood there like a wax figure. Dani was holding him so tight, he could hardly breathe.

Suddenly little Elizabeth woke up and started crying and Dani walked back to the bed and picked her up and held her to her chest, as she reached out for Shawn. Dani's face showed fear and shock, as she sobbed and begged the Mounties to let them go.

The young Mountie just smiled and said, "Ma'am, we aren't here to put anyone in prison, we are here to confiscate a truck load of valuables and to bring the McLeod family in to the local constable's station for questioning."

Shawn said, "I did it, my wife had nothing to do with it!"

The Mountie continued to smile and said, "We're not here to press any charges. To the best of my knowledge the only Canadian law you might have broken would be crossing the border illegally, a minor charge at best."

Shawn repeated, "I'm the one, I did it, my wife is completely innocent!"

The young Mountie said, "Maybe it would be a good idea to dress properly and we will drive you to the constable post and ask you a few questions."

Dani continued to cry and hold the baby in her right arm and Shawn with her left.

Uncle Hugh and Aunt Sue walked through the crowd of Mounties over to the cabin. As they reached the door, the Mounties stood to the side to let them enter.

As they entered the guest house cabin, Aunt Sue hugged Dani and said, "Don't worry; they said they just want the truck and to ask you some questions, not to arrest you."

Dani's face showed a touch of horror as she asked; "If they put us in prison, will they let us keep Elizabeth?"

Uncle Hugh spoke, "Nobody is going to prison, and you haven't broken Canadian law, so just calm down." Uncle Hugh looked over at Shawn and said, "Grab your clothes and get dressed, so we can go over to the house while Sue helped Dani get dressed."

Uncle Hugh winked at Shawn at the end of his statement, signaling don't argue, come with me.

Shawn grabbed his clothes, rushed over to Dani and gave her a big hug and said, "Don't worry; everything will be alright, we will just give them the gold and stay here till the statute of limitations run out!"

Tears are running down Dani's face as she said, "Oh my God, if only that will work!"

Aunt Sue said, "We can keep the baby."

As the cabin door closed, Dani handed little Elizabeth to Aunt Sue and said, "What have we done?"

Aunt Sue held little Elizabeth and put her other arm around Dani, trying to comfort her.

Dani continued to sob and said, "What were we thinking, to try something so crazy!"

Uncle Hugh and Shawn walked over to the big house and Shawn finished getting dressed while Uncle Hugh said, "Shawn, be careful what you say, they could be recording your interview and might turn the tape over to the U.S. authorities."

Shawn said, "Boy, did I screw up!"

Uncle Hugh placed his hand on Shawn's shoulder and said, "I have a feeling everything is going to work out."

Shawn said, "I just hope they won't punish Dani!"

Uncle Hugh said, "I don't think the Canadians will prosecute you. I can't think of any reason they would."

Shawn said, "Maybe they will just shoot me and let Dani go!"

Uncle Hugh just shook his head and said, "Regardless of how this turns out, nobody will shoot you!"

As Hugh tried to comfort Shawn and Sue tried to comfort Dani, the Mounties took possession of the truck. The Mounties took pictures of the truck and an officer wrote a receipt for it and its' contents, brought it to the big house, and knocked on the door.

Shawn jumped when he heard the knock and Uncle Hugh said, "Don't worry, I'll get it."

As Uncle Hugh opened the door, the Mountie handed him the receipt and asked for the keys.

Shawn looked at Uncle Hugh, because he was the one who parked it in the barn.

Uncle Hugh looked back at the officer and said, "I left them under the mat on the driver's side."

Uncle Hugh handed Shawn the receipt and Shawn told the Mountie the fuel tank is on empty.

The Mountie smiled and said, "A truck load of gold and no petrol!"

As the Mountie walked away, Uncle Hugh closed the door and said, "I'm going to call a lawyer."

Shawn decided to walk back over to the guesthouse to check on Dani. He gently knocked on the door and Aunt Sue let him in.

Dani was wearing a pair of jeans, one of Shawn's shirts and her western style boots sitting on the bed holding little Elizabeth.

As Shawn walked over to her, he could see the pain in Dani's eyes and he said, "I'm sorry, darling, for dragging you into this mess!"

Dani looked up and said, "You didn't drag me. We just made a foolish decision under extreme circumstances!"

Shawn said, "I'm going to tell them this was my idea and I will cooperate fully, if they will let you go!"

Dani hugged little Elizabeth as a tear dropped down her face and said, "It was a nightmare; I just keep hoping I'd wake up and none of this happened."

Shawn got down on his knees in front of Dani and said, "Please cooperate with me. You need to be free to take care of Elizabeth!"

Dani reached over and hugged Shawn and said, "I love you so much."

Suddenly, a knock at the door caused Dani to tremble. Aunt Sue went to the door and in walked Uncle Hugh.

Uncle Hugh said, "I talked to an attorney and he suggested that you should cooperate completely with the Canadian authorities and for you to ask for political asylum on the grounds you are young and impulsive and did something foolish under stress that you now deeply regret."

Dani looked up and asked, "Do you really think that will work?"

Uncle Hugh said, "I believe it would, because the Canadians would have nothing to gain by prosecuting you and besides the world is crazy about you!"

Dani looked at Shawn with a glimmer of hope in her eyes and asked him, "What do you think?"

Shawn said, "I think it's worth a try, besides we would only have to live here until the statute of limitations runs out, then we could go home!"

Uncle Hugh said, "I think it's time to go. You don't want to appear arrogant to these officers. What they think of you could make a big difference in the outcome of this situation."

Aunt Sue shook her head in agreement and said, "He's right, you need to be friendly and pleasant to the Canadian authorities, because they think the American government is a bit bossy and a little arrogant. If you are nice and friendly, it would help you tremendously!"

Shawn stood and reached out to help Dani stand and they walked toward the door. Aunt Sue and Uncle Hugh hugged them and told them they love them and Dani handed little Elizabeth to Aunt Sue.

Dani's voice was but a whisper, as she said to Aunt Sue, "If something goes wrong, will you see that she gets safely to Grandmother and Grandfather in

Russellville, Georgia."

Sue said, "Don't worry; you are going to be fine."

The young couple walked out the front door and was escorted to the rear door of one of the Mountie's Chevrolet Blazers. The same young Mountie who first appeared at the door of the guest cabin was the driver and an older Mountie with gray hair and a mustache was in the front passenger seat. A convoy of several vehicles followed them as they pulled out the front gate followed by their old faithful Ford moving van. The young driver introduced himself as Officer Wayne West and the older officer introduced himself as Mel McCayne.

Dani smiled and said, "I'm Dani McLeod and this handsome guy is my husband, Shawn."

Officer McCayne turned sideways in the front seat and said, "I want you to understand you are not under arrest and as far as I know the Canadian government has no plans to charge you with anything."

The younger officer, the driver, Officer West reached around with his right hand and he gave Dani a piece of paper and said, "Can I get your autograph. My kids will be so grateful."

Shawn looked at Dani and smiled.

Dani said, "When I was a kid my parents taught me that police, firefighters, emergency workers, and soldiers are the real heroes, because they risk their lives for their fellow man, so I should be asking you for your autographs instead."

Officer McCayne said, "Thank you for those kind words; we are very grateful."

Those kind words made the officers realize what a fine young couple the McLeods were and a feeling of mutual respect was formed between them.

The trip to the constable's station was pleasant and the officers were very friendly. Shawn and Dani were relieved to see how nice the officers were and the tensions and fears they had that morning began to fade away.

Officer McCayne said, "My mother was an American and I have a brother that lives near Atlanta, Georgia."

Dani explained that her mother's side of the family were Canadians and how her grandfather loved Canada so much that he returned to his homeland after living in the U.S. for over twenty-five years."

When the young couple and their convoy arrived at the constable's station, they saw a simple wood sided building with a stone facade, and a Canadian flag waving from a pole attached to the building. Officer West opened the door for Dani and Shawn, then led them up to the building.

Officer McCayne opened the front door of the building and led them to a conference room and said, "Just have a seat and relax; we will be with you shortly."

The young couple sat on a large sofa on the right side of the room and a young female officer brought them a cup of hot tea and introduced herself as Eleanor and said, "If you need anything, just let me know?"

Shawn and Dani had never had hot tea before, but they found it to be delicious. As they sipped the hot tea, they could hear voices in the hall.

Clyde Bostrum had spent the night in the barracks of the constable's station and was trying to get paperwork cleared through the American embassy to cover expenses for his two ill-fated cars. He wanted to proceed with his search for the McLeods. He had no idea that they were in the conference room sipping hot tea.

The Mounties informed him the McLeods had been picked up for questioning and that they were in the constable station. Clyde demanded that they be placed in his custody and that he be allowed to transport them back to the U.S. The Mounties had a good laugh over what he said.

Officer McCayne said, "You can't even transport yourself across the border. How do you expect to take the McLeods with you?"

Clyde got mad and demanded an opportunity to interrogate the McLeods, but he was refused access by the Mounties.

The young couple had waited about thirty minutes, but it seemed much longer before Captain McCayne and two other men entered the room. One of the men was a Mountie, wearing his red coat, but the other man was wearing a brown suit and carrying a leather briefcase.

Upon entering, Captain McCayne introduced the other Mountie, an older man and a little on the heavy side, as Captain Spillers and the well-dressed man, as Maxwell Holmes.

Shawn and Dani had stood up when the men entered the room and both men walked over and shook hands with them, as they were introduced.

Captain McCayne continued the introduction by saying, "This is Shawn and Dani McLeod."

The well-dressed man had gray hair and a mustache that turned up at the ends and he wore large black-rimmed glasses. He also had much more of a British accent than the others.

Captain McCayne asked everyone to be seated. He explained, "Mr. Holmes is the equivalent of your assistant Attorney General and the reason for this meeting is to go over the facts and try to rectify this situation. We need you to tell us exactly what happened. Your honesty is of the utmost importance, because if we find any deceptions or false statements in your story, we will be forced to turn you over to the American authorities, so be sure to be honest and straight with us."

Shawn said, "Yes sir, we understand."

Captain McCayne continued, "We will forward the information we receive to Mr. Holme's superior for the final decision by our government within the next forty eight hours."

Then Mr. Holmes stood and said, "The Canadian government does not plan to press any charges against you at this time and if you should ask for asylum, we would consider the merits of your actions and consider such a request, do you understand?"

Shawn said, "Yes sir."

Then Captain McCayne asked permission to record the hearing. He assured Shawn and Dani the recording was for the Canadian authorities only and no copy of it would be given to the American authorities. It is purely for our own reference as we study this case.

Shawn and Dani gave their permission.

Then Mr. Holmes said, "We need you to tell us the entire story and you can start at any point in time that you feel is necessary for us to get what might have caused you to commit such an act and how you got to this moment."

Shawn stood and started his story about how he was raised on a small farm in middle Georgia and about his parents and little sisters and about his school days and working at Mr. Peterman's grocery store. He went on to tell them about how he met Dani that first morning of their senior year in high school and about Dani's life on a small farm in North Georgia. He went on to tell them about how she lost her mother in an automobile accident, caused by a drunk driver. He told them they fell in love and got married after graduating and he told them about getting a job at Barton Manufacturing and buying a modest little home and rebuilding it. He told them about the birth of their daughter, Elizabeth, and about the death of Mr. Barton. He told them about Mr. Barton's son-in-law and how he gave Mrs. Barton so much trouble and about the fire at the plant. He explained about the gas pipeline letter and about the fire and explosion at their home and about how they barely made it out, and that Dani had miscarried in the process. He went on to explain how they left Russellville for Mountaindale hoping for a new start, but he failed to find a job. He painted a man's store for the use of a backhoe. He continued to tell them about how he accidentally discovered the treasure.

He explained about the pipeline crew working toward them and how in a moment of panic and desperation they swapped his pickup for the old moving van truck. He went on to explain how they loaded the treasure in the truck and took off for Canada where Dani has family. In the course of the story, the only small detail he left out was the night he took a walk in the park and buried about a ton of gold bars, but everything else he explained in detail. Shawn spoke for over an hour until the story brought them to this very room.

He then pleaded for help and mercy and said he was more than willing to return the treasure for he had realized the most important thing on earth wasn't gold or silver, but the love of his family and that he would give anything to undo what he had done. He also stated the blame was all his and that his wife and family had nothing to do with it. Shawn then apologized to Dani for dragging her and baby Elizabeth across the country and asked her to forgive him. Dani stood up and walked over to Shawn and sobbed in his arms.

The three men in the room were touched by the young man's story and how his wife reacted to it. Then Captain McCayne called for a recess and Shawn and Dani were left in the room alone. The three men exited in complete silence.

As Shawn held Dani in his arms, Eleanor entered the room and asked, "Would you like more tea?"

Shawn just shook his head and whispered, "No, thank you."

In a few minutes Shawn started talking to Dani, trying to get her mind off their troubles and they returned to their seats.

Later the three men returned to the room and Captain McCayne said, "Mr. Holmes would like to speak to you."

Mr. Holmes walked up to the front of the room. He stopped and for a second. He appeared to be in deep thought. He then raked his mustache with his thumb and finger and said, "In my twenty plus years of serving my country in my legal capacity, I have never heard a more moving story than yours." Then he stopped and looked at the ceiling and said, "I would suggest that you apply for political asylum to protect you from the American authorities. The American authorities want your heads on a platter, so to speak, but we can help you. I can all, but guarantee you that asylum status would be approved, but we can use the contents of the truck as a bargaining point, if you decide to return to the U.S."

Shawn stood up and said, "We appreciate your help and we would like to apologize for dumping this problem on the people of Canada."

As Shawn sat down Mr. Holmes said, "The American authorities can get a little aggressive and I think we Canadians have to teach them a little moderation at times."

Captain McCayne said, "You will be driven back to your relative's home, so you can be with them, while a decision is made by our government."

Dani stood and said, "Thank you, so much!"

Mr. McCayne continued, "You are not under arrest, but I must insist that you stay with your family until an agreement can be reached, and we will post a security detail to protect you from outside interference."

Then Captain Spillers stood and said, "You are a remarkable couple. I can't imagine how you two pulled off such a circus and while traveling with a baby, considering millions of people were aware of your story."

Shawn and Dani just looked at each other and smiled.

Captain Spillers continued, "I can only imagine what I would have done under the circumstances, but I don't believe I would have had the nerve to do what you did."

Captain McCayne said, "I just can't believe nobody saw you."

Captain Spillers replied, "I agree, it seemed like people all over the world were cheering them on, like they were folk heroes or something."

Chapter 30

Meanwhile, Clyde Bostrum, still waiting in the constable barracks for his paper work to clear, and fuming mad, because the Canadians wouldn't let him interrogate the McLeods, was having memory flash backs from his college days. He sat in an old wooden chair and propped his feet on a trash can as his mind took him back to 1960, when he was a junior at the University of Georgia at Athens. He had planned to elope with his girlfriend, but the transmission in his 1952 Chevrolet had gone south on him. He and his beloved had planned to drive to Franklin, North Carolina on the Saturday and be married and then spend the remainder of the weekend at a friend's cabin in Clayton, Georgia. The transmission failure would mean he would have to explain to the future Mrs. Bostrum that their elopement was off at least temporarily!

He walked across the campus to the ladies dorm to convey the bad news, when he saw an envelope blowing in the wind. He picked it up and read the words on the outside "To my beautiful granddaughter Sissy, from your Grandmother Powell" and noticed it had something in it. As he walked along, he opened it and found two hundred dollars in cash. He stopped just before he reached the girl's dorm. This would be enough money to pay the garage the one hundred forty dollars they wanted to repair his car's transmission, plus a little extra pocket money for the elopement and travel expenses.

It was at that moment, Clyde realized the devil had once caused him, in a moment of temptation, to do something he shouldn't have done. He thought about the McLeods; they also were tempted after having some financial problems and other setbacks. Clyde lowered his head in shame, as he remembered what he did. He decided to keep the money, fix his car, marry his beloved and figured in a few weeks, he would replace the money and return it to whoever "Sissy" was!

So old Clyde stole-er- I mean borrowed the money from the envelope, fixed his car, married his beloved, but lost one of his part time jobs for being gone that weekend. It took him a couple of months to replace the cash and return the envelope to the girl's dorm house mother, but he was told that the young lady known as "Sissy" had dropped out of college for financial reasons. Apparently, the money from her grandmother was to help her complete her studies, so she could become a school teacher like her grandmother.

The dorm mother told Clyde she would try to find the young woman and return the money to her. Clyde had tried to erase the bad memory from his mind, but over forty years later, it was still sitting in the middle of his brain like a big scar.

Clyde realized he had succumbed to temptation, and he wondered whatever happened to the "Sissy" who dropped out of the University of Georgia in 1960.

Clyde was so outraged at what the McLeods had done that he wanted to throw them in prison and throw away the key! Then he remembered John 8:7, "He that is without sin among you, let him first cast a stone at her." Now Clyde felt lower than a rattlesnake hole in Death Valley.

Clyde got up and walked down the hall to where the McLeods were being questioned. He was stopped by a young Mountie, Wayne West, at the conference room door.

Clyde said, "I've had a change of heart and I want to try to help the McLeods."

The Mountie said, "Sure you do and I rode my unicorn to work this morning!"

Meanwhile, the *World News Network* reported, "The young American couple have reached Canada and that the Canadian authorities have recovered the infamous truck, the golden treasure, and the McLeods, themselves, are being questioned by Canadian authorities."

Shawn's family back in Russellville, Georgia was relieved to hear they are alright, but still they are very concerned about what might happen to them. Dani's father had just arrived at the McLeod farm and had to work his way through all of the news media at the gate. He had driven from Montgomery, Alabama to visit the McLeods and try to figure out what they can do to help Shawn and Dani.

Back in Atlanta, Georgia, a crowd of people had gathered at the State Capitol supporting the young McLeod family. People felt that the young couple acted out of impulse and desperation! They demanded that the charges be dropped! People all over the world are flooding the internet with pleas for their release. At times, the internet itself began to crash. The President, the Governor of Georgia, and the Attorney General met in a closed circuit video conference call to arrive at a solution to the problem.

The Governor asked, "Could we just drop the charges and let them go, if we get the treasure back?"

The Attorney General said, "We must be careful. If we let them go unpunished, somebody will steal the Liberty Bell or try to steal the Statue of Liberty or the Washington Monument. We must punish them for what they have done."

The President leaned back in his chair at his desk in the Oval Office and said, "Why me? Why couldn't I just have had a simple problem like an alien spaceship landing in New York?"

The Georgia Governor said, "Mr. President, the American people are looking to us for leadership and the press is going to crucify us regardless of what we do!"

The President said, "What if, we make a deal to give him ten years and then

I'll pardon him when I leave office."

The Attorney General replied, "Do you remember what happened when President Ford pardoned President Nixon?"

The President raised his voice, "If you have a better idea, I want to hear it!"

The Governor spoke up, "Gentlemen, I have never seen so many people protesting in the streets like they are now. What if, we let the American people decide in a referendum? Just let them vote on it, and then they can't blame us!"

The Attorney General retorted, "That's what we don't want—mob rule!"

The President just rolled his eyes and placed his right hand over his face.

The McLeods have been driven back to the Davenport farm and have been reunited with Elizabeth. Tears of joy flowed like a river as the family reunited. Shawn and Dani decided to call their parents, considering everybody on earth probably knew where they are.

Uncle Hugh convinced them to wait for him to consult his lawyer who told them to be careful what they say, because it would most likely be recorded.

So the call was placed and for over an hour the family members on both ends of the call expressed words of love and hope.

The News Medias around the world converge on the Davenport's farm in Canada and the McLeods farm in Russellville, Georgia.

A thousand Canadians have filled the road in front of the Davenport's home and the two Mounties guarding the gate have now swelled to over fifty. They are there to show support for the McLeods. The next day so many people show up at the McLeod farm in Russellville, Georgia that local law enforcement had to call for help from the state to keep the crowds under control.

In the meantime, the Governor took a break after the conference call with the President and Attorney General. He walked from his desk over to the window. He refused to look down, because he knew the protestors are down there, so he looked up hoping for inspiration of some sort and suddenly he saw a blimp.

Its message board read, "Let them go!!!"

Suddenly, an aide entered the room and said, "Mr. Governor, can I get you something?"

He answered, "How about a one-way plane ticket to Tibet."

Chapter 31

Back at the Davenport farm Shawn and Dani tried not to worry about the decision from the Canadian government.

Early the next morning a Mountie came to the door with a letter addressed to Shawn and Dani McLeod. Shawn opened the envelope and removed the letter inside. The letter read: 'To the McLeods, after careful consideration, the Canadian government will give temporary asylum to the McLeod family. If you wish to be granted permanent asylum you will have to file the proper papers within thirty days. It is not the policy of the Canadian government to extend asylum to people who take possession of national treasures of another country and try to keep them for themselves. Because of your youth and desperation, not to mention that the treasure was found on your own land, we have decided to offer your family safe haven. The truck and its contents are being sought by the United States government, the State of Georgia, and even by the county where the treasure was found. However, the truck and its contents will remain in Canadian hands until the International Courts make a decision, as to the rightful owner. We wish to make this perfectly clear. The Canadian government does not condone what you did, but we have made a rare exception to our general policy by granting this offer. If you choose to seek permanent asylum and Canadian citizenship we must request that you forgo any desires, in the future, to become treasure hunters or to take the law into your own hands." Signed: Harold W. Gwayne, Adjutant General of Canada.

The Davenport home exploded in excitement as the family heard the letter. Dani and Shawn had spent the night on the sofa in the living room and little Elizabeth had slept beside them. The entire family had more or less held a slumber party of sorts waiting for the letter.

Dani's Uncle Hugh told Shawn, "I can probably get you a job at the lumber yard."

Shawn replied, "Sounds good to me!"

The excitement is so contagious, the Mounties and the crowd outside cheer along with them. Then as the excitement died down, Shawn decided to call his parents. Shawn's mother answered the phone and told Shawn that Dani's father had joined them. Shawn relayed the good news to his mom who immediately relayed it to the rest of the family. It's spontaneous joy for Shawn's family and then Dani's father said, "I want to speak to Dani."

As Dani and her father finally got to talk, they could hardly hear each other with all the happy noise in the background.

But in the moments of relief, sadness sat in as Shawn's parents realize that their son and his family will probably never be able to return to the U.S.

As Dani and her father talked on the phone, he began to realize that the good news also had a very sad side.

Shawn's mom sobbed uncontrollably. The girls realized something was wrong and asked, "Why is mother crying?"

Mr. McLeod just said, "It's alright, it's alright."

If all dark clouds have a silver lining, then this silver linings' dark cloud is that even though Canada has offered them asylum, that doesn't mean the United States government planned to just drop the charges and let them go free. The U.S. Department of Justice and the Attorney General's office exploded in rage at what the Canadians have done.

A task force was quickly formed to figure out some way of capturing and prosecuting the McLeods and retrieving the treasure. As the news hit the air waves, people all across America and around the world were overjoyed that they have been offered asylum in Canada. People turned out by the thousands in the big cities to celebrate. In the U.S.A. it was like this year had two Fourth of Julys.

Even freedom has its price, when you can't be with your family or ever come home.

After breakfast Uncle Hugh led everyone back to the big living room. He decided to avoid the television and instead turned the radio on to hopefully find some music to help Shawn and Dani relax. He turned the selection till he found a country station out of Grand Forks. A song was playing "If it wasn't for me and Jesse James who would thrill the women and rob the banks." As the music played the mood in the room improved, and an hour went by before they were suddenly jolted by the words "Bulletin-Bulletin!"

Everyone stopped and looked toward the stereo as the announcer said, "A bulletin just came into our news room as follows, "The F.B.I. had served arrest warrants on Shawn McLeod's father, Dani McLeod's father and a Mr. Peterman. They have been accused of aiding and abetting Shawn and Dani McLeod. Concerning the young couples escape to Canada with what is believed to be the lost Confederate gold. Stay tuned to KLRX and we will keep you entertained and informed. Now here's the latest hit by Toby Keith."

"Click!"

Uncle Hugh shut the radio off and tried to think of something to say, but the look on his face told the story for him. He was absolutely shocked.

Shawn and Dani couldn't believe their ears. It was absolutely insane. Neither of their parents had helped them or had any idea they were going to find a treasure and try to run to Canada.

As Shawn and Dani sat staring at each other, Uncle Hugh turned the television on and switched to the *World News Network* channel. The instant the picture popped on the screen you could see Shawn's father and Dani's father both in handcuffs being led to a Ford Crown Vic by several Federal authorities.

As the volume is turned up, they heard the reporter say, "And more arrests are expected as Federal authorities search for everyone involved in the young McLeod's escape to Canada."

Shawn and Dani could only watch in horror, as they saw their fathers led away in handcuffs, knowing they were completely innocent.

As the bulletin ended, the reporter said, "I'm James Dell reporting. Now back to John Preston in New York."

Then John Preston spoke, "Fuel prices are the highest since the '70's and no relief seems to be in sight."

Uncle Hugh turned the set off and just stood in front of it. Dani was crying in Shawn's arms. Everyone else in the room was shocked and quiet. Shawn tried to comfort Dani, as she cried uncontrollably.

His eyes looked like they were glazed as he said, "How did this nightmare start?"

Dani raised her head as tears dripped down her face and said, "I don't understand; they had nothing to do with it. Absolutely nothing!"

Uncle Hugh finally spoke, "I'm going to call my lawyer and ask him what's going on!"

In a few minutes Uncle Hugh returned and said, "My lawyer said he thought the American government wanted you so badly, they have filed charges against your parents hoping you will turn yourselves in to free them."

Little Elizabeth who had been playing with a couple of toys on the floor, crawled over to her mom and held on to her legs. She stood and reached for her mama. As Dani noticed her, she reached down and picked her up and hugged her.

Shawn realized that affection from someone you love is strong medicine.

As Dani held little Elizabeth, Aunt Sue appeared with a small glass of milk and a small blue pill.

She said, "Dani, take this. It's a mild sedative. It will help you relax."

Dani looked at Shawn, as if to get his approval and he said, "It's alright!"

Aunt Sue walked away to put the empty glass away, but returned in a few minutes with a pillow. She said, "Here, honey, just lay back and relax and don't worry!"

As Aunt Sue sat on the floor trying to comfort Dani, Shawn walked over to Uncle Hugh and whispered, "This had gone far enough. I want to talk to Mr. Maxwell Holmes to see, if he can help."

Uncle Hugh said, "I guess the Mounties at the gate would know how to reach him."

Shawn walked out the front door and walked over to one of the Mounties and requested, "Please help me contact Mr. Holmes."

The Mounties make a call and then gave Shawn the phone number.

As Shawn walked back toward the house, he realized what he must do to try to stop this disaster from getting any bigger. As Shawn approached the house, Uncle Hugh met him on the porch and asked, "What do you plan to do?"

Shawn said, "I'm going to see if Mr. Holmes can arrange a deal with the U.S. authorities to turn myself in, if they will drop charges against our fathers and everyone else to stop this nightmare."

Hugh said, "Are you crazy? They will throw you in a Federal prison and let you rot there."

Shawn stopped before opening the door and said, "I love Dani, but since we got married, I've caused her nothing, but pain and sorrow. ~~I'd rather be dead than to see her hurt again!~~"

Hugh said, "Son, maybe you need to think about this for a few days!"

Shawn said, "I'm going to see, if Mr. Holmes can negotiate a reasonable prison sentence, but my mind is made up.

When they entered the living room Aunt Sue motioned for them to be quiet. Apparently, Dani has drifted off to sleep. After being awake all night, the glass of warm milk and the sedative had done its job, and she was finally resting.

Uncle Hugh motioned for Shawn to follow him upstairs. At the top of the stairs, Uncle Hugh opened a door on the right, and as they entered, Shawn realized it's like a little office at home. The room had a desk, file cabinets, a couple of chairs and a phone.

Uncle Hugh said, "This is a place you can talk in private, but are you sure you want to do this. There is no rush!"

Shawn said, "No, sir. I've caused enough pain and trouble. I just want to see, if I can get this over with!"

Uncle Hugh said, "I'll be down stairs, if you need me. I just wish you would reconsider."

As the wooden door closed behind Uncle Hugh, Shawn never felt more alone in his life. He prayed for the guts to do what he had to do. Shawn's fingers were shaking, as he made the call. Mr. Maxwell tried his best to talk Shawn out of making such an offer, but Shawn is persistent.

Even though Mr. Holmes is against Shawn's decision, he finally agreed to put the offer before the U.S. authorities to see what could be done.

After making the call Shawn decided to go downstairs and check on Dani and Elizabeth. Shawn saw Marsha and David entertaining Elizabeth and he picked her up and kissed her face and then, he put her down. He then walked over to Dani, as she slept on the sofa. He bent down and kissed her face and he whispered, "Please forgive me. I love you!"

Shawn then sat on the floor beside her and reached out and placed his hand on her hand. Shawn's mind wandered back to that fall morning, only a couple of years ago, when he first saw Dani getting out of her grandmother's car in front of the old brick high school.

As he sat there, his mind played back to the fun times they had. Everything was so perfect. He felt like he was living a fairy tale. It all began to crash around him when Mr. Barton died suddenly and Buddy Strange started causing trouble. The Barton Manufacturing Company burned and a short time later, his home exploded and Dani suffered a miscarriage. Some people accused him of being an arsonist and on and on. He wondered how Dani would react to his decision. As he sat beside Dani, Marsha brought little Elizabeth over to him and he gave her a big hug.

As he held her close, he looked back at Dani and thought, how did I marry such a beautiful young lady and have such a beautiful child and then have everything on earth go wrong. Was it the gold? No, this series of disasters started long before he found the gold. He remembered a story from the Bible about a man that had everything and lost it all. Was this a test?

As Elizabeth crawled away, he wondered how he could have been crazy enough to think he could get away with a truck load of gold. The room was completely silent, except for the ticking of a large grandfather clock. He wondered why he had never noticed the clock before.

Meanwhile, Uncle Hugh and Aunt Sue went for a walk to talk about the situation and Uncle Hugh explained what Shawn is trying to do.

Aunt Sue said, "He should have called his mother and talked it over with Dani."

Uncle Hugh replied, "He tried to call his mother, but the phone had been disconnected. I figured it was a trick by the U.S. authorities to put pressure on Shawn."

Aunt Sue said, "Maybe he will change his mind after he gets his answer from the U.S."

Uncle Hugh said, "I hope so."

When Uncle Hugh and Aunt Sue returned to the house, they saw Dani still asleep on the sofa and Shawn sitting beside her.

Suddenly, the phone rang and Uncle Hugh grabbed it on the first ring. He then pointed to Shawn and whispered, "It's Mr. Holmes."

Shawn whispered, "I'll take it upstairs."

Shawn ran upstairs to the small office and closed the door behind him. He picked up the phone and said, "Yes, this is Shawn, sir."

Mr. Holmes said, "Well, son, the U. S. authorities have agreed to drop all charges against everyone involved, if you turn yourself in."

Shawn asked, "What kind of a sentence would I be facing?"

Mr. Holmes replied, "They said, three to five years, but only if you turn yourself in right away."

Shawn said, "Mr. Holmes, I'm ready to get the matter over. How will the surrender be handled?"

Mr. Holmes said, "I'll have one of my Mounties drive you to the border, if you are still determined to go through with it."

Shawn asked, "When will they release my dad, Dani's dad and Mr. Peterman?"

Mr. Holmes responded, "I have been assured they will be released immediately after you reach the border and turn yourself in."

Shawn said, "Mr. Holmes, I will never forget you and the Canadian people for being so kind to us and I want to apologize to all of you for causing you so much trouble."

Mr. Holmes said, "Shawn, we were just doing our job and we would be willing to help you even more, if you change your mind and decide to stay."

Shawn said, "I'm ready to get this nightmare over with as soon as possible."

Mr. Holmes said, "Why don't you wait just 24 hours and talk this over with your family?"

Shawn said, "I would rather go now."

Mr. Holmes replied, "Very well. I will contact the officers out front and they will be ready when you are."

Shawn thanked Mr. Holmes once more.

Mr. Holmes wished Shawn good luck and bid him farewell.

Shawn put the phone down and opened the desk drawer looking for a memo pad. He wrote, "To my darling Dani, Please forgive me for what I am about to do, but I believe it is the only way for us to get out of this nightmare. I don't understand why so many things went wrong, but I can't sit back and let them put your father and my father or anybody else in prison for something I did. I'm sorry for all the trouble I caused you and everybody else. I wish I could roll back the clock to the morning I first met you and start over from there. Please don't worry about me. I will think of you and Elizabeth every minute. My parents will help you and Elizabeth; they love you just as much as I do. Mr. Holmes negotiated a deal where I'll have to serve a three to five year sentence and then we can be free again. I knew this was the only hope we had to ever have peace and freedom. I'm sorry for letting you and Elizabeth down. I love you. Shawn"

Shawn walked quietly down the stairs and saw Elizabeth had gone to sleep next to her mother on the sofa. He bent down and kissed them gently on their foreheads and left the note beside Dani and walked quietly to the door. He hugged everyone good-bye and asked, "Uncle Hugh, will you help Dani and the baby get home?"

Uncle Hugh said, "I'll put then on an airline tomorrow."

Then Shawn took one last look at Dani and his child sleeping on the sofa and opened the big wooden door and walked away. As the big door closed, Aunt Sue broke down in tears and Uncle Hugh held her in his arms.

When Shawn got to the gate he told the Mounties, "I'm ready to go to the border."

The Mounties are saddened by his decision, but realized he's a brave young man trying to protect his family. They all pat him on the back and wish him well.

Officer Wayne West said, "I'll drive you to the border, if you are sure you want to do this, lad!"

As they left the driveway, Shawn looked towards the big wood house and silently said, "Good-bye."

Meanwhile, Clyde Bostrum's paper work had cleared and he was free to go, so he contacted the Attorney General and offered to escort Shawn back to the federal prison in Atlanta. Clyde's heart had been changed and he no longer had the contempt he once had for Shawn. As a matter of fact, he actually had begun to admire Shawn for his decision to face the charges like a man.

Clyde arrived at the border, courtesy of the Canadian Mounties, right behind Officer West and finally got to meet the man he had been pursuing for over a week. Clyde introduced himself and shook hands with Shawn.

Shawn apologized for all the trouble he had caused.

Clyde accepted his apology and said, "Believe it or not, I made a few mistakes when I was young."

Clyde had to sign a couple of papers and then they walked across the border marked only by a white line painted on the pavement.

Shawn was extended a rare privilege. Clyde allowed him to travel without handcuffs.

Shawn explained, "My father, Dani's father, nor Mr. Peterman had anything to do with the treasure or their trip to Canada."

Clyde said, "Shawn, I have no reason to believe they did." He explained, "Shawn, those charges came from the Department of Justice."

Shawn said once again, "I apologize for the trouble I have caused everyone."

Clyde responded, "Son, I'm not a perfect man; I did some things in my days that I'm not proud of, but at least you turned yourself in and I respect you for it!"

Shawn asked, "Mr. Bostrum, can you notify the agents in Georgia to release my father and Dani's father, as well as Mr. Peterman."

Clyde said, "I will do that as soon as we get into a Minnesota State Police car for a ride to the airport."

As they sat in the police car waiting for the border guards to return Clyde's pistol, Clyde saw a familiar vehicle, an old pickup, waiting in line to cross the border into Canada. He could recognize them anywhere, right down to their orange and green hair! As Clyde stepped out of the police car, the border guard handed him his pistol.

Perfect timing!

Clyde told the driver, "I'll just be a minute!"

The two punks sat in the old pickup playing their heavy metal music and they didn't see Clyde coming, until he knocked on the driver's side window with his pistol. The driver nearly freaked out as he recognized Clyde, as the person they scammed! The pickup was boxed in between the other vehicles, a cliff on one side and Clyde on the other. With nowhere to run, the punk rolled down the driver's side window and in a shaky voice said, "Yes, Sir?"

Clyde flashed his badge and asked, "Have you boys seen a couple of stupid looking punks that took a fifty dollar bill from me?"

The punks looked terrified, as they see Clyde's FBI badge in one hand and his pistol in the other.

Clyde said, "Give me your wallets!"

The driver quickly complied.

Clyde yelled, "Yours too, punk!"

The passenger quickly complied.

Clyde opened the wallets to find only seven dollars in one and two dollars in the other. Clyde removed the cash and said, "You guys seem to be a little short, but I'm willing to let it go, except for the carrying charges."

Then Clyde walked around the front of the ugly pickup and threw the two wallets over the cliff.

The two punks jumped out of the pickup and run over to the guard rail. The one with the orange hair yelled, "Hey, man, we can't cross the border without our ID."

Clyde replied, "Gee, boys, that's too bad. You know if you get right on it, you could probably climb down that ridge and find them by midnight!"

While the punks stared in complete shock at the bottom of the cliff, Clyde just smiled and said, "Have a nice day, punks!" Clyde got back into the Minnesota State Police car and told the driver, "Let's go, we've got a helicopter to catch!"

When Clyde said the word helicopter, it jogged Shawn's memory. He realized Clyde was the guy that he saw relieve himself after the helicopter landed next to Mr. Green's farm. He thought to himself, "I thought this man looked familiar."

They traveled about twenty miles until they got to a small airport and parked beside the helicopter. The blades were spinning and it was apparently ready for takeoff. Clyde placed his hand on top of Shawn's head, as they walked to the helicopter and Clyde said, "Stoop down, son!"

As they boarded the helicopter, the pilot and co-pilot turned sideways in their seats and shook hands with Shawn. The pilot, an attractive young woman with red hair said, "Good morning; we don't get many celebrities!"

As the helicopter lifted off, it was Shawn's first flight and he was shocked at how noisy the helicopter was.

Shawn removed a couple of pictures from his pocket. The pictures were of Dani and Elizabeth and of his parents and sisters. He realized it would be a long time before he would see them again. This flight was the loneliest hour of his life.

They landed in Minneapolis near a small jet for the flight to Atlanta, Georgia. As they boarded the aircraft, the crew met them at the door and they all shook hands with Shawn.

A young lady, the co-pilot, asked, "Shawn, may I have your autograph."

Shawn was happy to oblige, but he was afraid Clyde might be a little jealous of him getting so much attention.

After they take off and level off, the pilot left the controls to the co-pilot and stepped back to the small passenger compartment. Shawn's stomach was a little queasy, so the pilot gave him a pill and a small bottle of water to prevent nausea. The pilot explained that he flies VIP's for the government.

Shawn quickly said, "Like Mr. Bostrum!"

The pilot smiled and said, "Yes, Mr. Bostrum is definitely a very important person."

It seemed like forever, but in a few hours the small jet landed in Atlanta, Georgia. Then they boarded another helicopter that would fly them to the Atlanta Federal prison. Federal detainees are generally held in the nearest facility to the location of the crime. The helicopter circled and landed on top of the federal facility on a landing pad adjacent to the main guard tower. Shawn looked around, as he stepped off the helicopter at the drab surroundings that will be his home for several years. He wondered, if Dani is still sleeping. He felt badly that he left her while she slept, but he knew he wouldn't have gone through with it, if she cried and begged him not to.

Back at the Davenport farm Dani had awakened to find little Elizabeth asleep on her tummy. As she opened her eyes and looked around the room, she wondered where everybody was. She gently rolled Elizabeth onto her back, without waking her. Then she walked around the big room gently calling, "Shawn, Shawn, Shawn where are you?"

She looked out the front window to see Uncle Hugh, Aunt Sue, Marsha and David sitting on the front porch. She walked over to the big wooden door and opened it. Not a word was said, as she stared at them. She knew something was wrong. The heartbreak was written all over their faces. She just stared and finally said, "What's wrong, where is Shawn!"

Aunt Sue and Uncle Hugh rose and walked toward her with outstretched arms. Dani's heart pounded, as she waited for an answer. As her Aunt and Uncle wrapped their arms around her, and Uncle Hugh said, "Shawn made a deal to turn himself in so your father and his father could be released and the deal also meant neither you, nor anyone else will be charged."

Aunt Sue said, "He loves you with all his heart and he knew this was the only way this could end in peace!"

As Dani cried in her Aunt's arms, her cousins, Marsha and David, joined them in their family huddle.

The two remaining Mounties realized what was going on and removed their hats.

Dani cried, "Why, why, what happened to us? I can't live without him. I just can't!"

Uncle Hugh and Aunt Sue slowly walked Dani back into the house. They helped her to a big recliner and Aunt Sue sent Marsha for a pillow and a blanket trying to do anything they could to show her love and comfort.

Dani laid back on the recliner, looked up at the ceiling and said, "Why did this happen!"

Suddenly the phone rang and Marsha answered it. The call was from Shawn's father who said, "Dani's father, Mr. Peterman, and I have been released."

Uncle Hugh took the phone and told Shawn's father that Shawn made a deal to turn himself in, so they could be released, so no one else would be prosecuted.

Shawn's father was speechless. He just handed the phone to Shawn's mother and Hugh told her what Shawn has done.

As Shawn's mother cried, Shawn's father explained to Dani's father and Shawn's little sisters what has taken place.

Chapter 33

World News Network was reporting the latest developments in the Goldilocks story: The reporter said; "Shawn McLeod, after successfully escaping to Canada with a truck load of gold, had apparently surrendered to the American authorities in a deal to prevent his wife or anyone else from being prosecuted concerning the heist of valuables. According to sources presumed to be reliable, Shawn had been transported to the federal prison in Atlanta, Georgia where he will be held until he is formerly charged. Stay tuned; further details will follow. Now, back to New York."

People all across America are saddened by his arrest. They don't understand how he could be arrested for taking something found on his own land. Shawn was being held in a separate part of the prison. This was an area for people awaiting trial on federal charges, but who hadn't been tried and convicted.

After processing through the system and being humiliated beyond belief, Shawn was placed in a small cell with gray walls and a bunk bed. The only remnants of his past allowed are the two pictures of his family. As night fell over Atlanta, Shawn prepared to spend the first night of his life away from his family. The meal tray was slid through a slot in the door, but he was in no mood to eat. He just sat back on the bunk and placed his face in his hands and leaned against the cold gray concrete block wall. He tried to figure out why everything had gone so wrong!

As the news stories flooded the airways, millions of people felt sorry for young Shawn McLeod. They thought of him as one of their own. People said he's a fine young man who willingly gave up asylum in Canada to be sure no one else would be charged.

As the night drug on, Shawn had to deal with the loneliness of his tiny cell and prayed he would go to sleep and wake up in the morning and this would only be a nightmare.

Shawn's family, along with Dani's father, spent the night talking about what had happened during the last few days. Mr. McLeod couldn't understand why Shawn didn't call him before he left for Canada. He had always been very close to Shawn. Shawn's mother had cried until she couldn't produce anymore tears.

The room was quiet, as the sun came up and shined through the windows. When breakfast is served, Shawn drank the coffee. He thought the room looked smaller than it did the night before. He heard someone walking down the hall and the steps stopped in front of the door to his cell. He peeped through the slot in the door and saw a well-dressed man.

Suddenly the door opened and the man said, "Are you the celebrity?"
Shawn said, "I'm Shawn McLeod."
The man motioned for him to follow him and Shawn followed him down the

hall. The man said, "The federal prosecutor wants to talk to you."

Shawn is led into a room with a big long table and chairs. At the other end of the table is a small man with a black beard, wearing a dark blue suit. The man doesn't look up, but just said, "Have a seat, I'll be with you in a minute."

Shawn pulled back a chair, sat down, and waited patiently for nearly an hour. He began to wonder why he was led to this room, just to watch a man read paper after paper. Finally the man looked up and said, "I'm Ben Brantley, Federal Prosecutor for the Northern district of Georgia and I've been reading over the case we have against you, and an agreement made by the Attorney General's office."

Mr. Brantley scratched his beard with his fingers, as he looked up at the ceiling and said, "If you are willing to come clean completely and name everyone that conspired to help you, I can make you an offer of twenty years."

Shawn stood up, very excited, and yelled, "Twenty years. I was told three to five."

The man said, "Three to five is for jay walking."

Shawn said, "But the treasure was on our land and I willingly turned myself in and I was told I'd get three to five years and no one else would be charged!"

The prosecutor said, "Regardless of whose land it was on, it is of historical significance and it belongs to the United States government. As for the three to five years, that agreement was made under duress and unless you come clean and name names, you'll get thirty years or more!"

Shawn was completely shocked as he said, "I don't understand. I willingly turned over the gold. Why should I get such a long sentence?"

The prosecutor said, "We don't have the gold. For all we know we may never get it."

Shawn replied, "They told me it would be held until the World Court decides whether it belongs to federal, state or county."

The prosecutor said, "And how do we know, if they'll return it, or if we get all of it?"

Shawn responded, "I know how much we had."

The prosecutor sat back in his chair and said, "What possessed a basically good person like you to become a world class thief?"

Shawn just looked at the floor and said, "I don't know, sir, I just don't know!"

The prosecutor said, "Was it that little cutie pie wife that drove you to do it?"

Shawn jumped to his feet and yelled, "I love my wife and she did absolutely nothing wrong. It was all my idea. There's not a kinder sweeter person on earth!"

Then the prosecutor sprang to his feet and yelled, "Well, unless you can give me a good reason for stealing a national treasure, I'm going to throw the whole damn book at you, and you'll be so old when you get out of prison, that you won't remember what women look like!"

Shawn fell back in his chair and placed his hands over his face and said, "We should have stayed in Canada. The Canadians were so nice to us."

The prosecutor snarled, "If you had stolen as much from them as you did from us, they would have been on your butt just like us."

Shawn looked down at the floor and said, "I want a lawyer."

The prosecutor replied, "You can't have a lawyer until you have been formerly charged and even then a lawyer won't do you any good. It is twenty years, if you talk and thirty, if you don't."

Shawn mumbled, "I'll take my chances with a jury."

The prosecutor smirked and said, "You won't get a jury. In such a case you will be tried before a federal judge."

Shawn replied, "Why can't I have a jury?"

The prosecutor said, "When you stole a national treasure and then ran to a foreign country, you lost your right to a jury trial."

Shawn felt like his life was over and his faith in a fair trial seemed to dissolve. Shawn just looked at the floor and spoke in a whisper, "I was told, if I surrendered I'd get a short sentence."

The prosecutor said, "If you talk, some of the conspirators can serve some of your time; otherwise, it is thirty years or more."

Shawn didn't say another word; he just looked at the floor.

The prosecutor said, "I can't waste all day, son. So while you think about it. I'm going to send you back to your cell with a pencil and pad, in case you get smart and want to write a full confession."

The prosecutor pushed a button on his desk and a guard opened the door and escorted Shawn back to his cell. ~~The guard opened the door and Shawn took a final look around, before he walked into the tiny cell.~~ As the big steel door closed behind him, he felt like an electric shock ran through his body. Shawn just stood there and realized this could be his home for the rest of his life.

Suddenly the guard returned and slid a writing pad and pencil through the slot in the door. As Shawn opened the pad, he saw an envelope. He picked it up and looked at the guard, still standing outside the door.

The guard said, "You can write a letter to your family, but don't seal it, it will have to be read and approved before it can be mailed."

Shawn said, "Thank you."

The guard walked away, whistling.

Shawn's cell had a small window, but he had to stand on his tiptoes to see through it. All he could see was a rundown part of Atlanta and of all things, a McDonald's. ~~Shawn thought, right now I would do anything to be able to go to that McDonald's with his wife and daughter. But then he~~ realized ~~it could be thirty years before that could happen~~. He thought in thirty years Dani would be nearly fifty and Elizabeth would be over thirty years old. It would be much too late for them to have another child.

As his heart sank in his chest, he realized it would be a tragedy to ask Dani to wait for him. She was beautiful and she could remarry and hopefully have more children, so Elizabeth wouldn't be lonely. As a lump formed in his chest and a tear dropped down his face, he picked up the pencil and pad and began to write a letter to Dani.

"To My Beautiful Darling Wife! I want you to know that I love you with all my heart and that I am sorry for the disaster I made of our short life together. I'm sorry for taking the coward's way out by leaving, while you were asleep. I knew I wouldn't have the strength to go through with the plan to turn myself in, to prevent anyone else from being charged or jailed. I realized we could never go home to see our families or even to visit your mother's grave. I realized I would have to pay for what I did to be sure our families and friends wouldn't be prosecuted. I had Mr. Maxwell Holmes negotiate a deal so I would only serve as few as three years and then we could spend the rest of our lives together. Unfortunately, now I am told by the federal prosecutor that they won't honor the deal and it will be thirty or more years before I could possibly be free again. By the time I get out of here, the majority of our lives will be over. I'm not sure I can survive thirty years in this tiny cell. I could never stand to see a bird in a cage or a fish in a bowl. I don't think after thirty years in here, I would be any good for anything. I love you and want what is best for you and Elizabeth. You are so young and beautiful. You will find somebody else to spend your life with. Maybe next time you will find somebody who's normal. You need someone to love and care for you. My life is over and my future is hopeless. I don't want you to suffer for my mistakes; therefore, I request that you file divorce papers at your earliest convenience and please forgive me for hurting you and Elizabeth.

I have nothing left to give you, but your freedom. My parents will help you; they love you just as much as I do. Fate dealt me a beautiful blessing, you! But now it has taken away everything. Even though I will always love you, I know it's in vain. So I must painfully request you divorce me and get on with your life. If I die in this miserable place, please don't tell Elizabeth what happened to me. She is so young she won't remember me. Hopefully in due time you might also erase any memory of me from your mind. Please honor this, my request. I got you into this mess and this is the only way under the circumstances I can get you out! I will always love you in my dreams. Shawn."

After writing the letter to his wife, he folded the pages and put them in the envelope. He then laid the envelope on the ledge at the bottom of the slot in the door. Shawn walked back to his bunk and laid down. Shawn had no food or sleep for over forty eight hours. He tried to find the strength to face his miserable life as he sat in his cell.

Shawn's mind went back to when he was five years old and caught his first fish. He thought about his grandmother who died when he was six. He thought about his parents and little sisters and Mrs. Poole, his first grade school teacher. He thought about his first pony ride. He thought about his grandfather. Everybody said he died of a broken heart after the death of his grandmother. He remembered the night their barn burned down. As his mind put on a show of his past, he wondered what would happen to his family.

Then suddenly the big steel door opened and in walked a guard with a lunch tray and said, "Here's your lunch and I'll need that pencil and pad."

Shawn handed the guard the pencil.

The guard knew that Shawn was distressed; he had seen it before. He said, "Son, don't give up hope. These people are trying to break you down and get you to agree to the easy way out for them."

Shawn ~~continued to sit on the bunk, but he~~ listened to every word the guard said.

The guard looked up and down the halls to make sure no one else is around. Then the guard said, "Just hang in there, the American people think you and your wife are heroes. They will help you, just don't give up."

The guard picked up Shawn's tray and realized he hadn't touched his food. He turned toward Shawn and said, "Son, you have got to eat something. Trust me; I have a feeling something is going to work out for you."

Shawn said, "Yes, I got a great future ahead of me!"

Shawn was being sarcastic, as he sat there drowning in sorrow.

The guard said, "Son, you can't give up. You have a beautiful family who loves you and millions of Americans demanding your release."

Shawn looked up and said, "Sure and in a few months nobody will remember us!"

The guard responded, "Are you kidding? Even people in foreign countries are protesting at the American Embassies and here in the States petitions are being signed by the millions!"

Shawn sat up and said, "Are you sure!"

The guard said, "Look, I have a deal for you. You eat this food for me and I'll come back in a few minutes to pick up the tray and I'll take you to the infirmary, because you have a stomach ache!"

Shawn asked, "What?"

The guard winked and said, "While you wait to see the doctor you can watch the *World News Network* on the television in the waiting room!"

Shawn looked shocked and said, "Will that work?"

The guard grinned and said, "Sure it will, the average wait for something simple, like a stomach ache, could be an hour or more!"

The guard helped restore Shawn's hope and he said, "You have a deal."

Then the guard said, "You have to eat every bite. That's the deal."

Shawn agreed and opened the tray and for the first time in nearly three days he felt hungry. The meal consisted of a slice of ham, a roll, potato salad, carrots and jello. Shawn finished his meal in two minutes flat and oddly enough he did have a little bit of a stomach ache.

The guard returned and asked, "Are you ready to go?"

On the way down the hall, the guard had to put a waist band around Shawn and put his hands in the cuffs. He explained that he had to wear them when visiting the infirmary.

Shawn felt humiliated, but he tried not to think about it.

When they arrived at the infirmary, Shawn had to sign in, and a nice young lady held the patient's log book for him to sign.

Then the guard signed after him.

The young lady smiled and said, "We don't get many celebrities in here."

Shawn suddenly looked around the room trying to see who she is talking about.

She laughed and said, "I'm talking about you!"

The guard said, "I'll be back in a few minutes to check on you."

Shawn walked to the back of the waiting room and took a seat. Eight other people are ahead of him and they stared at him. The *World News Network* is reporting on the upcoming Chinese Olympics, and then went to the record high gas prices. Finally, after about ten minutes, they gave an update on the Goldilocks story.

The reporter is standing out front of the Atlanta Federal Prison and said, "Shawn McLeod, husband of the now famous Goldilocks, had been held here at the Atlanta Federal Prison since yesterday and authorities said he will be charged in the morning with pirating in connection with the theft of gold found on his wife's property. The federal prosecutor was apparently going for the term of thirty years according to reliable sources. We have been told that bail could be as high as fifty million dollars. So, unless Shawn has a rich uncle, he will be held here until his trial, probably sometime next spring, before a federal judge. This is John Clements reporting from the Federal Prison in Atlanta, Georgia."

Then, the news channel returned to its studio in New York with Martha Steele reporting, "The Goldilocks story just keeps rolling on as Dani McLeod and her baby girl have returned to the home of her grandparents in Russellville, Georgia. According to federal authorities, her husband has accepted full responsibility for the removal of the gold and no charges will be placed against her at this time. However, not only nationwide, but worldwide, the story keeps growing. Millions of Americans have signed petitions demanding the young man, Shawn, be released. The petition can be signed online at (www.FreeShawnMcLeod.net). Politicians are being warned, if Shawn is convicted, they will be voted out of office. American Embassies all over the world are being swamped with angry crowds who are demanding the young man's release. Even the President, when asked at a news conference this morning if he would consider a pardon for Shawn McLeod said, 'I would consider it, if Shawn would be willing to help him pass the stimulus package.' This caused a thunderous round of applause. Something the President had not achieved in the earlier part of his remarks.

Millions of Americans feel he should be set free, because the gold was on their land and, because of the fact, so many bad things had happened to them prior to the discovery of the gold. The loss of Shawn's job and their home exploding in the middle of the night, causing his wife to lose an unborn child and then being unable to find a new job was what started this predicament."

As Shawn listened to the report, he had renewed hope that he might get a pardon or maybe have a chance of a more lenient sentence. Eventually, he got to see the doctor. The doctor told him the stomachache was probably from stress and gave Shawn a couple of Rolaids and told him to come back the next day for a follow up.

As a matter of fact he told Shawn, "I'll call you to come back every day for a while to check on you." He then whispered, "That waiting room out there is a lot bigger than your cell."

On the way back to the cell, Shawn thanked the guard for his encouragement and help.

The guard, a middle age man with blonde hair in the buzz cut and a few extra pounds said, "I'm glad to help you, son."

As they walked along, the guard stopped and showed Shawn a big window where you could see the street out front of the prison, and he saw several hundred people protesting for his release. Shawn could see the signs that read 'Shawn, a prisoner of love' and 'it's their gold, let them go' and still another that said 'Shawn

McLeod is a political prisoner!'

Shawn felt much better after seeing such strong support, but he realized his sentence would be handed down by a federal judge, and not the everyday people on the street. As Shawn reached his cell, the guard removed his handcuff belt and said, "I'm Bill Keys," and reached out to shake hands with Shawn.

Shawn shook hands with Bill and again thanked him for the encouragement he had given him. Then Shawn asked, "Do you still have that letter I wrote?"

Bill pulled it out of his shirt and said, "You mean this one?"

Shawn was relieved the letter had not been mailed, he had written it in haste at the lowest moment of his life. It had been a long day and the guard did his best to keep him company, even dropping an *Atlanta Journal* newspaper through the slot in the door. He figured if Shawn could read some of the editorials and news stories it might give him even more encouragement.

About five o'clock Bill brought Shawn's food tray to him and Shawn was asleep when he came back by to pick up the empty tray. As Shawn slept his mind sought a place of peace and he dreamed he was a kid again back on his family's farm in Russellville.

Early the next morning as daylight broke over Atlanta, Shawn woke to the reality of his life. He sat up in the middle of his bunk and just prayed for help from above for him and his family. A guard came by and brought him some clothes and escorted him to a private shower and dressing area. This area was off limits to prisoners, but it was available to guards or suspects being held for trial.

Shawn showered, shaved, and got dressed and was escorted down the hall for his arraignment before a federal judge. He was charged with piracy and pleaded "not guilty." The judge set his bail at twenty five million dollars. Shawn knew he could never raise that much money and was escorted back to his cell. The news of his arraignment was telecast across America and around the world. Shawn's parents and Dani's father had wanted to attend the arraignment, but they were told to stay away by their lawyer.

Midmorning the guard who had been so good to Shawn the day before came by to check on him and told Shawn the crowd of protestors outside the Federal Prison was even larger than the day before. Bill realized Shawn was depressed again so he said, "Cheer up. Something will work out, don't worry!"

Shawn said, "My bond was set at twenty five million dollars. Do you have an extra twenty five million I could borrow?"

Bill laughed and said, "No, I'm afraid my checking account and savings accounts are closer to twenty five dollars." Bill asked, "Have you ever been in trouble before?"

Shawn shook his head and said, "No, never."

Bill said, "Not even in school?"

Shawn said, "No, I did really well in school and even managed to make mostly A's."

Bill said, "I came from a broken home and I was getting drunk when I was fourteen and when I was sixteen, I stole a new car from a local dealer."

Shawn asked, "What kind of car did you steal?"

Bill snickered, "A gold Mustang!"

Shawn said, "So we have something in common. We both stole something gold."

They both laughed.

Shawn hadn't laughed in so long, he couldn't remember the last time he did.

Bill said, "Son, don't give up. You have too much to live for. And this turkey shoot ain't over yet!"

Chapter 34

Meanwhile, ~~Dani and Elizabeth had been driven across the border by her~~ Uncle Hugh and Aunt Sue ~~and they~~ paid for airline tickets to send Dani and the baby back ~~to Atlanta. Dani's father picked them up at the airport and drove them~~ home. Dani begged her father to take her to the prison to see Shawn, but her father said, "It was too risky, because the US authorities weren't living up to the agreement Mr. Maxwell Holmes had made."

Her father warned her they would all have to lay low for a while until they could put a lawyer on the case.

Dani broke down and cried, but her father said, "Shawn's father had gone to see Max Asbell, a lawyer that he had tremendous faith in. He had agreed to take the case for whatever they could afford to pay."

When they arrived at the McLeod farm, they entered from a gate on the back of the property to avoid the press, law enforcement people, and supporters at the front gate. They were told that the lawyer had said he was preparing a fight that would make news around the world.

Dani hugged Mrs. McLeod and told her, "I'm sorry. We had no idea what we were getting into!"

Mrs. McLeod said, "Mr. Asbell, the attorney, said he would start negotiations for Shawn's release on bond and to try and get the charges dropped within a few days."

When they entered the house the *World News Network* was reporting that Shawn had been arraigned on piracy charges and that his bond was set at twenty five million dollars. The room was so quiet you could hear a cotton ball drop.

Then Dani started crying and Shawn's mom tried to console her.

Then the *World News Channel* showed an interview with the prosecutor and he said, "We have an iron clad case against Shawn McLeod and regardless of how much the public yelled and protested; he will spend the next thirty years in federal prison. We have got to show these hoodlums they can't steal from our government."

Instantly, Dani fainted.

Shawn's mother and Dani's father grabbed her before she hit the floor and helped her to the sofa. Fortunately, little Elizabeth had been handed off to the twins at the front door. Total mayhem broke out as Shawn's mom ran to the kitchen and quickly poured a glass of ice water and ran back to the living room. She quickly splashed ~~a handful of the~~ cold water in Dani's face. Dani came to and looked horrified trying to figure out what is going on.

Her father ~~hugged her and~~ said, "Don't worry, darling. We will straighten out this mess, if it is the last thing we ever do!"

As the excitement took place in the McLeod's living room, the *World News Network* reporter speaking to the federal prosecutor said, "Considering the fact Shawn McLeod is young, has a family and no criminal record, are you telling us that you are still going for a maximum sentence?"

The federal prosecutor faced the camera and pointed his finger at the lens and said, "He will be given no mercy and he deserves none."

Dani's father raced across the room and shut the television off and said, "Oh yea, if they want a fight, they will get one!"

~~While Shawn sat on his bunk trying to figure out a way of getting help in the legal fight he realized he had nothing of value.~~ The house fire destroyed what little ~~they had and they even lost the equity, because they only bought enough insurance to cover the mortgage. So the money Dani's father had given them had been lost.~~

As Shawn sat there on his bunk ~~going over his options~~, he heard a strange sound. He soon realized ~~what it was~~. It was a helicopter landing on the roof of the prison. He remembered the sound from when he arrived and wondered who the new arrival could be. Then a cold chill came over him, as he realized they could be going to transfer him to another prison, because of the protestors. His heart sank at the thought of being transferred further away from his family. ~~If only he could talk to his family!~~

A short while later Bill Keys, the guard, came to the door and said, "Well big boy, you have a visitor."

Shawn said, "A visitor. Are you sure? Who would come to see me?"

Bill unlocked the door and led Shawn to an elevator, and in a few seconds they were on the fourth floor. When they arrived, at the visitor center, Shawn asked the tall thin guard, at the door, who the visitor was?

~~As the guard shuffled through the papers, Shawn asked, "Is it my wife or father and mother~~?"

Then the guard said, "It's a surprise."

Shawn wondered, "Was it, his wife or parents?"

Shawn was led into a small room with a table and chairs.

The guard said, "Just sit here and wait!"

Shawn thanked the guard and wondered who would come to see him, especially considering the trouble he was in. Then Shawn heard someone entering the room.

Shawn looked toward the door and couldn't believe his eyes. The well-dressed man entering the room was none other than Kenneth Grayson Koonce, the United States Attorney General. Shawn's mind went into a tailspin, as he wondered why the Attorney General would come to see him. Should he have fear or hope?

Shawn .rose to his feet, as the Attorney General's smile put his mind at ease, as he reached out to shake hands with Shawn.

The Attorney General said, "Mr. McLeod, I am pleased to meet you." He placed his briefcase on the table and motioned for Shawn to sit down.

Shawn was trying to think of something to say, but he was too overwhelmed to respond.

As the Attorney General opened his briefcase, he said, "I am here on behalf of my boss, Edward E. Hamilton, President of the United States of America." He looked toward Shawn and said, "To say that you have caused an international crisis would be putting it mildly. The President is coming up on his re-election campaign and he wanted to settle this little matter concerning your little treasure hunt and trip to Canada as quickly and quietly as possible. The President is offering you a deal to settle this little matter, once and for all."

Then the Attorney General removed a letter from his briefcase and said, "I'm going to read you his offer.

Greetings, Mr. McLeod,

I must say that your story has been a sensational event for us and the world, and I, myself, have been somewhat fascinated by your little adventure. I have tried to put myself in your shoes to see, if I could have overcome the temptations you faced. I can only imagine what it must have been like for you and your young wife and child over the course of a few weeks. Then, to be tempted by such an enormous amount of wealth and to have a pipeline crew barreling down on you must have been more stress than any normal person could stand.

Now, let me say, at this point, that regardless of my sympathy concerning your difficulties, to take a national treasure, even though it is found on private property for one's own use, cannot be allowed.

So, I am faced with a historically unique situation. My mind needs to be on leading our country, as we face many challenges at home and around the world.

Last night, I met with leaders from both parties from the House and Senate and they unanimously endorsed my recommendation.

Mr. McLeod, I am willing to give you a conditional pardon, so that your family and the nation can move on with our daily lives. The conditions will be as follows:

1.)   You are to sign a press release that we have prepared for you that expresses your gratitude to me, the Vice President, and members of Congress for your pardon and apologize to the American people for your transgressions!

2.)   You will not directly or indirectly get involved in a book or movie deal about your adventure.

3.)   You must refrain from guest appearances on radio or television or to even converse with the public over the internet.

4.)   You and your family must make every effort to return to being normal everyday Americans.

5.)   You must not leave the USA or become involved in politics, regardless of the circumstances.

6.)   You will be given a well-paying federal job in Washington, DC, so you can support your family.

7.)   You will cooperate with American officials in an effort to convince the Canadian government to release the treasure you transported to Canada.

8.)   You must keep the terms of this agreement completely confidential.

Mr. Mcleod, if you agree to the terms of this agreement and are willing to sign a sworn deposition that will be witnessed by the Attorney General, your pardon will become effective immediately, and the Attorney General will hand you a check for $10,000.00 to help you settle any obligations you may have incurred and the balance should be used for your travel expenses. A very nice townhouse apartment, we generally use to house foreign dignitaries, will be made available to you and your family, and we will give you a nice federal job with the State Department. Your salary will be $100,000.00 and your first assignment will be to assist the Attorney General in his effort to retrieve the treasure you transported to Canada.

We need you as soon as possible, so spend a few days with your parents and we will send a State Department jet to the Macon Airport to transport you, your wife, and child to your new home and job. As soon as you and your family have settled into your townhouse, the First Lady and I will invite you to the White House, so we can meet your family.

Very Sincerely Yours,

Ed E. Hamilton
President of the United States"

Shawn quickly agreed to the terms and signed the papers without any hesitation.

The Attorney General said, "Thank you, Mr. McLeod. I am looking forward to working with you."

Shawn said, "I don't know a single thing about the operations of the State Department, but I'm willing to try anything."

The Attorney General said, "You have won the respect of a great majority of the American people, as well as, people all over the world, and you will be a great asset to the State Department."

Shawn said, "I don't believe this is really happening!"

The Attorney General said, "I have one more surprise, just as soon as you can get a shower and get dressed. I'm going to personally escort you back to your family in Russellville in this nice Marine helicopter I have parked on the roof!"

After his shower and shave, Shawn is offered his choice from several very nice expensive suits, but Shawn decided to wear his western style shirt, jeans, and boots. These were the same clothes he was wearing that morning when he first laid eyes on Dani.

As the helicopter lifted off from the helipad on top of the federal prison, it then circled and set a course for Russellville. Shawn was seated directly across from the Attorney General.

The co-pilot opened the door to the cockpit and asked, "Mr. McLeod, does Russellville have an airport?"

Shawn said, "No, it's just a small town."

Then the co-pilot asked, "Does it have a large parking lot?"

Shawn said, "Yes, the high school parking lot and the adjacent football field cover several acres."

The co-pilot said, "Thank you. I'll call the local Sheriff's Department and have them check for utility lines and guide wires and to direct us in."

The Attorney General thought, "This is a Cinderella story; everything but a glass slipper."

He handed Shawn his cell phone and said, "Here, call your family and tell them you are on the way home."

Shawn said, "Thank you" and dialed his parents' phone and hoped that Dani was there. He dialed several times, but the number was busy. His parents had taken the phone off the hook, because of the calls from the press and pranksters. Then, Shawn dialed Dani's grandparents' house.

Meanwhile, Dani had finally drifted off to sleep in her grandfather's recliner after being awake for several days.

When the phone rang, Dani's grandmother grabbed it on the first ring and said, "Hello."

Shawn had to yell, because the noise of the helicopter was so loud.

Dani's grandmother could barely understand what Shawn said, nor could she tell for sure, if the caller actually was Shawn. She hung up and then took the phone off the hook.

The phone call woke up Dani and she walked toward the kitchen and asked her grandmother about the call.

Her grandmother said, "Some guy was screaming on the phone and he said he was Shawn and for you to meet him at the high school parking lot."

Dani said, "Are you sure it was Shawn?"

Her grandmother said, "No, there was so much noise, I could not tell who it was. It's probably another prankster."

Dani looked down at the floor and said, "Yes, you are probably right," and then she returned to the recliner. As Dani tried to go back to sleep she thought, "The high school parking lot is where she and Shawn first met."

Suddenly, she got up and walked to the kitchen and said, "Grandmama, can I borrow your car for a few minutes?"

When she arrived at the high school, no one was around. It was Saturday and the school was closed. Dani thought, "How could I have been crazy enough to think the call was real?"

As she drove around the parking lot to make sure no one was there, she saw a Sheriff's car pull into the parking lot with its emergency lights flashing. Then she heard a big helicopter circling just above the parking lot.

The Sheriff's deputy circled the lot and then parked next to the school house.

Dani got out of the car and watched, as the big helicopter landed. The blades continued to slowly turn, as the side door opened and the steps lowered themselves to the ground. Dani thought, "It must be the Governor coming for a visit."

Then she saw Shawn run down the steps and she screamed and run toward him. They collided and fell to the ground and start rolling around on the grass, as they are locked in a big kiss.

Then suddenly, Dani wound up on top and said, "How did you get out?"

Shawn said, "The President gave me a pardon and a job with the State Department and we have a townhouse waiting for us in Washington, DC!"

Dani kissed Shawn again and then she whispered, "But what if a

country boy like you and a country girl like me can't handle living in
Washington, DC?"

Then Shawn winked and whispered, "If all else fails, I guess we will
just have to go for *A Little Walk in the Park*!"

The End

Proof

Made in the USA
Charleston, SC
18 July 2014